AJOS

A SCI-FI ALIEN REBEL ROMANCE

A.G. WILDE

Ajos

Ajos © A. G. Wilde 2021

This book is dedicated to my mother. You taught me how to fight and never give up. You've always been fighting...and you still are. You have one last battle. I know you will win.

DISCLAIMER

This work of fiction is intended for mature audiences only.
All sexually active characters portrayed in this book are eighteen
years of age or older.

AJOS

Penance.

It is the only thing on his mind.

He merely exists as a tool, a weapon for the Restitution till the gods are satisfied he has suffered enough.

He has no dreams for a different future, until...

...a human, one he rescues, falls into his arms.

For the first time in a long while, something stirs within Ajos. But this unknown feeling is not the only thing that stirs.

Maybe taking the human on a secluded planet had not been the best idea...

Now, instead of fighting the enemies that plague them, the person he has to fight the most...is himself.

1

THE DARK SPIRITS OF TONVUHIRI WERE WORKING HARD THIS DAY.

Ajos stretched, cracking the bones in his neck as he gripped his spear in one hand.

He could feel the unease—as if it was floating through the air itself.

Cocking his head, he glanced at the skies, his gaze searching the nothingness above. In the distance, only the sky tower marred the otherwise cloudless expanse.

Nothing was out of the ordinary.

Nothing except the huge metallic structure that stood in front of him.

A stasis hold.

The brown dirt and dust that settled over everything hardly stuck to the surface of the huge structure, causing it to almost glisten in the star's light.

It was...expansive...otherworldly...from a different time, even though...that was far from the truth.

"How many do you think are inside?" he asked.

"Well over two stleks of humans are within," V'Alen answered.

Ajos' gaze narrowed slightly.

More than twenty-four...

That was a lot. More than he had expected.

"All female." It wasn't a question, for he knew the answer even before his comrade replied.

"Affirmative."

A breath left his lips as Ajos scanned the structure.

This was one of the largest rescue missions any team in the Restitution had ever pulled off.

The structure in front of him was carved from one of the rarest metals. Built to withstand the harshest impacts. Engineered to carry out a singular purpose.

He'd never seen anything like it before.

Only one set of beings on this side of the universe could afford to construct such a thing.

"Ajos." A voice caught his attention and Ajos turned to see the commander who'd retrieved the stasis hold approaching.

"Xul," he greeted the male.

"I appreciate your assistance today, brother, and V'Alen's as well."

Ajos jerked his head in acceptance.

Commander to commander, he knew Xul was a fighter who cared about the Restitution probably as much as he did.

"I've only given a few rebels clearance to assist in opening the stasis hold with us," Xul continued.

Ajos jerked his head once more, his gaze moving back to the large, dark structure. "I consider myself honored to be one of them," he said.

Even with extra minds on the task, though, their machines had no impact on opening the structure. It had forced them to brainstorm different ways to get inside.

Today was their thirteenth attempt.

The commander ran a hand through his long filaments to scratch the base of one of his horns.

Only three members of his team were within the secured area today, an Arois named Yce and two others.

The Arois was surrounded by four human females—four that were rescued long before Xul and his team found the stasis hold.

They fussed over him, for the Arois was the only link between the beings within the stasis hold and those outside its walls. He had mind-melded with the trapped ones—so much so it activated the neurons all across his body.

Ajos eyed the females with a sideways glance.

He'd heard stories of how they'd fought alongside his brothers to reach safety.

He wondered whether his brothers had stretched the truth.

Small beings the humans were, even smaller than he'd expected them to be.

Not one cleared the height of his shoulders.

"They worry," Xul said, noticing Ajos' gaze.

"So they do," he replied, flicking his gaze back to the structure before them. "They want their people out."

And he knew exactly how they felt.

Ajos' nefre stiffened, unease making his pulse beat through the delicate dorsal fin that ran down his neck to disappear into his spine.

He knew exactly how the humans felt—because he'd lived through something like this before.

THE NEW MACHINES he and V'Alen had engineered rolled toward the stasis hold, breaking the pull of his memories. Their wheels crunched the soft gravel, crushing it to dust as they moved to the side of the huge structure.

They'd tipped the rotary saws with talix metal—the same metal that the High Tasqals had used to engineer the entirety of the hold.

If this didn't work...if they didn't break through the metal structure on this instance...he didn't know what would.

"Just where did you procure talix metal?" Xul's gaze settled on V'Alen.

Ajos kept his eyes on the stasis hold as the machines began to cut, their saws whirring in the stillness of the space.

He'd wondered the same.

The only beings that had access to talix metal were the Tasqals themselves. Yet, V'Alen had been able to get some.

"I have a friend," was all V'Alen said.

Xul grunted, his eyes narrowing a bit.

It was a conversation for another time.

In silence, they watched the machines work and when he looked over at the human females, it seemed as if they were all holding their collective breaths.

The machines whirred for ages before the undeniable sound of a saw breaking through resistance and meeting air filled the area.

For one moment, it was as if they all held their breaths.

Relief shot through him, though he did not show it.

One of the humans jumped in excitement, her joy barely contained, while the other three gripped each other in elation.

The commander's shoulders lost some tension as he released a breath.

They'd done it. On the thirteenth try, they'd done it.

Yet, within himself, Ajos' unease grew.

Rolling his shoulders, he frowned.

This was not like that time—that time that threatened to invade his consciousness with memories of old.

This was different. Nothing was going to hap—

V'Alen stepped forward suddenly, his eyes flashing. His cybernetic limbs glistened in the light.

"Wait," he said, and his voice caused the humans to hush. "Something is wrong."

Without realizing it, Ajos' hand stiffened on his spear.

He could feel his life organ speed up...feel the memories returning, the doom surrounding him.

He uttered a silent prayer underneath his breath.

May the gods of Tonvuhiri prove him wrong.

"What do you mean?" one of the humans asked.

V'Alen raised his hand, his head tilting slightly. "There is a signal."

"A what?" another human asked.

V'Alen paused, his head slowly tilting as he looked up into the sky.

"A signal," he repeated. "One that began broadcasting as the hold was breached."

Ajos followed his friend's gaze, his eyes searching the nothingness once more.

"The signal grows stronger," V'Alen muttered.

"What signal? Speak, brother," Xul pressed. The sudden tension in his voice was clear.

V'Alen hesitated and Ajos knew he was scanning. "A signal." He paused again, reading the information they could not see. "One whose origin is from within the stasis hold itself. Its destination..."

It went unsaid.

They all knew who the signal was for.

It was heading straight to the High Tasqals—the same terrible race that had enslaved so many beings for so long and the same race they'd defied to retrieve the stasis hold.

"We have to get inside, get the women out, and kill that signal. Now!" One of the humans, one with long, pale filaments, touched Xul on the arm, insistence in her eyes.

Xul grunted. "Athena is right. If they find us—"

Ajos growled softly.

The humans might not know it, but all the brothers did.

It was too late for that.

The signal was already out there.

The strange feeling growing in the pit of his stomach...this was what it meant...

"Qrak," someone cursed.

As the machines continued whirring again, Ajos made up his mind.

"We cannot wait." He was moving before he even finished speaking.

The commander met his gaze and jerked his head in agreement.

Nothing was said, but they both knew what needed to be done.

If they didn't kill that signal, whatever it was, it wouldn't be good for any one of them.

"Xul." The Arois' eyes glowed. He was deep in the mind-meld, so much so that his voice didn't come from his lips. It sounded otherworldly, as if it echoed in the open space. "The humans..." the Arois said, "they're all waking..."

Ajos froze.

No.

"What do you mean they are all waking?" Xul turned to the Arois.

The Arois staggered somewhat and the humans by his side grabbed on to him to steady him.

"All awake. So many minds." The Arois grimaced. "Terrified. Panicked."

No.

Not again.

Ajos could hardly breathe.

The gods could not be so cruel to make him relive the one thing that had torn him apart from the inside out.

He knew how this ended.

The roar that cut through the space sounded like it came from his body but Ajos didn't think about it as he charged against the metal hole the machines had already outlined.

He lodged his spear into the outline, but there was hardly any give. As he moved back to slam his shoulder against the outline in the metal once more, he hardly heard the concerned cries of the humans behind him.

His mind was on one thing, the females within the hold. The same ones waking up from cryo-sleep only to find themselves trapped with no way out.

He didn't want to hear their cries...he didn't want to hear their screams.

If he had to relive this again, he wasn't sure he would survive this time.

"Status!" he shouted over his shoulder as he took another few steps backward to charge at the hold once more.

"The pods..." the Arois spoke and his voice halted. He sounded strained, and when Ajos turned to look back at the male he saw why.

Yce was overloading his neurons. So much so that his blue skin was like a shining white beacon. He was sure the male couldn't keep it up for much longer.

"The pods are failing..." Yce spoke and the world disappeared from around Ajos.

Suddenly, he was back on that ship, back in that time, the same words ringing in his ears.

"The pods are failing!"
Screams for mercy filled the ship's hold.
"Save me, Ajos. Please!"

"What do you mean the pods are failing?!" one of the four humans shouted and the fear in her voice snapped Ajos back to reality.

"The pods are shutting down," the Arois repeated. "The humans are all awake."

"But that's okay, right?" asked another one of the humans. "It's okay if they wake up, right? *Right*?!"

"No..." Ajos stepped back, staring at the structure.

The dark gray of the huge metal box hardly had a dent in it from his efforts.

"They will not be okay." He swallowed hard as he backed away even farther to charge forward again. "This is the work of the High Tasqals."

"Breaching the hold's integrity has created a sort of self-destruct. And that signal was the first trigger." V'Alen delivered the news.

The sharp gasp of one of the humans caught Ajos' ear but he didn't need to turn to see the distress on her face.

This had to be a curse, for he couldn't believe it was happening again.

Pledging his life to the Restitution was no penance for his failure. The gods had no mercy on him...and he deserved their punishment.

"Stop the robots! Stop drilling the hole!" One of the humans rushed forward, her eyes haunted.

She was only pulled back by one of the commander's team members, who caught her by the waist and held her tight as her body shook with emotion.

"That won't stop it," Ajos heard himself say and the human

turned her haunted eyes on him. "It's already been triggered. They will wake and slowly..." He trailed off.

Slowly, the ones inside would suffocate—the stasis pods, the things that kept them alive through the journey from their planet, would be the thing to kill them.

He couldn't say it out loud.

If what his brothers said was true, these females had already seen too many horrors in their lifetime. He wouldn't add to their nightmares.

And the females trapped inside the stasis hold...

His life organ wrung with the pain of old—of seeing this happen before.

For a moment, he stood frozen, unable to move. It felt as if he'd been sent back to a time when he'd been helpless...

Ajos' muscles tensed.

But that was then...

He'd been young...inexperienced...untrained...

This time was different, and he refused to see the same thing happen again.

"They're dying," the Arois spoke, his voice still thick with that ethereal feel. "Losing oxygen."

Cracking the bones in his neck, Ajos charged forward once more, slamming his entire body into the large outline the machines had made.

As his body collided with the metal, he was sure he heard a creak.

There was hope yet.

Between his efforts and that of the machines, maybe, just maybe he could save the females this time.

Maybe, just maybe, he'd be successful this time.

As Ajos backtracked a few steps, the huge commander took his position and charged forward to hit the same spot.

There was another creak.

As Xul backtracked, one of his team members crouched and sprung forward and against the structure, hitting the same spot.

A look passed between them and there was agreement.

To his right, Ajos heard a hum, and he looked to see V'Alen charging his systems.

"Follow Ajos. We'll force it open," Xul said. "Whatever it takes, get the females out. They are the priority. We'll deal with that signal later."

V'Alen shot forward, his cybernetic limbs carrying him quickly as he slammed his body into the hold.

There was another creak.

They could do this.

"Crank the robots up to full power. Overload their systems!" Ajos shouted before charging forward again.

The ache that filled his bones from crashing his body against the metal was nothing.

He could deal with temporary pain. He could always heal himself. What he couldn't do was breathe life into those who'd lost it and if they didn't get inside the structure, that's exactly what would happen.

"Oxygen levels are critical," the Arois said. "Their panic grows."

A strained cry left the lips of one of the humans as she fell to her knees. "No."

Her cheeks became wet—something that possibly meant she was so overcome with emotion she was losing control of her bodily fluids.

It only renewed Ajos' vigor.

Once, twice, three times, he slammed his body into the side of the stasis hold.

May the gods of Tonvuhiri be on his side.

May they hear his plea.

He'd begged them only once before, and they'd denied him, but may they grant him this one thing.

It felt like minutes passed as they took turns slamming their bodies into the side of the hold, and as his shoulders ached and Ajos charged forward once more, he hit the side of the hold with all his might.

Gravity gave and he lost his balance as a part of the hold bent inward.

Triumph.

But they couldn't celebrate yet.

He didn't need to hear the cries of encouragement as he squeezed his body through the opening. The metal pressed against him, cutting into his skin, but as before, he ignored the pain as he forced himself into the hold.

It was dark but his eyes didn't take long to adjust. The only lights were the dim blue strips that ran along each pod's perimeter.

And there were many of them.

V'Alen had been right.

Over two stleks.

So many trapped humans.

In the back of his mind, he was aware that V'Alen had also managed to enter the hold.

Glancing behind him, he caught the eyes of Xul.

The female with the pale filaments on her head rushed by the commander's side.

"Please," she begged. "Please do everything you can."

Ajos jerked his head in confirmation even as the female began squeezing through the hole as well.

Time was ticking.

V'Alen was already at a pod, his systems scanning the code pad to crack the key that would unlock the device.

Within seconds, V'Alen's integrated AI returned a result.

"Code X—▸□ (ex -ash zim por)," V'Alen said, as he punched in the code. The cover of the pod he unlocked began to retract as V'Alen moved to another.

The deep inhale of the first female reached Ajos' ears before her scream ripped through the hold.

Qef.

This wasn't how they'd intended to wake these females up.

The pale-filament female rushed to the woman. They'd been adamant about making the transition for the new females as smooth as possible.

Now, it wasn't going to be that way.

He'd wasted enough seconds. With that thought, Ajos moved to the stasis pod closest to him. He didn't even look at the being trapped inside, he just got to work.

X—▸□.

The pod's cover retracted and he barely registered the gasps of the human inside before he moved to another.

X—▸□.

Another.

X—▸□.

He didn't know how many he opened; his only focus was on getting as many of them open as quickly as possible.

On the other side of the dark stasis hold, V'Alen worked even faster than he did, his robotic fingers flying as he entered the code and moved from one stasis pod to another.

When he reached the end of the line and glanced behind him, he realized V'Alen had already opened the last stasis pod on his side and was helping a female to step out of it.

Now, there was only one left to open.

Punching in the code, Ajos focused even as the loud exclamations and screams from the awakened humans filled the stasis hold.

That was expected.

Their planet knew not of life outside their world.

They were like lost infants.

Terrified and unsure.

The code pad below his fingers flashed but nothing happened.

Punching in the code once more, Ajos frowned, urgency making something akin to fear tingle in the pit of his spine.

The code pad flashed again.

Something was not right.

Small five-fingered palms hit against the inside surface of the pod and for the first time, Ajos' gaze moved to the being trapped inside.

Trele!

His life-organ ceased thumping for a few seconds.

Terrified light-brown eyes stared back at him as the female slapped her palms against the pod's transparent lid.

She was shouting something he could not hear, but he didn't need to hear her words to know exactly what she was saying.

Ajos!

It was just like that time.

This was a level of, ixfre—deja-vu—that he had never experienced.

There was fear in the human's eyes.

Raw, unfiltered, terror.

It wasn't over.

In an instant, he was there once again, staring down at Nama.

She'd had that same look in her eyes.

The coincidence...

No.

This was no coincidence. The similarities were too stark.

In the few seconds that passed by, the female before him began to change to a rosy color, her eyes watering.

Losing air.

She was suffocating.

A deep chill settled through his nefre as he punched in the code again, his forefinger trembling.

X—▸□.

Denied.

X—▸□!

DENIED.

"V'Alen!" Ajos' voice carried over the commotion of the newly freed humans, but he did not hear nor see them. Vaguely, he was aware that the rebel fighters that had been stuck on the outside had managed to breach the stasis hold and were also stepping inside to calm the terrified humans.

But he couldn't focus on that.

The only thing he could see was the light-brown eyes of the female before him.

Pleading.

She was pleading with him just as Nama had on that horrible day.

This female didn't know him. She'd never seen his kind before.

Yet, in her shock, he doubted she even realized that she wasn't looking at a human.

The need for survival overrode all of that. This female was begging him to do something to save her.

"V'Alen!" he shouted again.

V'Alen was taking too long.

If he had to smash the pod to bits just to get inside, then so be it.

He didn't know this female, but he couldn't let her down.

Clasping his hands together, he made a double fist that he brought down with force against the pod.

"V'Alen!" Ajos repeated the action, lifting his arms to bring them down in a punch that should shatter the transparent surface.

The female's gaze locked with his, and her eyes became glassy.

As her hands stopped pounding against the surface and fell limp by her sides, time stood still as he watched her eyes close.

No.

"Hold on!" The words tore from his throat.

But her eyes remained closed.

By the Shum'ai gods of Tonvuhiri...NO!

Not again.

2

———————

Ajos wasn't even sure when V'Alen arrived and began interfacing with the stasis pod.

He'd seen him do it before, override circuits with his own input, so he knew the cyborg could do it.

But he could focus on nothing else except the female dying before him.

She was limp...lifeless.

"Hurry!" His voice did not sound like his own.

It sounded like the young male he'd been many moons ago—the one who had let his sister die like the helpless Shum'ai he had been.

Painfully slow seconds passed as he looked down at the female. He pressed his palm against the surface, staring in, and the pod's cover slid partially open.

The mechanism stirred, jerking a little, but the hatch would open no farther.

Qef.

He couldn't let that deter him.

With all his might, Ajos braced his entire weight on the lid, pushing against it.

The muscles in his arms screamed and the tendons in his neck tensed with the effort. With a roar, he pushed the lid fully open.

Without a pause, Ajos reached inside the pod to take hold of the female. His life organ was hammering against his chest as he reached in, and at that first contact, the organ skipped a few beats before regaining its rhythm.

She was soft...so incredibly soft. He hadn't expected that.

He noted immediately that she wasn't as small as the humans he'd met before—this one's limbs were longer—but she was not nearly as sturdy as a Shum'ai female either.

Even in the urgency to have her regain consciousness, he could feel how delicate she was in his arms.

Breakable.

He could feel there was no strength in her bones—as if one wrong move and he could snap her in two.

Someone handed him a breathing apparatus, he wasn't sure who, and he slipped it over the female's face and activated the device.

The seconds that ticked by felt like hours, and in that time, there was no change.

She was still limp.

Still lifeless.

Moving quickly but with care, Ajos lifted the female from the stasis pod and into his arms like something he was afraid to hold too tight.

Stooping to the floor, he held her against him as he placed a palm to the back of her neck.

What was he thinking? She had no nefre.

He knew nothing about human physiology, so he had no idea how else he could check the female's life force.

Seconds ticked by as he held his breath, searching her neck for the pulse of her life-organ.

Nothing.

He could feel nothing, and even with the breathing apparatus, she wasn't stirring.

Panic gripped him, Nama's face swimming before his eyes, and Ajos gripped the female tighter, willing her to wake up.

Still nothing.

He was just about to remove the breathing apparatus and

perform resuscitation on his own when V'Alen spoke.

He had forgotten his comrade was there. He had forgotten everything that was happening around him.

The stasis hold...the screams and cries of the other humans...it had all melted away.

"She is breathing," his comrade said, but even to Ajos, who was so close to the female, it didn't seem that way.

"You are positive?"

"Yes. I can sense her airflow." V'Alen paused. "Initial scans tell me the female is in a state of unconsciousness, possibly as a result of the low oxygen." V'Alen's gaze probed the human. "It was not enough to cause permanent harm. No cerebral damage detected. She should revive soon."

Ajos jerked his head in confirmation. He trusted V'Alen. His comrade had resources he didn't, and he was sure V'Alen was right.

"The signal," V'Alen suddenly said, "it has stopped."

Ajos met his friend's gaze.

"Since when?"

"Since just a moment ago."

"Is everything all right?" The human with the pale filaments, Athena, rushed over. Her gaze locked on the female in his arms.

"Is she..."

The female was so limp in his arms, he knew exactly what Athena was thinking.

"She lives."

Athena released a breath.

"Thank God," she said. "So far, we've had no casualties."

Xul moved up behind his mate, his gaze set on V'Alen.

"The signal?" he asked.

"It has ceased."

Their gazes crossed, and Ajos saw the unease in the back of the commander's eyes.

"Maybe it was just an alarm because we broke into the hold?" his mate asked.

"Maybe," the commander replied, but his gaze said something else.

They all knew—him, V'Alen, the commander—the signal was much more than a simple alarm.

It was a beacon.

As soon as they cleared out the humans, they had to deal with whatever the signal had hailed.

It should strike fear into him, but this was the life he had chosen —or rather, the life the gods had chosen for him.

Turning his attention back to the female in his arms, Ajos was vaguely aware of the others moving off to help the rest of the rescued humans.

It felt as if he was in another space as he looked down at the small creature cradled against him.

His gaze moved over the female's pale skin to land on the streaked filaments that fell across her face. They were a mixture of light strands mixed in with dark ones, a bit wavy, and falling down her shoulders.

His people were fur-less, but it seemed all humans possessed a mass of filaments on their crowns, based on the few he'd met.

Tentatively, he moved a finger forward to brush the strands away from the female's face.

A small mouth was revealed, resting underneath an even smaller, pointed nose.

She didn't resemble Nama in the least...yet...the look that had been in her eyes...

That memory was burned into his brain.

Running a finger across the female's cheek, Ajos brushed away a few more stray strands and gazed upon the female.

Her skin felt like flower petals underneath his fingertips. Soft and easily broken.

He'd never touched a human before to realize this. Were they all this soft?

He was almost afraid to touch her. A delicate creature she was...

Sure, he'd been around the other humans that had been rescued first, long before they'd been able to open the stasis hold, but never had he been this close to one.

They were all mated, after all; betrothed to other members of the

Restitution, and he would never disrespect his brothers in such a way.

One of them was even carrying a fighter's young.

The female's breaths picked up a little and Ajos released the tension that had set his shoulders rigid.

His throat moved as he swallowed hard, unaware that he'd been holding himself so rigidly, waiting for some sign of life within the female's limp form.

Her mouth opened slightly with a breath and as Ajos removed the transparent breathing apparatus, he found himself tensing for a whole other reason.

She was beautiful. Perfectly formed and delicate.

It had been many moons since he'd been this close to a female, even one of his kind. He had not allowed himself the pleasure.

To be holding one so close now...

Something stirred within him, but now was not the time.

He should put her down.

She would wake soon and probably scream in terror if she found herself in his arms.

However, as he made to move, a soft voice had him frozen mid-motion.

"Don't leave me."

Ajos' eyes widened, his gaze moving to the female's lips.

She'd spoken. He was sure of it.

"Don't leave me...please."

A plea.

Ajos blinked, his gaze moving from the female to the chaos around them.

He should put her down. But...

Eyes falling back to the female, he settled on his haunches, his gaze moving over her features.

More strands of her strange filaments had fallen over her face, and he brushed them away with his finger.

She was soft. Warm.

He could stay for a little while.

Maybe he could hold her for just a bit longer.

3

She should have known something was out of the ordinary when she twisted in her sleep and encountered hardness.

"Goddamnit," Kerena mumbled, her voice muffled by the hard thing she was pressed against.

Blasted mahogany.

She had to get rid of this old chest of drawers. It had been a mistake putting it so close to her bed.

Somehow, she always managed to hit her head against it when she had particularly restless nights, and this was one of those nights.

Annoyed, she tried to snuggle farther into the warmth so she could return to sleep.

Her sheets smelled good. Like fresh winter air. So much so that she inhaled deeply and groaned.

Well, she *had* used that new fabric softener she'd bought. She'd have to look at the scent and write it down.

She'd been in such haste as the supermarket, she'd just grabbed the nearest bottle.

But whatever it was, this scent was utterly relaxing.

Snuggling farther into the warmth, Kerena stretched out her arm for her blanket, but her fingers grasped air.

Kerena groaned.

No doubt Cindy Clawford had pulled it off her in the night.

Her Maine Coon had the attitude of a supermodel—hence her name—and she seemed to be of the idea that the double bed was hers and that Kerena was the one who had the habit of sleeping in it.

That darned cat.

The bed was warm, but the air felt chilly. She needed that blanket! She wanted to snuggle and get a few more minutes in before she had to head to work.

Note to self: Lock the bedroom door before you go to sleep. DO NOT open it! No matter how Cindy begs and paws at the door at five A-frickin'-M. You are the boss! Not the cat!

The sound of screams and a lot of noise also slammed into her consciousness all of a sudden.

That darned cat probably turned the TV on again.

Don't ask her how Cindy did it; she just did. Cats did what they wanted *when* they wanted.

You know, if she sat and thought about it, Cindy owned the apartment and she was the cat's roommate.

"Cindyyyy," Kerena groaned again.

"Nee wekda ji nee foofre xiteeklu."

Huh?

That didn't sound like Cindy at all.

She kind of had a deep meow for a female cat, but her arguments never sounded like actual words before—regardless if it came across as utter gibberish.

God, she must be extremely tired.

Granted, she had been putting in a lot of work at the lab.

Going in early, leaving late, and repeat days of overtime. Maybe she'd overdone it.

With a huge sigh and another curse, Kerena squeezed her eyes tight.

Even her bed felt hard, not just the dresser she was pressed against.

Yep, her body was protesting. And not only her body, but her mind as well.

She'd been having the weirdest nightmare—one straight out of an experiment gone wrong.

She'd left the lab a little later than usual, but she'd headed straight home instead of picking up a meal at the 24/7 McDonald's near her apartment. She hadn't been far from home when she'd seen a huge alligator.

And get this—as if seeing an alligator in the middle of the city wasn't strange enough—it had been standing on two legs...and it had been holding a gun.

She'd laugh if it hadn't felt so real, it'd been terrifying.

Groaning, she cursed underneath her breath again.

Her sleep was broken. There was no falling back into the clutches of much-needed rest.

She was awake.

Fuck that useless dresser. She knew she shouldn't have bought it at that yard sale. Her friend was the one who'd talked her into it.

Moving to California with nothing, they'd both tried to save as much as they could on almost everything.

LA was an expensive city and the huge pharmaceutical company they worked for paid two months behind.

It'd been tough starting up life in the City of Angels, but it was going to be worth it in the long run.

Yawning, she froze.

Wait a minute.

The dresser wasn't by her bedside anymore.

She'd moved it two days ago because of the same problem of bumping her head into it at night.

Frowning now, Kerena squinted as she opened her eyes.

Her vision was blurry, but not blurry enough for her not to notice that her face wasn't pressed into mahogany.

Instead, she was snuggled against something the color of mint mixed with teal.

Huh?

"Nee wekda ji nee foofre xiteeklu."

The...fuck?

The voice was male, not Maine Coon, and it was coming from above her.

Stiffening, Kerena didn't want to look up.

"Ji kludanee nee."

No.

It couldn't be.

The dream...

It was coming back to her now.

Vividly.

So vividly, it felt as if her soul was slowly leaving her body.

Waking up in a casket, a see-through casket.

The panic that flooded her not knowing where she was or what was happening.

The dull sound of screams and shrieks on the outside of the casket.

The sudden realization she was finding it hard to breathe.

Not being able to get up, not being able to escape...

Then the face...

Taking care not to make any sudden movements or move her head, Kerena looked upward and terror filled her soul.

That same face was above her, and golden eyes locked with hers.

Blinking, she couldn't move—*refused* to, as if keeping still would make her disappear.

The man looking down at her was *not* human.

That thought registered quickly.

Minty-teal skin. Golden eyes that shone from a sclera that was the same color as the person's skin.

This...was not real.

She was still dreaming, right?

She'd dreamt about aliens before, but this one looked so...*real.* And handsome.

Whenever she'd dreamt about aliens before, the little green men looked nothing like this green man she was seeing now.

They were all big heads and huge dark eyes—you know, the way they drew them in cartoons.

Such a simple description could not describe the alien in front of her now.

His irises alone were rich, like spun gold.

Minty-teal leathery skin covered every inch of his body she could see—even his lips.

Firm cheekbones, a strong jaw, a straight nose...his face was mostly humanlike.

But his head...

Apart from the fact that no hair covered his crown, there were two protrusions on either side of his head and they seemed to run to the back, leading from his temples. They were pale yellow and the only thing that broke the uniform color of his minty-teal skin.

Her hand moved in her peripheral vision as she frowned at the alien looking down at her.

Her fingers touched the alien's cheek and he jerked away a little, his gaze registering shock as he stared back at her.

For a few moments, he did nothing.

Instead, he kept staring at her as if expecting her to scream and run away. Then, when it seemed he realized she wasn't about to do that, he leaned toward her outstretched palm.

His skin was like soft leather and her mouth fell open a little as she stared at the contrast between her hand and his cheek.

His skin was such rich minty-teal, it seemed like body paint or something.

Blinking several times, Kerena slowly became aware that there was some sort of commotion around her.

Screaming, crying, words of comfort, orders being shouted—and words she couldn't understand.

Turning her head, she looked across the room.

It wasn't her TV that was on.

Well, duh!

She wasn't in her room as she'd thought.

There were several people close by. Women. Some on the floor, some standing, but the general similarity was that they all looked terrified.

But that wasn't what made her eyes widen.

There were...*beings*...even more aliens and different ones from the one that held her—she was realizing—*in...his...arms.*

"What—" Kerena began, and the arms that held her tightened a little.

This was some kind of costume party, wasn't it?

Had to be.

Though, the guy across the room that dressed like C3PO definitely went all out on his costume.

How much did he pay for that?

"Klufoo kluer oh freem kluer neejiem," the man that held her said.

Kerena's eyes widened some more.

This one was even talking gibberish to sound like an alien.

Yet...his costume was so...*lifelike.*

Man?

Alien?

She wasn't sure now.

If this was a lucid dream...it was really, *really* convincing. She hadn't even known she could imagine an alien language that sounded so...*real*—as if the alien was actually saying something of meaning.

"Ajos!" A blonde woman rushed forward. "You've been over here for a while. Is she all right?"

The woman stooped down. "Oh, she's awake!"

Kerena was mildly aware that the woman was touching her cheek and turning her head so she could look at her face.

"She looks ok. You removed the oxygen mask. She didn't need it anymore?"

"Neg. Er er negelde. Wek fre frede erix fre quwekix qu oh freix ji elix," the man, or alien, or alien-man said.

"Yes, but that could just be her way of processing this. Most of the others are hysterical, but we'd prepared for that. Maybe she is the type that doesn't spook easily."

Okay. None of this made sense.

Weren't dreams supposed to be manifestations of her subconscious? It didn't feel as if she was in control of any of this.

You know what, time to wake up.

Squeezing her eyes shut, Kerena willed herself to wake, but when she opened her eyes again, they were met with the same golden eyes of the being that held her.

Fear began crawling up her spine.

Again.

Try again.

So she tried again.

But no matter how many times she closed then opened her eyes, the being before her always came back into view.

She never woke up in her bed. Cindy Clawford wasn't by her feet hogging the blanket...

"No," she managed to utter.

As she tried to scramble away, she almost fell to the floor, and she would have if it weren't for the strong arms that held her.

"Er be' ee. Wek neg negix el ji enerfooel elqu negfre."

Kerena's eyes shot to the alien.

"It's okay. I know this is a lot to take in, but try to remain calm. Just try to focus on me," the blonde woman said. "We'll explain everything to you soon."

The woman's words made her pull her terrified gaze away from the male that held her.

"Wh—where am I?" Kerena's eyes darted from the woman back to the alien leaning over her—and the more her brain came online, the more terrified she became.

He looked too real to be a figment of her imagination.

It wasn't a costume.

This...was...real.

"You're on the Restitution's base. You are safe," the blonde woman answered.

"The what?"

"The Restitution. I know you don't know what that means, but the alliance is the only reason you're alive." The woman glanced at the... the *alien.* "It's the reason we all are alive."

She'd heard her the first time, but the second time didn't make it any clearer.

She turned the words over in her head.

The Restitution.

It sounded like a military base.

And the alien...

Area 51?

How the hell did she end up in Nevada?

Looking down at herself, she frowned even more.

She was dressed in the exact outfit she'd been wearing when she'd left work—a short sleeveless dress and her boots. They'd taken her on her way from work and brought her to Nevada?

And all the rumors about them hiding aliens...those rumors were real?

What kind of government bullshi—The fuck did she get herself into?! And how?

The only thing she could think of was the fact that she worked for one of the biggest bioengineering companies in the US. They conducted classified experiments the government might have been interested in.

But she was a botanist!

What did they need her for? Man-eating alien plants?

She wasn't a part of the secret experiments she knew the company she worked for conducted. Her work comprised the more "ethical" experiments on which the company built its name and which the public knew about.

This didn't make any sense!

The blonde woman had fierce eyes but a kind smile. She looked like the type of person who told it as it was. Possibly the type of person she could trust.

"I—" Kerena licked her lips and tried to keep her gaze from sliding back to the alien. "I don't understand."

The woman smiled.

"I know. First, let me introduce myself. My name is Athena."

"Okay, Athena." Kerena licked her lips again before her eyes darted to the tall mint-colored alien once more. "I'm Kerena."

The alien's golden eyes were still on her, and it didn't take her long to realize he'd been watching the movement of her tongue against her lips.

"Um, Athena..." she whispered. "I don't know if you noticed but... I think there's an alien holding me in his arms." She paused. "Tell me I'm wrong."

Athena's shoulders rose and fell in a low chuckle before a sad smile twisted her lips.

"I don't know how to break this to you, so I'm just going to come out and say it."

Kerena froze. Those were not the words that usually came before good news.

"You were abducted..."

Everything within her stopped moving. She was sure even her heart stopped beating for a few seconds.

"And..." Athena continued.

Wait, there was more?

"There's no way of going back home."

4

———

KERENA STARED AT ATHENA, WILLING THE WOMAN TO SMILE AND POINT some finger guns at her in a "gotcha" moment, but that didn't happen.

Instead, Athena seemed guarded, as if she was waiting for her response to the news.

Kerena's gaze darted back to the alien and then to the many people, humans and obvious aliens alike, who were in the room.

"Look..." she said as she tried to rise, but the arms around her wouldn't budge.

Turning her gaze to the alien, Kerena frowned slightly.

"Can you, uh," she gulped, "can you put me down?"

Holy fuck, she was speaking to an alien!

Lock that up and put it in the safe for later deliberation, Kerena.

"Oh negklu negji neg negix erix. Er fre fredenigr neg ix oh neg."

Okay. She hoped her captors had free dictionaries because she was going to need one.

Turning her questioning gaze to Athena, Kerena raised her eyebrows a little.

"Oh, I keep forgetting you all don't have translators yet." Athena gave an apologetic smile. "He said that you were without oxygen for a little and he is afraid to let you go lest you collapse," the woman translated.

"I won't collapse." Kerena motioned to the floor. "Please, put me down."

The alien's hairless eyebrows moved a little as he set her on her feet, and his gaze was wary as he eyed her.

Not a second passed before a bout of dizziness passed through her.

Maybe she'd overestimated herself.

She must have swayed because the alien's huge hands were quick to steady her.

A little nonplussed by the alien's contact, Kerena took a deep breath.

"Th-Thank you." She blinked rapidly as she stared into the alien's chest.

Shouldn't she be terrified right now? Panicked?

Was it strange that what she was feeling wasn't fear, but confusion?

"You said I was...abducted?" She needed answers. That would determine how she should feel about this.

Athena nodded. "Unfortunately."

"But you said there's no way to go home?"

Athena nodded again.

The woman paused as if waiting for her to ask more questions. As a matter of fact, both Athena and the alien beside her seemed guarded.

They were looking at her as if waiting for something to happen.

Kerena frowned and wrapped her arms around herself.

She suddenly felt cold, and she wasn't sure if it was because of the atmosphere or if it was the fact that she had woken up in this distressing situation.

"I mean..." She focused on the woman, trying her best not to let her eyes drift to the tall alien standing beside her. Maybe if she didn't look at him, she could pretend an extra-terrestrial wasn't standing RIGHT...FRICKIN'...BESIDE HER.

Clearing her throat, Kerena continued, "I live in California. That's like, right beside Nevada... Surely, after this government experiment or whatever this is, I'll be allowed to return to my normal life...right?"

Something within Athena's countenance fell...something that made a sickly feeling develop in Kerena's stomach.

"We're not on Earth anymore." Athena's voice was calm and measured, as if she'd had to say those same words several times.

"We're...what?" Kerena held herself tighter.

It wasn't like her to ignore the data in front of her, so she guessed she had to face it.

As Athena remained silent, giving her space to process what she'd said, Kerena's gaze moved from the woman to the alien standing beside them, then to the rest of the room.

The several aliens...the distressed females...

"You're serious..." Kerena whispered and Athena's pause then nod almost made her belly bottom out.

Kerena stood in disbelief as she fought to comprehend and accept this reality.

"I must say," Athena said, "you're taking this news well."

In another situation, she would have said, "Sike!" But there was no time for her to say anything before her legs gave out from beneath her.

If not for the alien's quick movements, she would have fallen to the floor.

"Bring her over here."

Athena's voice blended into a new series of cries that echoed in the room. Someone else was freaking out.

"Neg, wek freix erix fre quwekix qu uufrewek ix nee wek freix," the mint-colored alien spoke, his voice a deep vibration as he lifted her effortlessly.

He took her in his arms, cradling her like something precious, as he rested her on what she assumed was a gurney.

She wasn't sure if it was one because the thing was floating mid-air, it seemed, on its own.

As he put her down, his hand settled on her midsection and Kerena realized only then that she was trembling.

Shock.

This only happened when she became too overwhelmed.

She was having an episode.

One breath in and another one out.

The alien moved something toward her that looked like two small bicycle handlebars connected to a V-shaped transparent piece and Kerena pulled away from the device.

"It's an oxygen mask," the blonde said, but Kerena only shook her head.

She didn't need an oxygen mask. She just needed to calm down.

One breath in and another one out.

She repeated this to herself as she took huge breaths in through her nose and exhaled through her mouth.

"Esfre er wek negde?"

"It's a breathing exercise," Athena replied. "It helps to calm us down."

"Negix elfre ixji neg?" the alien asked, and Kerena's gaze darted to him.

There was a skeptical look on his face, but concern in his eyes.

"Yes," Athena answered. "It works. Trust me. Just give her a few seconds."

It dawned on her then that the woman could understand the alien.

"Wait," she spoke between breaths. "You can understand him? *How*?"

Athena tapped the back of her ear and turned slightly so Kerena could see. There was an almost imperceptibly raised area there, about half a millimeter across.

"Translator implant," Athena said. "You and the others will each get one."

Kerena's gaze moved to the other people in the room. Several of the human women were huddled in groups on the floor.

"Many of us were taken," Athena spoke up. "You are not alone."

"I don't understand how this happened..."

Athena smiled again. "We'll explain everything to you. It's a wild story, though. Might take some time."

Another tremor went through her and the three-fingered hand of the alien pressed against her gently, as if to steady her.

Kerena froze, her gaze locked unto the contact as she processed the feelings within her.

Don't freak out. Don't freak out.

"Neg neg ix fredenigr. Er fre neg ekde oh erix."

Kerena blinked, not understanding.

"He said you shouldn't be afraid. He's not leaving your side," Athena translated.

As Kerena looked up at the alien, she was slightly taken aback by the intensity of his gaze.

His words were comforting...

So why was it that, deep down, she was still terrified?

AJOS STARED AT THE FEMALE.

Keh-reh-nah was her name.

Contrary to what he'd thought, his proximity didn't seem to be freaking her out as much as he'd thought it would.

She hadn't screamed.

She hadn't tried to run away.

And...

She'd touched him.

Of her own accord, she'd laid her hand against his skin.

The faint brush of her fingers against his cheek was still there like the touch of a phantom and now that she was no longer in his arms, he felt a strange loss that was as irrational as the fact that he was still standing by her side.

He was frowning at this particular thought when V'Alen glanced his way.

His cybernetic ally was speaking to Xul, who jerked his head when Ajos caught his gaze.

They wanted to speak to him.

That prompted another confusing feeling, and Ajos moved his gaze back to the female.

She was looking around the stasis hold, her gaze widening ever so slightly with each passing moment. Still, she didn't react with hysterics the way Athena had briefed them most of the humans would behave.

His gaze moved over her face and he realized he didn't want to move from where he stood.

This irrationality was surprising, and it made his brow dive toward his nose.

"Ajos," Xul took a step toward them and paused, "a moment."

Jerking his head in confirmation, Ajos' gaze never left the female before him.

Keh-reh-nah was looking at him now, those brown pools of hers moving over every inch of his face and for the first time in all his years, he wondered the silliest and vain thought he'd ever had in his life.

Does she think I'm strange-looking? Hideous?

The female continued to study him.

...Handsome?

His shoulders stiffened as he regarded her.

She probably didn't understand him, but he spoke anyway.

"I will be back," he said, wondering at the same time why he was telling her that, before he forced his legs to move.

Xul's voice was low as he approached, but Ajos still caught some words the commander spoke to V'Alen.

"...before we could terminate that signal." Xul looked his way.

"The signal?" Ajos asked.

"It terminated on its own, but I suspect," V'Alen lowered his voice, "that it has already reached its target."

"It was a beacon," Ajos said, and he could feel a coldness settle over the room.

A beacon that had most likely transmitted their exact location.

A full-on attack from the High Tasqals was something they always feared and something they'd learned to live with. But with rebels manning the heavens, they would alert everyone on the ground in time for them to escape.

Still, an attack wasn't something that anyone wanted to happen. Life on the base was...good.

Safe.

However, they still had to take precautions.

"We must alert the sky towers," he said. "Put them on high alert. If anything is out of the ordinary, we need to investigate." Ajos glanced around. "Today has been a strange day."

"If the stasis hold transmitted the location of the lost humans, the Tasqals will retaliate," V'Alen said. "There is an eighty-five percent chance of that."

Ajos swallowed hard.

The problem with V'Alen was that he was usually right in his calculations.

This was horrible news.

So many beings within the stasis hold, and a whole population of other beings on the base itself.

So many lives were in danger.

Xul became silent, and when Ajos looked at him, he realized the male was staring at his mate. There was something in the male's eyes that he'd never seen in the many years that he'd known him.

The commander feared what this would mean.

Ajos' gaze flicked to the human he'd rescued, the one who'd told him not to leave her, and he found her brown eyes on him.

There was a feeling within him, fueled by the intensity of her gaze.

If the signal had indeed transmitted their location, the entire base was in danger.

She was in danger.

And possibly, it was his past experiences still haunting him, or maybe this was some cruel plan of the creators, but he had the urge to do all he could to save this strange being.

This Keh-reh-nah...

To do all he could to protect her.

5

For the next few minutes, or it could have been a full hour—
she didn't know—the noise level within the strange chamber slowly
receded.

There was still some sobbing from a few of the women. Kerena
even saw a dark-haired lady who'd crawled behind one of the stasis
pods and refused to come out.

For the first few minutes, she'd tried to find a familiar face, but
she knew none of these people. Every single one of them was a
stranger.

Of the entire group, though, four women seemed to work along-
side the aliens.

Those four were all dressed in similar outfits: dark trousers and
white tops.

Despite the chaos, there was still some organization there with
the females in black and white seeming to be running the operation.

That made little sense. Had Athena been lying about them not
being on Earth?

Why would aliens abduct us then have us order them around?

There was a huge alien with horns, one with blue skin and long
white hair, and the C3PO—and they were passively observing.

For the most part, they didn't interact with the humans.

Instead, they allowed the women in the black and white to take charge.

That's when she let her gaze wander to her side.

The minty-teal alien was still by the gurney. He'd surprised her when he'd returned to stand beside her, and she didn't know what to think of it.

Should she be concerned or was this his post and she was the one in the wrong spot?

As her gaze moved from his torso and went higher, she had to tilt her head a little so she could look at him.

He was tall—possibly the tallest person in the room—and she knew that for a fact because she was a solid six feet and he would tower over her if she stood.

He was dressed in a pale-colored shirt and dark pants. There was a sort of crude leather armor that protected his shoulders and upper arms, sort of like what she'd expect gladiators to wear minus the chest plate.

A three-fingered hand grasped a wicked-looking spear by his side, and she noticed that the same pale yellow that colored the protrusions on his temples was also present on his palm.

As her gaze moved downward, she almost fell off the gurney as she reached his legs. That's when she noticed he was standing on entirely alien feet.

He was barefoot and two-toed. Balancing on the balls of his feet, he looked like he was standing in seven-inch heels, only without the actual heels.

He had hooves—that's the closest thing she could compare them to.

It was impolite to stare, but as her gaze moved upward once more, she knew her eyes shone with marvel.

He was...absolutely magnificent.

He stood now, leaning against the wall but unlike the other aliens, who were keeping their distance and trying, she supposed, to appear as non-threatening as possible, this guy didn't seem to get the memo.

After all, he wasn't keeping away from her. If she reached out, she could easily touch him.

As her gaze reached his face, the alien's golden eyes held on to hers.

They were captivating, and it was incredibly difficult to look away.

They were reptilian, yet not. Humanlike, yet not.

As she stared, it took her more than a few moments to realize that he wasn't looking away.

Why was he looking at her so...so intensely?

Her mouth fell open as she finally pulled her gaze away.

Slipping off the other side of the gurney and away from him, she adjusted her dress and tried not to glance behind her. However, thanks to her peripheral vision, she could see the blurry outline of the alien as he leaned off the wall at her movement.

Maybe he thought she was going to fall again and was just making sure she didn't introduce her face to the floor.

With a deep breath, she tried to ignore him and moved over to one of the cryogenic pods.

Her hand trembled slightly as she touched the pod's surface.

"So, this is a cryogenic chamber..." she murmured, more to herself than to anyone else in the room. It felt strange touching the thing.

It felt even stranger that she had been inside one.

The craftsmanship was impeccable, the curves a little too smooth. She didn't know what it was, but something about the way they made the device caused it to look unearthly. Alien.

A few companies back on Earth were experimenting with such pods, with the first person being put to sleep way back in 1967. There were even people who paid to be frozen and preserved, but as far as she knew, the thawing process was still a work in progress.

This technology, however, was already leagues above Earth's.

After all, if all this was true and she wasn't on some prank show, they'd frozen and thawed her with no complications—she hoped!

With another few steps, she reached a large group of the rescued women huddled together on the floor. Athena's voice rang out in the chamber.

"Now, that everyone is settled enough to listen, we're going to answer your questions. You've taken this all pretty well so far and I have to say, I'm surprised. This isn't easy to digest." She took a breath. "However, outside, there are many more than, Xul, Yce, Ajos, and V'Alen here." She jerked her head toward the aliens and the robot.

A bout of murmuring ensued and Kerena looked toward the three aliens who stood together.

Was it just her or did they seem...tense?

Possibly, the humans weren't the only ones who were under stress.

"The Restitution has instructed that all non-humans clear out this section of the base. However, I'm pretty sure you will see more than a few other beings as we transition from this room and you take your first steps on alien soil," Athena continued.

"Sounds like a frickin' vacation ad," someone murmured and Kerena almost chuckled.

"You mean there are more aliens out there?" A woman with short curly hair spoke up. Her eyes shone as if the prospect excited her, to which some of the females around her looked positively disturbed.

Athena nodded. "Yes...there are *several* other species of aliens out there."

Of course, there were. Kerena had expected as much. In this room alone there were three different species of alien, maybe four if she counted the robot guy.

She wasn't quite sure if he was a robot or a man in a suit.

A string of questions rang out as the women began murmuring and anxiety grew thick in the air.

"How did we get here?"

"And how do we get back home?"

"Are the aliens dangerous?"

The questions kept coming and Athena raised a hand to quiet the group.

"I will try to answer as many of your questions as possible. But for now, I will give you a quick breakdown of what has happened to you...to *us*." She motioned to the other three women wearing the same type of clothes as her.

They all stood at the front of the chamber now, close to what looked like a hole in the wall.

Athena continued. "A few months ago, I and four other women woke up on an alien ship." There was dead silence. The woman suddenly had everyone's attention. "Five members of the Restitution rescued us. Two members of that team are here today. Xul..." she motioned to the alien with horns, "...and Yce." She motioned to the alien with long white hair and frickin' glowing eyes.

"We destroyed the alien ship. We didn't know there were more of us, but the guys had a hunch. So they went back looking for any signs of a stasis hold in the wreckage, and that's when they found you." There were a few gasps and more murmuring. "The stasis hold, *this hold*," she motioned around them, "was built to survive such crashes and we knew you were safe. We only had to try to get you out, which we managed to do today without any repercussions."

The aliens glanced at each other and, once again, Kerena got the feeling that they were tense—or hiding something.

She hoped it wasn't the latter.

Kerena moved her gaze to the group of women around her.

Most were young or looked of similar age as her. There were only a few women who looked more mature. There was nothing that was distinctly similar between them.

Except...

"Why are there only women?" The question spilled out of Kerena's mouth almost immediately. When some of the women turned to look her way, she gathered her composure and continued. "Is there a cryogenic hold containing men as well?"

Athena's gaze darted to the alien with horns that she'd referred to as Xul, and when the woman's shoulders stiffened a little, Kerena knew she would not like the answer.

"Flelix elix neg ji." A deep voice spoke from so close to her, she jumped.

She hadn't realized the minty-teal alien had moved to stand by her or that he'd been so close.

Either she didn't feel threatened by him or her instincts were dull as hell.

Craning her neck, she looked up at him. At the same time, she could hear the females around her shuffling away.

He looked imposing, so that didn't surprise her.

"I'm sorry, I can't understand." He was speaking a language that sounded like utter gibberish to her. She knew that wasn't the case, but every word sounded alike to her ears. And it wasn't because he was speaking something alien either. She'd always been shit at languages. She was barely competent in her mother tongue, English, much less something foreign...er, *alien*.

"What did he say?" she asked.

"He said," the robot began, "there were no men on board."

Whispering ensued, but Kerena didn't miss a beat.

Her gaze zoomed in on the robot and it felt as if she was looking into the eyes of the most advanced AI in the universe.

"You...you speak English?"

In her peripheral vision, she saw Athena and the other women exchange glances.

The robot's face showed no emotion. Only a slight nod told her he understood her question. "I do. The human language designated as Een-Glish has been uploaded to the servers. Every being on the base now knows your language."

That caused a lot of murmuring, and Kerena's eyebrows shot up a little.

"So, everyone can understand us?" she asked, her gaze moving to the minty-teal alien. "*You* can understand me?"

"Ix." He was still looking down at her and, for some reason, his strange golden eyes made her feel...calm.

She guessed that meant "yes."

She looked back at the robot guy. "I don't understand. How can you speak English, but he can't then?"

"I am an artificially enhanced life form," the robot answered. "I can do many things that others cannot." He paused. "I was very... excited to meet a new species from a Class Four planet so far away— one that holds such similar biological characteristics to my people." He paused again and Kerena realized it was so quiet, a pin could drop and the sound would ring in the air. "My name is V'Alen. I am told I must say it is a pleasure meeting you, though I feel no such emotion."

That made Kerena stiffen a little, but the robot guy, V'Alen, didn't appear hostile.

"What do you feel then?" It was the curly-haired woman again. Her eyes were wide as she looked at the robot, but it wasn't fear in her gaze, it was utter admiration.

The robot's gaze slid to the curly-haired lady.

"Interest," he said. "I am delighted by the prospect of the data our interactions will bring."

Kerena's brows shot up even farther.

Depending on how one looked at what the robot said, he could either be saying he was an ally or he could be their worst enemy.

Most people didn't trust AI even on Earth. *I, Robot* kind of made people super nervous about humanoid robots.

But this was amazing.

However, it was clear some of the other women didn't think so.

Someone started saying prayers, and another woman burst into tears and began talking about the apocalypse.

Despite that, she hadn't forgotten where the conversation had been going before the robot dropped those bombs.

"Why were there no men on board?" she asked. She watched the women at the front for their reaction, and it seemed that the answer wasn't one they wanted to say outright.

"Foodo ki Tasqals daji teefa laji gahvu teefoo vu dafoo nee foolala," the mint-colored alien growled.

The sound was so chilling, Kerena looked up at him immediately.

The alien's eyes flashed anger as he crossed his arms.

His voice only seemed to make the females huddled on the floor tenser and Kerena had to admit, it was sending a shiver down her spine too—only, she was pretty sure it wasn't fear that led that feeling.

The more time she spent in his presence, the more interesting the alien became.

Her curiosity pushed the feeling away as her gaze darted to Athena and then to the robot. "What did he say?"

Athena seemed to hesitate.

"He said the Tasqals are sick beasts who like to rape—" V'Alen started.

"V'Alen!" Athena cut the robot man off.

But it was too late.

Another wave of cries ensued and Kerena could acknowledge that was the last word anyone wanted to hear.

She didn't need to be a genius to get the drift. There was only one reason she could think of why an alien race would abduct only females.

Still, the robot's unfinished words made her shiver.

Athena had to raise her voice to talk over the noise and bring order back to the group.

"That will *not* happen. Here, you are safe from those hideous beasts' atrocities. But we know it was not your choice to be here. And while I and the others," she motioned to the women close by her again, "have embraced this new life, we know some of you might not want to do the same."

There was murmuring as everyone tried to come to terms with what they were hearing.

"How do we know you're not in on this?" someone asked. "How do we know you and those three women with you are not using us as guinea pigs in some grand scheme of yours?!"

"Yea!" someone else joined in. "I was thinking that! How do we know you aren't working with these *aliens* that abducted us?!"

The women's exclamations caused the group to go crazy. Everyone began whispering, arguments began to form, and there were so many people speaking at once that the noise level grew immediately.

Athena's face fell, the look in her eyes was one of utter heartache, as if the accusation was one that hurt her deeply.

Behind Athena, the alien named Xul looked positively enraged. He stalked forward to stand in front of the Athena, dwarfing her.

"How dare you suggest that my Athena would do such a thing?" Xul looked furious, and his image alone made a hush pass through the group of females before him. "To conspire with such despicable beasts—*scum*—!" He spat the word.

Athena placed a hand on the alien's arm and stepped in front of him once more.

"It's okay, hon." Her voice was low, but in the quietness of the room, it still carried. "They have the right to be suspicious. I would be. It's hard to come to terms with this." She patted his arm. "It's okay."

The large horned alien seemed to relax a little, but his furious gaze was still directed at the woman who'd voiced the opinion first.

Kerena took a deep breath, her eyes moving over the group.

This wasn't a time to throw accusations around, especially when none of them knew what the hell had happened to get them to this place or how to navigate this unknown world.

They all needed more information.

"I think we should all take a few breaths and calm down." Her gaze moved from one woman to the other. "We don't know anything yet and it's best we all try to learn as much as we can before we start making assumptions."

A few of the women nodded.

"She's right," the curly-haired woman said as she ran her hand through her hair. "But they are right too." She motioned to the two suspicious women. "So let's just calm down. No need to get hysterical until we know for sure what the hell we're dealing with here."

There were a few more nods, and Kerena smiled slightly at the curly-haired woman.

"Elfre er erneighborix," the minty-teal alien above her said, and Kerena glanced his way.

She wished she could understand his words.

"What now? Is there no way to go home?" someone asked.

All eyes went back to Athena.

"Unfortunately not," the woman confirmed, raising her voice before the protests began. "For that reason, we give you two choices."

"Choices?" Kerena pulled her gaze away from the alien beside her. She hadn't realized she'd even been staring at him.

Athena sighed and the redhead standing beside her took over.

"You can try to make the most of this new life the Tasqals have thrust us into, or you can choose to go back into cryogenic sleep until they find a way to return to Earth in the future." The redhead was straight to the point.

Kerena appreciated that.

"I want to go back to sleep. Wake me up when we get out of this nightmare!" someone said, to which some others agreed.

The prospect sounded like a good one. But Kerena was a scientist. She knew it wasn't that simple.

It never was.

"And how long will that take? Worst case?" she asked.

V'Alen's eyes flashed. Literally.

"Worst case?" he asked then continued without stopping. "I calculate the worst case would be that you return to your planet after twenty million of your Earth years have passed."

She knew her eyes bugged out, but she couldn't help it. Someone began crying once more.

"What would be the point of that?" Kerena finally asked.

"Fooda," the minty-teal alien said, and despite herself, Kerena smiled inwardly.

She didn't need a translator for that. It sounded as if he agreed with her completely.

"He said, 'Exactly.'" The robot spoke up.

The room became loud once more with protests and cries and Kerena bit on the tip of her finger as she thought about this predicament she'd found herself in.

Twenty million Earth years meant humans might not even exist when, *if*, they made it back to Earth. Everything she knew would be gone. Everyone she knew would have long ceased to exist.

Her mom, her dad...Cindy Clawford!

Her heart suddenly ached for her beloved pet.

Images of the little furball meowing by her bedroom door almost crushed her, and she sagged a little.

Strong arms were quick to support her, but she didn't even need to look up to see who it was.

She knew it was the tall alien.

Her chest heaved with the pain of withheld emotion.

Her poor cat.

She felt like the worst mother, not having thought about Cindy sooner.

She could only hope that her lovely elderly neighbor stopped by to bring her some stew and saw that Cindy was alone. The woman had a key and could get into the apartment without trouble—something her mother had forced her to do should there be an emergency. She wasn't more grateful for that advice than now.

Easing off the huge alien, Kerena swallowed hard.

"Thank you," she murmured to him, and she wasn't sure he even heard her from the noise and cries of the other women around them.

Kerena took a deep breath as she considered the situation.

This wasn't a desirable experience; it was certainly not one she'd ever considered would happen to her, and because of that, she had no backup plan.

BUT, and that was a big but, this was a once-in-a-lifetime experience.

She could approach this in two ways.

She could cower and be afraid, wishing that she could turn back the hands of time and return to her life on Earth.

Or, she could grab this opportunity and make the most of it.

Out of seven billion humans, she was one that had the chance to interact with and possibly even study alien life.

What would the scientists at NASA give to switch spots with her?

"I want the chip," Kerena finally said, talking over the din. "The translator chip. I want it."

Her words brought an instant hush across the group.

"What the hell did she just ask for?" someone murmured.

"I don't know, but I'm not letting them inject me with anything," someone else whispered.

Athena's eyebrows moved up a little before she smiled and nodded. "I was just about to bring that up." The woman turned her gaze to everyone else. "We have translator chips for those who do not wish to go back into cryogenic sleep. The chip is a small device that goes behind your ear. V'Alen here has volunteered to install them, as he is the most capable of doing so."

The robot tilted his head slightly before stepping forward.

"Are you sure?" One of the women touched Kerena's leg before cowering back. Glancing behind her, Kerena realized why. The impossibly tall alien was still there, his eyes now on the woman. He was looking at the woman as if he would slice her hand off for touching her.

Kerena's brows furrowed.

She must be reading that wrong.

Alien emotions. Different facial muscles.

Confused, Kerena pulled her gaze away to answer the cowering woman. "I'm sure." She forced a smile. "I want it."

The curly-haired woman raised her hand. "I want one too. No way I'm going back to that God-forsaken planet. I gladly volunteer to stay. This is too...awesome." She grinned.

Some others murmured that they'd also want to get the chip installed.

As the robot approached, Kerena took a deep breath.

She was going to do this.

What was the point of being around aliens if she couldn't understand them? If this was real, if this was her new life, then she needed all the advantages she could get and communication was central to all of that.

If she was going to advocate for herself, she didn't want information coming to her second-hand.

"Okay." Athena smiled and continued addressing the group. "As V'Alen administers the first chip, I'll just tell you a bit more about the Restitution. I'm pretty sure you have a lot of questions."

As the conversation droned on in the background, the robot spoke as he reached by her.

"This will only hurt a little," he said, and she was sure the minty-teal alien said something in response.

"Yes, Ajos. I will take care. I am aware her skin is fragile and easily broken."

Kerena's eyes darted to the minty-teal alien.

Ajos was his name.

It suited him well.

He was frowning at her skin as V'Alen touched her ear.

He must have noticed the difference in their skin when he'd held her earlier.

Memory of that experience flooded her, and she felt her cheeks warm.

Looking back at it now, her response when she'd initially regained consciousness had been inappropriate.

"I and three other humans are sort of leading this transition, but we don't want you to feel like we're your overlords or anything." Athena's voice pulled Kerena's thoughts away for a moment. "We've just been here longer than you have and have formed relationships with the aliens here. We trust them and we want you to know you can trust them too. My husband and his team have worked really hard to make sure all the females will be comfortable here."

"Husband? I thought you said no men were taken," one woman spoke up immediately.

Athena's cheeks grew pink. "He's not exactly human…"

Oh…

There were more gasps and shocked expressions in the group.

Only the aliens in the room didn't seem surprised by this.

It must be usual out here…in this open universe. Different species must form bonds where it was reproductively possible to. Obviously, Ajos, V'Alen, and Athena's husband were different species. There was biodiversity…an open economy too?

It would make sense.

The cold tips of V'Alen's fingers touched her ear, interrupting her thoughts, and Kerena inhaled sharply.

"Esfre freem oh negde?"

"I have not installed it yet. Patience, brother." The robot turned his gaze to her. "I will install the chip in five, four—"

A sharp pain sprung up at the side of her head that made her yelp in pain.

All eyes turned on her and she realized Ajos stepped between her and V'Alen.

There was a pulsing behind her eyes and it felt as if her head was heating up. But the feeling only lasted for a few seconds.

"I told you to be careful," the minty-teal alien said.

"I was. The deception was necessary. I have logs that humans prefer deceit when being administered medical jabs."

Kerena blinked. She knew exactly what he meant, but how he knew that was a surprise to her.

"I'm okay." At her voice, the minty-teal alien turned. His gaze searched her face even as he ignored the hushed mumbling around them.

As she rubbed the area behind her ear, she could feel the raised surface under her skin.

It only hurt a little. It was more the surprise of it all than the pain that had caused her to yelp.

"Are you sure?"

"Yes." Kerena nodded then froze. "I can understand you," she breathed. She hadn't expected it to work so quickly.

The tall alien took a step forward then, towering over her.

There were more whispers and a few gasps.

But despite that, Kerena all but forgot that there were other people in the room. All she could do was stare at the alien before her.

He filled her space and this close, he was absolutely mesmerizing.

"So, you can...Keh-reh-nah," he said.

She didn't remember telling him her name...and the way he said it...nobody had ever said her name like that before.

His tongue caressed the syllables as if it was moving over her skin.

A very inappropriate thought indeed—even if it did make her heart quicken a bit.

"I am Ajos, Commander of Reku 2," he continued, his eyes moving over her face slowly. "I am here to take care of you."

Something must be wrong with her because that last sentence sounded loaded with insinuation.

Shaking her head slightly, she stretched out her hand for a handshake, ignoring the gasps around her.

Ajos' eyes fell to her hand before he pressed his three-fingered palm against hers in a not-so handshake.

For that moment, she stared at the contact of their hands.

His skin felt cool against hers, and when he caught her eyes again, his mouth twisted slightly.

"I will be by your side, Keh-reh-nah."

That was just a mixed-up translation, wasn't it?

Still, why did it make her smile?

As the alien's lips twisted slightly into a smile of his own, something suddenly changed within him.

For a split second, she saw terror in the alien's eyes.

"Take cover!" She was sure it was the robot guy, V'Alen, that shouted the instructions, but she didn't get the chance to investigate why.

She was suddenly pulled into a hard chest, as Ajos gripped her and plastered her face against him.

She made to protest but something happened that made her so confused, it felt like she lost control of her mind and body.

There was a bright flash.

So bright, it lit up the inside of the dim space like they had placed the sun inside. In horror, Kerena realized she could see right through the alien standing before her.

For a few moments, it was like she was pressed against a living x-ray.

She'd never seen anything like it before.

All his bones, his blood vessels...it was all lit up in front of her eyes. There was a sudden unexplainable warmth in the room, a heat she'd never felt before, but Ajos didn't let her go. He shielded her from the light and pulled her closer to him before a loud sound erupted. Loud enough to deafen her as the ground shook beneath them.

For a moment, she couldn't hear anything—there was a high pitch ringing in her ears and all she could feel was Ajos holding her against him as he brought them to the floor.

Realization slowly hit as his heavy body pinned down hers.

Another explosion seemed to hit close by because the ground shook once more.

This was all strangely familiar.

Suddenly, her grandfather's stories didn't feel like old war tales anymore.

They'd been hit by something big, and there was only one thing it could be.

They'd been bombed.

6

———————

Staring wide-eyed, she saw Ajos' mouth move. He was shouting something, but she couldn't hear any words.

Her ears were still ringing, and she wasn't sure if he was speaking to her or to everyone else in the room.

He was still covering her, his body pressed against hers, shielding her, but despite the ringing in her ears, she was vaguely aware that chaos had erupted all around them.

Women were screaming and clamoring behind and between the stasis pods for cover, everyone trying to save themselves.

A fear she'd never known crept deep inside her.

Her grandfather had talked about it so many times—of being a young man who'd been sent out to Christmas Island, being told nothing except that they were going to test bombs. He'd said they'd been told to shield their eyes with their hands or to bury their face in the crook of their arm.

And then the light.

A bright light that made him see his bones through his flesh. Then the heat. A heat that felt like someone on fire had walked right through him.

It was all too similar.

"What's happening?!" she screamed, but her words were not answered as another explosion hit the hold.

The entire structure tilted, and the world went topsy-turvy. In the back of her mind, she knew the building was flipping over—either that or gravity had shifted and the planet had turned on its axis.

Strong arms gripped her as Ajos pulled her toward his chest and secured her there. With the entire structure falling over on its side, she didn't know in which direction they went, only that their bodies were thrown as if they were dolls.

In front of her, some women were still trying to find cover, but without the strength of someone holding them down, they flew effortlessly across the room.

Some of them hit the hard stasis pods lined up against the wall, and Kerena was sure she saw blood.

Behind her, she heard Ajos grunt as his back collided with something hard. He'd taken the brunt of the impact, saving her from injury.

Her heart felt like a brick hitting against her chest as the huge stasis hold stopped moving and the ringing of her ears subsided enough that she fully heard the screaming occurring around her.

There was dust in the room now, coming through the hole that was in the wall, and Kerena coughed as she covered her nose, her eyes watering as she searched for any survivors nearby.

Her eyes landed on the body of someone about a foot away. In the dust that was now circulating in the room, she could hardly see, but she was sure it was the curly-haired woman who'd spoken up earlier.

There was blood on the woman's forehead and her eyes were closed.

Wriggling, she tried to free herself from the Ajos' arms, but he held her even tighter.

"I have to help her." She turned her brown eyes to gold ones.

"It is not safe. We might get hit again."

She didn't even have to think about it. She could never live with herself if that woman died and she didn't help when she had the chance to.

"I don't care," she said. "Let me help her."

Ajos searched her gaze for a moment before he released her enough for her to slip from his arms.

Screams, cries, groans of pain—she could hear it all now, as clear as she could see the dust that choked the air.

Coughing, she covered her nose and mouth with one hand as she crawled over to the woman.

Her legs couldn't carry her, they were too weak from the shock of it all, but luckily, the woman wasn't too far away.

She checked the woman's pulse, and relief flooded her when she felt the faint movement in the woman's neck.

"We have to get to safety," a deep voice said over her shoulder.

She hadn't realized Ajos had followed her over to the woman.

"I have to move her. Can you help me?"

Ajos jerked his head before grasping the woman as if she weighed nothing.

He looked around the hold—apparently he could see better than she could in the dust because she couldn't see shit. Everywhere else must be chaos, because he moved the woman to the spot where he and Kerena had just moved from.

He turned to look at her then, and in the lessening dust, she saw there was a sort of film over his eyes.

A nictitating membrane.

Mild shock made her stare at him for a few beats. She wished she had one of those. It felt like there were grains of sand trying to get into her eyes and she was squinting so hard, she could hardly see her hand in front of her face now.

Nodding to him, she kept her nose and mouth covered as she scrambled over to where he'd placed the woman.

As she touched the woman's cheek, noting the thin line of blood running from the woman's forehead, Kerena was sure she saw the lady's eyelids move.

"Hey! Can you hear me?"

The woman frowned and groaned, her eyes opening a little.

"I can't see..." the woman groaned.

"Hey! You're ok. We're going to be all right." Fuck her if she was lying to herself as well.

Her heart was still hammering in her chest and she was frickin' terrified. But she needed to surpass her fear. Survival was paramount, and she needed to check if the woman had a concussion.

"What's your name?"

"Alaina," the woman said, raising her hand to touch her head. "What the hell happened?"

The woman answered fast and her speech wasn't slurred...that was good.

Kerena glanced at Ajos and he was looking at her with a grim expression on his face.

Possibly he knew what happened because she had no true idea. If they'd really been bombed...

"I need to help the others," he said.

Kerena was nodding before she even could form the words. "Of course. Do what you have to do."

The alien hesitated for a second, his gaze traveling over her, and Kerena realized he was checking whether she had injuries.

"I'm fine," she smiled. "You saved me."

The alien's throat moved as he regarded her some more before he jerked his head and disappeared into the lessening dust.

"What happened?" Alaina groaned again. "I can hardly see anything."

Kerena gulped. She wasn't sure if Alaina was referring to the dust or the bright light that had almost blinded her.

Ajos had shielded her from the light. How he'd known in that split second that the bomb was coming, she didn't know.

She'd seen his face change, seen the terror that had transformed his features suddenly. If not for his quick thinking, she would have been suffering more than a few broken bones.

She'd possibly have lasting effects on her eyes as well.

"I'm not sure what happened." Kerena looked over the woman. Choosing to keep her thoughts to herself, Kerena focused on Alaina instead. "Do you feel pain anywhere except your head?"

Alaina shook her head. Her face had a pained expression and she was squinting hard as well, but she seemed to be in her right mind.

"Okay." Kerena looked behind her. There were a lot of women

who needed help. "I have to go see if I can help the others," she murmured.

"Go." Alaina grimaced but sat up straighter to lean against the stasis pod behind her.

Pushing strength into her feet, Kerena stood.

The dust had settled somewhat and she could see better now, but despite what she'd been expecting, she still wasn't ready for what she saw.

THERE WERE PEOPLE STREWN EVERYWHERE, over and under the stasis pods.

Above them was another row of stasis pods and Kerena realized the stasis hold had indeed fallen unto its side.

At the front of the hold, she spotted Ajos and the other aliens moving the injured humans toward what was now the floor at the front of the room.

She headed that way.

She'd had to take a first-aid class as part of her new job and now was the time to use that knowledge.

Dust covered everyone and the pained cries she heard as she moved toward the front pulled at her heartstrings.

Athena was there tending as best as she could to the injured females, and Kerena joined her to check the pulse of the next woman in line.

The woman was alive, but from the way her arm was set, it looked broken.

"Is there a hospital? Can we get them to it?" Kerena asked.

"There's a med bay. We've sent word. They'll be coming as soon as they can, but I'm afraid they're already overwhelmed with casualties." Athena glanced her way as she moved to another victim.

Her words puzzled Kerena for a moment before realization dawned. Still, she asked, "What do you mean?"

Athena's look was grim. "Those fuckers bombed the entire perimeter. There were people—there were other beings out there.

They didn't have the cover of this stasis hold. They hit them directly and without warning."

Kerena swallowed hard, her eyes moving to the hole in the wall.

The hole was above them now because the stasis hold had flipped, and she was looking up into a cloudless, brownish sky.

Dust.

Outside was filled with dust.

"How will the doctors get in?"

Athena glanced up, her gaze focusing on the hole in what was now the roof.

"They'll find a way."

As she spoke, the head of an alien popped into the hole and his dark eyes flicked over everything before he seemed to find his mark and jumped down.

Kerena noted the shark-like fins on his back before her eyes widened as an angel followed behind him, floating down on huge iridescent wings.

They rushed over to two of the women in black and white and she couldn't help but stare.

One of the women was pregnant, it seemed. She was gripping her belly, her gaze worried as she met the alien's eyes. The alien with the fins crouched to place his face against her baby bump, but his dark eyes seemed murderous.

Alarm bells rang in Kerena's head.

"Are they—"

"They're friendly," Athena said. "They're their husbands."

Oh...okay.

Someone groaned beside her, and Kerena pulled her attention away from the couples before quickly moving to the injured woman.

This one definitely had a concussion.

Her words were slow, slurred, and she didn't answer any of Kerena's questions.

Gulping, Kerena's gaze traveled over the stasis hold. The dust had settled enough for her to see, and she watched as Ajos and the other aliens moved to help the humans.

There were so many injured people, she could only hope they didn't end up with any casualties.

As Ajos and his comrades brought the women from wherever they'd fallen, she worked with Athena checking vitals.

She didn't know how long she and Athena worked, but it felt like time moved slowly.

Medical supplies were lowered inside as the aliens worked to cut another hole into the side of the stasis hold.

The medical supplies consisted of a bunch of small packets she didn't how to use, but with Athena's help, they managed to tend to most of those who were the least injured.

However, there were those they couldn't immediately help.

There were broken legs, broken arms, a few people seemed to have concussions and there was one woman who couldn't move at all.

She didn't even want to think about what that could mean.

The angel alien airlifted the emergency cases out through the hole in the top. Meanwhile, they did everything they could to tend to the women before the hole in the side was open and more aliens rushed in with floating gurneys.

The curly-haired woman she'd helped, Alaina, had been the last one to be pushed away on a gurney and as they took her away, Kerena sank to the floor.

She was more exhausted than she'd thought. Adrenaline had been what had kept her energy up.

A shadow fell over her immediately and, for some reason, she knew exactly who it was without even lifting her gaze.

"It is your turn to go."

Her eyes met Ajos'. "Go where?"

"To the med bay. You must get checked for injuries."

Kerena couldn't help but smile. "I think *you* should get checked. You're the one that took all the beating while you protected *me*."

"Beating?" Ajos' head tilted a little and Kerena opened her mouth to explain, but she only ended up staring at him instead.

His eyes were back to their normal golden color now, the nictitating membrane gone.

"You got damaged because of me," she finally said. "You protected me when you didn't have to."

"It is my oath," he said.

His response was a little cryptic, and she was about to ask if all of them took oaths to fight with the Restitution, but a conversation between Xul, Athena, and the robot caught her ear.

"—was a warning. They know we have them and they want their humans back," Xul said.

She didn't mean to eavesdrop, but she couldn't help but cock her ears.

"I believe they targeted the stasis hold, knowing the explosion wouldn't destroy it," V'Alen said. "The perimeter, however...they killed those beings on purpose."

"But bomb the stasis hold? What if they'd killed everyone inside?! It could have crumpled on us," Athena said.

"Negative," V'Alen answered. "They made the hold of talix metal. It is bomb proof."

"Still..." Athena suddenly sobbed, and her next words were mostly muffled as the bull-alien pulled her into his chest. "...they killed so many people outside."

"We have what they deem as theirs and they are irrational beings," V'Alen said. "It was indeed a warning."

"What warning?" All eyes turned on her and Kerena felt mildly embarrassed. She doubted it was a conversation that she should have been listening in on.

"A warning that the second Great War has begun," Ajos said from above her.

War?

Her worried gaze met his and the resignation in his eyes chilled her.

He wasn't joking.

He was dead serious.

Ajos' words seemed to pass through the others like a bad omen, and even though she'd just been thrust into this world, Kerena could feel the tension as if it was in the air itself.

"They are not safe," V'Alen said. "The humans are not safe."

"We *all* are not safe," Athena corrected.

"Nor will we ever be..." Ajos' golden eyes bored into hers.

A feeling she'd never felt before passed through Kerena, one of complete trust as she looked up at this tall alien being, and Kerena wasn't sure what to make of it.

He'd saved her twice, but it wasn't even that. The short time she'd spent around him felt like it had been stretched out over many days.

She felt like she'd known him for more than just a few hours, even though that wasn't the case.

Kerena held his gaze, unable to look away.

She knew what this was—it was the mysterious power of near-death experiences.

It could draw people closer, even strangers...it could even bring an alien and a human together.

The thought made her eyes widen a little as she stared up into the alien's eyes.

"So what do we do now?" she whispered.

"There is only one thing to do..." Ajos said, his gaze moving from hers to focus on the others.

"...We fight."

7

"We should leave this area," Ajos said before glancing down at her. "And you need to go to the med bay."

"I'm fine." Kerena forced a smile.

Granted, she was a bit shaken, but she didn't feel physically out of sorts.

To be fair, she was surprising even herself with how well she was taking this entire situation.

Not only did she wake up among aliens, but she survived a bombing not long after.

Her mind should be frazzled.

"You should both go to the med bay," Xul said, his eyes on Athena.

Athena nodded, her shoulders sagging a little. She'd kept her emotions firmly in check for the entire time they'd been working to patch up the few women they could assist. It was the first time Kerena saw an ounce of exhaustion reflected on the woman, and it reminded her it must be hard for Athena and the others who'd been rescued first.

They probably felt like the wellbeing of all the humans that had been trapped in the stasis hold was on their shoulders—and then this happened.

The already terrified females were now even more traumatized.

"Do you need me to carry you?" Ajos' gaze flicked over her and though his voice sounded firm, Kerena realized he wasn't being rude. He was looking at her as if he was genuinely concerned that she wouldn't be able to walk.

She shook her head. "I'm fine. I can walk."

As the group began walking from the stasis hold, Kerena looked back. Ajos was behind her and she had to look around him to see the place she was leaving.

Brown dust had settled over the pods inside, and their pristine appearance was no more. Her gaze traveled over the entire thing before she swallowed hard and looked toward the light coming through the hole in the structure's side.

This was going to be her first step on alien soil.

Outside, the entire area was bathed in bright sunlight that kissed her skin.

The air was dead, there was no movement, and an unnatural stillness permeated the space.

The hue was different here, different from on Earth.

The sun's light was whiter, brighter.

Below her feet was hardened orange-brown dirt, and the buildings close by were of a similar color—but that wasn't what struck her the most.

First, there was rubble...everywhere, and as her gaze adjusted to the brightness of the outside, horror gripped her as her hands flew over her mouth.

Athena's sharp intake of air reflected her feelings.

There were bodies strewn everywhere. Non-human bodies. Aliens.

Piling those bodies into huge carts were other aliens, their faces grim.

It looked like pictures she'd seen of the Aleppo bombings.

She'd known the bombs had dropped. She'd known there'd be damage, but nothing she'd imagined came close to reality.

V'Alen had been right when he'd said their enemies had known they'd be safe within the stasis hold.

Glancing back at the huge structure now. It looked mostly untouched, but everything around it had been completely decimated.

"My God..." Kerena muttered, her feet pulling her over to one of the carts.

She didn't want to look. She didn't want to face it. Yet, it was as if she couldn't pull her eyes away.

The dusty face of an alien with round protrusions on its head stared back at her with lifeless eyes.

She didn't know she was shaking till she felt a strong hand on her shoulder.

"You don't have to face this," Ajos said. "Not now. Not after what you just endured."

Tears filled her eyes as she pulled her gaze away from the dead being in front of her, but everywhere she looked, she saw another and another.

So many.

They'd been killed so viciously, snuffed out as if their lives meant nothing.

All these aliens, these sentient beings, died because another group saw their lives as inconsequential.

All because the Restitution had rescued her and the others...

"Who—" Her voice broke. "Who could do something like this?"

Ajos gripped her and turned her away from the carnage so she was looking at him.

"The same beings who took you away from your home. They are a scourge across the universe that will be eliminated. Be strong, Keh-reh-nah." Ajos gripped her a little tighter. "Vengeance will be ours... and it will be yours. The Tasqals will pay for what they've done."

Kerena nodded, but her mind couldn't help going back to the carnage around them.

How could she ignore it?

If there were innocent children here that died...

Forcing away the sudden pain she felt inside, her gaze moved to the others and she realized they had been watching the exchange between her and Ajos.

There was pain in their eyes too, and she knew they were prob-ably thinking the same thing she was.

Keeping her gaze averted as much as she could, she walked along-side Ajos as he led her with a hand on her shoulder.

The bull-alien, V'Alen, and Athena walked in front, while she and Ajos followed behind in silence.

There was that brown dust everywhere, and she tried to imagine what the place had looked like before the bombs had dropped, just to keep her mind off things.

Judging from what was left of the buildings, the place had prob-ably resembled somewhere like Cairo possibly, and it looked like it had been teeming with life.

It took a few minutes, but soon, most of the destruction was behind them.

"Who's going to bury them? Their families?" she asked, her mind still on the carnage.

She supposed the aliens had family around.

"Most of those beings were refugees like you are," Ajos answered. "Most have no blood relations on the base. Only a few, like me, are lucky to have relatives with us." He paused. "We all are family here. The Restitution is all most of the beings on this base have."

Kerena nodded.

She guessed that applied to her as well.

The Restitution was all she had now too.

She'd lost everything.

Her family. Her friends. Her job. Cindy Clawford.

Everything.

Craning her neck to look up at Ajos, her heart skipped a beat.

She kept forgetting he was a completely different lifeform. When she wasn't looking at him, it felt as if she was speaking to a regular person, a human.

Talking to him came so easily.

It wasn't how she'd expected first contact would be.

"You have family here? You are one of the lucky ones then," she said, forcing a smile.

Ajos' golden eyes flicked to hers and as she craned her neck so she could study his face, she didn't miss the fact that he seemed to stiffen somewhat.

"Some would say so," he finally answered.

He stopped walking suddenly, and she realized the three others had stopped in front of a large, rectangular building.

There was a glowing sign etched into the wall in a language she couldn't read, but when the doors slid open, it was obvious what the building was.

The hospital.

As they walked in, the moans and whimpers of the people being treated reached her ears and Kerena tried not to wince.

It seemed as if it was an emergency room.

They'd lined the walls with floating gurneys holding humans on them.

Guilt flooded her as she looked at the faces of her fellow humans.

Muddied, dirty, bloodied—some were in hysterics while some were crying silently.

Others looked numb.

Almost every one of them had devices covering their eyes, possibly to help with the exposure to that bright light.

Those who weren't unconscious looked like they were in pain, and she couldn't help but feel as if she'd been given a cheat code by not having any injuries at all.

As they walked past a room on their way to the front of the emergency area, a door slid open and an alien that looked like a huge fly walked out.

He was about five feet tall and had huge bug eyes at the side of his head. At least, she assumed they were eyes. There were no pupils, only two rounded, textured sacs.

But that wasn't the thing that caught her attention.

The sight behind the alien did.

Inside the room, a dark-haired woman sat on a floating gurney and it was immediately clear that something was off about the woman.

She was staring straight at Kerena, but it was like looking into the eyes of someone dead.

There was nothing there.

The door slid closed, but not before Kerena noticed two more things.

The woman didn't look dirty or beat up like the rest of the injured humans, and she was in a private room alone.

It seemed as if they had placed everyone else in the huge emergency area.

What had warranted that the woman with the dead eyes be placed in a room by herself?

Call it her "spidey" senses, but something immediately felt out of place.

The fly-looking alien was about to buzz by her when Ajos stepped in his path.

"Aker."

The alien had to tilt his head almost ninety degrees to look Ajos in the face.

"Commander Ajos, how surprising to see you here." The fly guy's voice was normal. She didn't know why she'd expected him to buzz a little when he spoke. "You are injured to the point of needing medical attention?"

"I am here to assist with the humans." Ajos turned to her. "Please run diagnostics on this female."

The fly alien turned to her and outstretched his hand. He had six fingers that looked slightly hairy.

Kerena took his hand, and he squeezed it so firmly, she winced a little.

"Oh, my apologies." Aker didn't have any lips. At least, she couldn't even see his mouth. His nose was like a relaxed ball sack that hung down his face and moved as he spoke. It was difficult not to stare. "I am still learning human customs. The human named Piper taught me the shaking of hands. Did I not do it correctly?"

Kerena smiled.

She was good at judging people within the first few moments of meeting them, and this alien seemed like a good enough being.

"Just a little too hard on your grip there." She smiled.

The doctor nodded. Or, at least, she thought he did.

"I will work on the pressure I place on my hand." He moved his head, and she assumed by the angle that he was looking up at Ajos. "Show her to the scanner. I will be right with you."

Ajos jerked his head in a nod as the short, little doctor hustled over to Athena and Xul, who were waiting a few steps away.

She watched them converse and noticed their gazes kept moving to the room with the strange woman inside, but she couldn't pick up what they were saying.

Between the general noise of wails and sobs within the emergency room, the three were speaking in hushed tones.

"This way," Ajos said, and when she looked up, she realized he was studying her like he always seemed to be doing.

Forcing a smile and pushing away her apprehension, Kerena followed him over to a machine that stood against the wall in the room.

It looked like one of those ring lights photographers used in their studios.

"Stand here," he said. "It will scan you, let you know if there is anything of concern."

When she didn't immediately step forward, Ajos made a sound like "hmm" in his throat.

"I will show you," he said as he stood under the ring light and Kerena watched as the thing moved to adjust itself to his height.

A green light formed a circle around his head and proceeded to move down his body.

"This is technology we scavenged from a Tasqal ship," he said, and Kerena realized that the entire time, he'd still been studying her.

He had the advantage to do that. She had to look up every time she wanted to look at his face.

"The Tasqals..." She'd heard the name so much now, she could almost imagine what they looked like. Probably a huge warrior race that went around plundering. "Is there not much access to technology on this planet?" She paused. "Which planet are we on, anyway?"

"You are on Murn GZ and no." The green ring of light had almost reached his knees now. "The Tasqals restrict the movement of goods to planets that do not form treaties with them," he said. "Murn GZ is not eligible for any treaties." His facial muscles stiffened. "Not that we'd want them."

"So it's like an embargo?"

Ajos' head tilted slightly as his hairless eyebrows knitted.

"I do not know what an em-bahr-goh is," he said, stepping from under the machine just as the green light disappeared.

As he moved, a full-body 3D image appeared in the space he'd just stepped out of.

Kerena's eyes widened.

The image spun as he moved it with his fingers and her eyes widened some more.

It highlighted an area at the back with a glow, and Ajos stepped behind the image of himself to look at the area.

He did something to the image, tapped a setting, and suddenly, the clothes on his 3D self disappeared.

It took less than a second for her to realize that she was looking at a full-3D representation of Ajos naked and her eyes widened in their sockets.

Was this normal?

Should she look away?

Kerena cleared her throat, but her eyes wouldn't move.

For science.

She was observing for science.

That was her job, wasn't it?

Well, it had been.

Ajos had a broad, firm chest and memory of how she'd snuggled into him without knowing what she was doing came back to her immediately.

Despite that his skin was such a strange color, nothing about him made her squeamish. Instead...he was so very interesting.

Without realizing, she took a step forward toward the image.

Out of respect, she should probably turn and give him some privacy as he checked out the injury on his back but, instead, her gaze fell farther, moving down the muscles etched in his chest and lower.

He was a fighter, and it showed.

His body was fit, carved impeccably, and not an ounce of fat was present.

Muscle. Pure muscle.

Because of his height, her gaze didn't even have to fall far before she was looking at his crotch.

And...

This time, her eyes bugged out when she realized where she was looking.

There was nothing there.

Apart from a noticeable bulge, his crotch was smooth.

What the...

Kerena released a breath at her stupidity. Of course, the image wouldn't be anatomically correct. Why would they make it so it displayed the genitals for all to see?

"It seems I have sustained a minor injury to my posterior when we fell during the explosions." Ajos' voice reached her ears and Kerena pulled her gaze away, the warmth in her cheeks giving away the fact she'd been doing something inappropriate.

"Oh, I'm sorry." She cleared her throat. He'd gotten hurt that time when he'd grabbed her and shielded her while they'd been thrown around like rag dolls. "Do you need to have the fly doctor check it out or..."

As Ajos stepped from behind the 3D projection, she couldn't meet his gaze and looked everywhere except at him.

"Fly doctor?"

Oh, of course, he wouldn't know what she meant. There were probably no flies here...also what she'd said could be taken the wrong way. This was a whole other culture. She'd have to mind her words so she didn't offend anyone.

She had so much to learn.

"I mean the doctor guy."

"Aker," he said. "No. My cells will fix themselves." He paused. "Now, it's your turn."

Clearing her throat again, Kerena nodded and stepped underneath the light-ring thing.

"Do I have to do anything or will it—" Just as she spoke, the machine began scanning her.

She didn't feel a thing as the green light ran over her body.

The entire time the machine scanned her, they stood in silence, the sobs and groans of the other humans that were being tended to by more fly-like aliens filling the space.

That sobered her a bit.

She couldn't forget what was happening around them and with that thought, her gaze flew to the door where she'd seen the woman with the dead eyes. What had happened to her?

As the green light shut off and she stepped from underneath the machine, a 3D image of her sprung up in the space.

It was strange seeing a life-size image of herself, and it was at that moment that she realized how frazzled she looked.

It had captured her exact image.

Her eyes looked drawn and haunted, and her hair was a mess.

Reaching forward, she tried to touch the image, but her hands went right through.

It was amazing technology.

"So, this thing scanned my entire body?"

"Everything. Your entire anatomy down to the last cell."

Safe to say, she was impressed.

"Wow, nothing like this exists on Earth," she murmured, turning her hand, and the image turned as she did that action.

"And nothing like this exists in Sector 3 regions. We were lucky to retrieve this scanner while on a mission."

"Sector 3?"

"Like Murn GZ," he said. "The undesirables."

Kerena's eyebrows rose a little as she looked at her image.

"The bad guys, the Tasqals...they really keep these things to themselves?"

Withholding technology, healthcare, to retain their power? They sounded like sick beings and she was happy she was rescued from them.

"It is how they became so powerful...how they've been able to invade and control so many cultures."

As she flexed her hand, she must have activated something within the image because one moment she was looking at a clothed image of herself and the next, she wasn't.

Fuck it. She'd been wrong.

It was VERY anatomically correct.

"Shit."

Her breasts...her nipples...her crotch with the singular line of hair she'd left unshaved! Everything was RIGHT THERE.

Kerena gasped, fanning her hand inside the image to make it change back, but instead of re-clothing her or shutting off, she somehow caused it to zoom in on her breasts.

"Shit, shit, shit!" she cursed underneath her breath.

She could *feel* Ajos staring and the fact that he said nothing only made it worse.

When she finally gathered the courage to look at him, she paused for a moment, blinking at the look he was giving the image.

Her mouth fell open slightly as she stared at him.

The look in his eyes was both one of wonder and...well, that other look was something she hadn't expected to read so clearly on an alien face.

Lust.

It shone in those gold eyes like they were glazed.

With wide eyes, she jumped in front of the image, blocking his view.

"Uh—"

Ajos blinked at the sudden intrusion, and his eyes finally focused on the real version of her.

His throat moved, and he touched the machine, causing the image behind her to disappear.

"You do not appear to have any injuries," he said.

So they were going to ignore that she'd just shown him her naked body?

All right.

She wasn't complaining. She was actually thankful for that.

"You should still get some rest," he said, and it seemed as if he was concentrating hard on looking her in the eyes.

There was a slight frown on his forehead and she wasn't sure if it was because he was confused or disturbed.

Kerena didn't know what to think.

"I'll try and help the others instead of resting." She glanced at the hustle and bustle happening around them. "These doctors look overwhelmed."

As she looked over the emergency room, her gaze found the curly-haired woman, Alaina.

The woman was sitting upright on a gurney and was looking around the room.

It was the perfect option to get away from the tension suddenly swimming around her and the tall, minty-teal alien. "Be right back."

She shot him a glance and Ajos jerked his head in a nod.

AJOS WATCHED KEH-REH-NAH GO.

She moved quickly from him, her small feet taking her across the white flooring towards another human, and he immediately felt a loss at her not being by his side.

Ridiculous.

It was not like him to...bond—if he could even call it that.

His nefre pulsed.

It was probably because the female reminded him of Nama.

He'd loved his sister, and memory of her had been strong this day.

Keh-reh-nah's small feet took her over to the other female quickly.

She was embarrassed.

The change in her skin coloring told him that.

He hadn't meant to stare at her bare flesh but, at the same time, he hadn't been able to stop himself.

Something had stirred within him when he'd seen her, and his nefre pulsed again.

He took a few steps towards her before he realized what he was doing.

Why was he following her?

Squeezing his eyes shut to clear his thoughts, he opened them to glance around the room.

There were so many other humans that needed help—all injured, some crying, some unconscious.

Even though they'd been protected by the stasis hold, so many of them had been hurt badly.

It didn't seem as if any of the humans had regenerative qualities either.

Not surprising. The Tasqals went for planets that had little to no defenses against them, only to steal as many resources as they could by sheer force.

The Tasqals may have thought the humans had still been locked in the stasis pods and, therefore, protected from the explosions.

But that hadn't been a surety.

They were cruel beings.

Maybe they intended all this to happen, for the humans to hurt, for rebels' lives to be lost, for the entire base to go into disarray and quake with fear.

"You already scanned?" The medic, Aker, interrupted his thoughts and Ajos looked down at the small Taiq'ud.

"Yes, and the human scanned as well." Ajos' gaze flicked back to Keh-reh-nah. She was smiling with the other human she was speaking to, her white teeth showing in her small mouth. As he stared at her, his nefre stirred again, and once more, he had the urge to plant himself by her side. He frowned and shook away the feeling. "The human is well."

As he said this, one human at the far end of the room let out a high-pitched sound, her arms thrashing as she tried to fight the Taiq'ud tending to her.

The intern, shocked by the sound, fell back, scattering trays upon trays of medical items that were behind her.

Aker winced. "The humans' pain tolerance is remarkably high for their simple bodies. However, they are scared urgless of us." Aker winced again as the woman continued with the high-pitched noises. "We have given them the standard dose of anesthesia, and it seems to work for the pain. It would be unethical for us to give them more just to make them calm."

Aker's nose flexed, the round fleshy bits bunching up as he sighed. "There is much to do. Almost all the humans are injured. If you are not busy, we could use your help."

Ajos nodded and pulled his gaze from Keh-reh-nah. Somehow, his eyes had found her again, despite the chaos in the room.

"What do you need?" he asked as his frown deepened.

"We need help to lift and move the humans. The machines we usually use are out of service. There was a magnetic blast with the explosions. Most instruments are not working." He looked Ajos up and down. "That human seems comfortable around you. Your presence may calm the others as well." Aker's nose moved again—a sure sign he was distressed. The medic looked around the room.

Funny that Aker should think his presence would calm the others.

His gaze moved over Keh-reh-nah.

There was a strange pull to her, a strange energy, and he wondered for a second if that's why she'd been so calm around him. Did she feel it too? Maybe it had nothing to do with him personally.

Maybe the gods were trying to tell him something else...lead him from this path of penance...

He stopped the thought right there.

There was no other reason.

Yet...

Something was strange...

He didn't feel nearly the same pressing urge to protect the other humans as he did with her...

With Keh-reh-nah, this strange human female he'd just met, it felt as if he had to protect her and nothing else mattered.

With the others, it was more a sense of duty.

He frowned deeper at this.

This felt like bonding...but he couldn't be sure.

After all, he'd never experienced bonding before.

Still, that didn't mean that he wouldn't do what he joined the Restitution to do.

His duty came first.

Ajos touched Aker on the shoulder to steady the medic, who was now quaking with pent-up stress.

"I am here, Aker. I will assist."

ALAINA'S SMILE grew brighter as Kerena walked over.

"Girl, you look better than all of us and I thought *I* was lucky."

As far as Kerena could see, the wound on the woman's head was almost healed already—possibly another medical advancement that Earth didn't possess.

"No." Kerena returned the woman's smile. "But, I can admit, I *was* lucky."

Alaina's gaze drifted to somewhere behind her.

"Does that tall guy have something to do with it?"

Kerena turned to look behind her, and her gaze immediately landed on Ajos. He was standing beside the doctor and they were engaged in what looked like deep conversation.

"Something..." she murmured in answer to Alaina.

"He seems friendly. Friendlier than the others. They all keep their distance from us, like they don't want to spook us, but he's been by your side. Luckily too, or you'd probably be tending a broken arm or something right now." Alaina's grin grew even wider when Kerena's eyes reached her again. "Ugh, I envy you right now."

Kerena couldn't help but laugh. "To be fair, I'd envy you too if you were the only one uninjured."

"Ha! That's not what I'm talking about." Alaina's gaze followed one of the fly doctors. "You're the only one that can understand them AND one of them is actually being friendly with you."

Ajos *was* friendly.

Friendlier than she'd expected him to be. "He is friendly, isn't he." She studied the woman before her. Alaina seemed so unperturbed by it all—a stark contrast to some of the other women in the room.

To Alaina's right, a brown-haired woman lay looking straight up into the roof, her eyes glassy, but no tears fell down her face.

"Hey." Kerena made sure her voice was soothing. "Are you okay?"

As soon as she asked, she felt stupid.

Of course, the woman wasn't okay. None of them were.

The woman turned her head slightly, her green eyes focusing on Kerena.

She nodded, but it was obvious she was holding her tears back.

"I only have a broken arm," she said. "I was lucky."

Kerena smiled a little, one of consolation more than mirth.

"You'll be okay." She certainly hoped that wasn't a lie. "What's your name? I'm Kerena, by the way."

"Constance," the woman said.

"Nice to meet you," Kerena smiled again, "even under these circumstances."

Constance nodded again and smiled a little too, a note of sadness pulling down her lips.

"Nice to meet you too," Alaina added.

Kerena's gaze flicked back to the woman.

Alaina was following everything that was happening in the room, soaking up every bit of detail, it seemed.

"Aren't you wondering what happened back there?" Kerena asked.

"Not, one of the women in the black and white came over and told us not to worry, that it was a bomb but the threat is gone, for now at least."

"They didn't even seem shaken up about it either," Constance added, her voice low. "The way they look, it's like they've seen so much shit before, the bombs were nothing."

She wiped some tears from her eyes as she grimaced while sitting up straighter.

"I've only seen that look on the faces of women I work with." Constance's face fell. "*Worked* with," she corrected herself. "I was a therapist."

"Well, maybe you'll have a job here too. So much shit has happened, I'm sure we'll all need therapists," Kerena joked and Constance smiled a little.

Kerena looked around. None of those women were there now. Athena was the only one she could see of the four, and she was in deep conversation with the bull-alien by that door with the strange female inside.

Kerena's eyes narrowed.

"Did they say anything else? Like anything about more females being rescued before us?"

Alaina frowned slightly. "No, why? Are there more of us?"

Kerena looked toward that room that held the strange woman.

"I'm not sure. I just... There's a woman in that room. I don't remember seeing her before or after the bombs went off."

Alaina's voice dropped to a whisper.

"So you saw her too?" Alaina asked. "I glimpsed her when I was brought in here. She looks...strange."

Kerena let out a breath. She was glad she wasn't the only one who'd seen the woman.

"It is strange," she agreed.

"Do you think..." There was a note of apprehension in Alaina's voice, and when Kerena met her gaze once more, the unease was evident in the woman's eyes. "Do you think something strange is going on here?" Her voice dropped even lower. "The bombs, that woman... What if this is all an elaborate plan to get us thinking they're the good guys?"

Kerena took a moment to think about it, and her eyes found Ajos once more.

He was helping the doctor with one woman, lifting her effortlessly as the doctor directed him where to bring her.

Alaina could be right, but she wasn't sure.

The aliens seemed genuine.

Ajos seemed genuine, even if he was a bit strange.

Furthermore, why would the aliens' plan involve killing so many of their own?

The bombs hadn't been planned.

She doubted it.

"We have to be careful. We don't know anything yet," Alaina whispered. "This is like the best thing that's ever happened to me and I get overexcited about things but, yea, we need to be careful."

Kerena nodded and agreed.

Until she knew more about this new world, she had to remain smart and alert.

It was probably also best to stay out of the aliens' way and keep a low profile.

As the thought crossed her mind, Ajos turned and looked directly at her, as if he'd heard the words in her head.

Their gazes locked and neither of them looked away.

Biting the inside of her lip, Kerena considered the alien.

Something told her that keeping a low profile was going to be harder than she thought.

8

Three days later

Kerena's head lolled backward, and she caught herself, jerking upright from her position against the wall.

She'd slipped to the floor to rest, not wanting to use up a gurney that might be needed.

Apparently, there was another side to the medical center where they'd placed the aliens that had been injured in the blast—a precaution so they didn't traumatize the injured humans even more—and resources were stretched.

For days, the doctors had been busy tending to the injured, and now, the med bay was finally quiet and the lights were low.

Most of the females were asleep, and some were resting, but the shock of the bombing had mostly worn off.

After she'd spoken with Alaina that first day, she'd gone off to assist the fly-like doctors as much as she could.

It turned out that most of them were interns and that the main one was called Aker.

Taiq'uds, they were called, from a planet that was caught in the middle of a war between the Tasqals and another more dominant race.

They'd fled with the help of the Restitution on a ship that had almost crashed, and they ended up on the base.

Back on their planet, Aker was a renowned medical expert and as thanks to the Restitution, he was contributing his skills to healing the wounded the rebels brought in.

From what she'd learned, it seemed to be that way for most of the aliens on the base.

In whatever way they could contribute, they were a collective force that fought against the beings that had taken her away from Earth.

So, instead of standing around, she'd hopped right in.

For three days, she'd worked non-stop, helping in the clinic, not taking a break.

Part of it was guilt that she'd been unscathed, another part was the fact she knew this was tough on everyone included.

The work was good, though. It took her mind off things and she could almost imagine she was back on Earth, working tirelessly at the lab.

The only thing was, at night, she didn't get to go home and cuddle with Cindy.

Instead, she found a quiet corner and settled in with a blanket.

As her head lolled back again, strong arms grasped her, and she was suddenly being lifted.

The scent of fresh winter air filled her nose, and she knew who it was but she was so tired, she could hardly even open her eyes.

She'd overworked herself. Again.

"I can walk," she murmured.

"Nonsense." Ajos' voice reached her ear, and she noted he sounded a bit pissed.

For the three days, he'd hovered around, and whenever she'd caught his gaze, he'd been frowning in her direction.

They began moving and Kerena opened one eye halfway to see where they were going.

They were heading toward the door.

That confused her a bit.

She'd heard earlier that the accommodation they'd prepared for the rescued humans had been destroyed in the bombs and that they would keep them in the medical center till they could figure out what to do.

Most of the humans didn't want to live in the bomb zone anyway. Kerena included.

It reeked of death and destruction, and the memory of what happened was too rich.

"Did they fix the homes?" Her voice sounded tired.

"No," Ajos said. "I am taking you to mine."

Kerena's eyes widened, and she opened her mouth to protest.

Ajos cut her off. "It is much more suitable than the med bay floor. I cannot stand watching you rest there another night."

He was being incredibly nice, but she could stay in the hospital for as long as necessary. She wasn't fussy.

"I don't want to put you out," she said.

Ajos grunted. "I don't intend to be put out. I will be staying there with you."

Kerena opened her mouth again, and it closed on its own accord.

Was it safe to go off with him? And did he mean that she'd be sharing a room with him?

"You will be safe there," Ajos said, and it felt as if he read her mind. "I will not harm you."

His words felt true, but he hadn't needed to utter them, she realized.

The entire time she'd known him, granted it hadn't been for that long, she hadn't once felt unsafe around him.

"Rest, Keh-reh-nah," he said. "It is a bit of a walk from here."

Another protest died on her lips as she looked up at the alien holding her close.

Her gaze traveled over minty-teal skin, up his collarbone to his firm chin. He had full lips that were pressed together and the look on his face didn't change as the door slid open and they stepped out of the medical center.

Ajos didn't pause but kept on walking.

It was dark, but the night air was only slightly chilly. Still, he walked with haste, weaving through alleys and streets she didn't know.

Now and then, she could hear the brush of feet around them as they passed other aliens going about their night business, but not once did Ajos stop.

He just kept moving forward, his forehead set in a frown, his lips pressed into a thin line, and those golden eyes of his piercing forward.

It took him a while before he looked down and caught her staring at him, and Kerena noticed that his features softened a little when he realized that she wasn't asleep.

"We will be there soon," he said.

"Okay."

She couldn't help herself or pull her eyes away from him, and even when Ajos tore his gaze away, she still stared.

This had been a helluva few days.

In such a short time, she felt as if she'd experienced more than most humans ever would in their entire lives.

It was no wonder she was so exhausted, and maybe that exhaustion was clouding her judgment.

Despite what her instincts were telling her, she still needed to keep her eyes open in case anything questionable was happening on this base.

There were a lot of questions she still needed answered.

Ajos stopped walking in front of what looked like a bunker.

It was literally a door set into the rock face, like a hobbit hole but larger.

"We're here." As he said this, he pressed his hand on a panel by the door and it slid open.

Kerena turned her head to see where they were going and as Ajos stepped inside, she realized the place was already lit.

It was white. Everything was.

It looked like a room decorated with modern, minimalistic furnishings and there was a lot of space.

The sleek furniture, the walls, the floor...it was such a contrast from the brown of the outside.

"Wow."

"This is our dwelling."

As she scanned the interior, V'Alen turned a corner and stopped. His gaze landed on her immediately before moving to Ajos.

"Ajos?"

Ajos didn't pause. "She is staying here."

V'Alen blinked as Ajos walked forward and passed him, but he said nothing more.

He was looking at her though and she wasn't sure if it was because he was a robot or not, but she couldn't read his gaze.

Was there a problem with her being there?

Ajos walked into another room and the door slid closed behind him. Before long, she was being placed on top of something hard.

Kerena began looking around, and it didn't take her long to realize that this must be Ajos' bedroom.

There were two spears against the wall in the corner, another piece of armor like the one he wore hung on the wall, and there was a pair of male boots against the wall by the door.

Apart from the hard thing she was on, there was a singular table in the corner.

This was his personal space, and she was in it.

She wasn't a virgin, but she suddenly felt like one—not that she thought they were about to have sex...or anything.

She cleared her throat at that thought, and when she finally looked at the alien in front of her, she saw him fidget a little.

He too was looking around his space, his frown growing even deeper by the second as if he didn't like what he was seeing.

"Nice place." She smiled. "It's great." *And spotless!*

Sheesh, her apartment didn't look like this even after she cleaned for an entire day.

Ajos' gaze slid to hers and she glanced around the room again. "It's certainly better than sleeping on the hospital floor."

That hard thing that he'd put her on was the only flat surface in the room and she assumed it was the bed, though, it was so hard she couldn't imagine anyone having a good night's sleep on such a thing.

Ajos made a sound in his throat and when she looked back at him, he was frowning at the bed too.

It was cold as well, she realized, and she wrapped her arms around herself. It seemed to grow colder as the seconds went by.

"Computer, turn off sleep cycle and adjust," Ajos said.

"Noted, Commander Ajos," a female voice suddenly said. It was hardly robotic. It sounded natural. "Settings, please."

Ajos studied her for a second. "Adjust for the female life-form in my quarters."

There was a pause before, "Adjusting for the female life-form. Species: human."

Kerena's eyebrows lifted. The temperature in the room began rising almost immediately.

"Wow, that's..." She didn't have the words.

"I apologize for the cold. It should be perfect for your rest now."

"Thank you," she said. "You don't like it warm?"

Ajos set down his spear and removed the armor that sat across his shoulders. The shirt he wore underneath had no sleeves and his biceps bunched as he moved.

"I am Shum'ai," he said. "We can only rest if the temperature is low. On my planet, it is not this warm."

Oh. Of course, he wasn't from here. He was from somewhere else, just like she was.

"What's your planet called?"

Now unladen, he turned to face her. "Tonvuhiri."

Yet another world she'd never heard of before, although, if some scientist had discovered it, they'd have dubbed it something else anyway.

"So these Tasqal guys destroyed your planet too?"

"No...at least, not yet."

"So..." Kerena frowned slightly, trying to understand. "Why did you leave?"

Ajos' mouth formed a thin line once more and his shoulders visibly stiffened.

Damn, was that too much of a personal question?

For a few moments he said nothing, and it seemed as if his gaze wasn't even focused on her anymore.

"I left," he finally said, "because I had to."

Kerena clamped her mouth shut.

There was awkwardness in the air, and she wasn't going to question him about something that obviously touched a sore spot.

He moved then, stepping around her toward another door that was set in the wall.

The door slid open, and the room lit up.

"This is the room for cleansing."

Kerena nodded, her gaze following him as he stepped toward the main door to the room. He turned once more, and he frowned at the bed.

A yawn stretched her lips before she could stop it. She really was tired.

Ajos jerked his head. "I will leave you to rest," he said, his gaze moving over her. "Rest well."

He was leaving?

Kerena moved forward, and in her sluggishness, she almost stumbled into him.

Her hand grasped his bare arm and Ajos froze.

That thing that ran from his head down his back like a thin, soft fin seemed to pulse.

Kerena swallowed and removed her hand.

"Thank you," she said.

He didn't have to do any of this, and she was truly grateful for it.

Ajos jerked his head, but no words came from his lips, and with that, he stepped out of the room.

As the door slid closed behind him, Ajos took a few steps down the corridor before leaning his head against the wall.

What the qef was he doing?

This was more than an urge to fix what he had failed to do in the past.

This wasn't about penance.

He'd brought the female into his space and why?

Because he felt sorry for what had happened to her people? Or was it that he felt sorry for *her*, specifically?

While he'd carried her to the bunker, the walk had been almost painful.

It was clear she felt safe with him.

Would she feel so safe if she knew that he'd failed to protect someone and it had cost them their life?

He'd never get Nama back, and for that, he had no right to lay claim over this female when he'd failed at the basic duty of every Shum'ai male that ever lived.

Ajos stiffened at that thought.

Claim?

He wasn't thinking of laying claim on anyone.

But even as he thought this, he couldn't deny that the walk to the bunker had been painful for another reason.

His nefre kept pulsing, and every movement of the female in his arms had sent tingles straight to his genital pouch.

He could feel the blood causing the area to throb even now. That touch she'd landed on his arm had caused a fresh wave of pulses.

Ajos groaned, his hands fisting at his sides as he tried to control the confusing feelings.

A shadow fell at the end of the corridor to the sleeping quarters, and Ajos looked up to see V'Alen standing there.

Pushing himself off the wall, he composed his features and walked forward.

Brushing past V'Alen without a word, he headed toward the door.

"Brother?" V'Alen's voice stopped him, and Ajos clenched his fists.

"What is it, V'Alen?"

He knew his comrade was about to speak some revelation that he didn't want to hear, and that only made him tense more.

For a being that had no emotions, V'Alen sure as qef knew how to identify them in others.

"Your nefre," was all V'Alen said.

"What about it?" Ajos frowned and turned to look at his ally.

He wasn't in the mood to chat about his body parts right now—especially when it seemed like he was losing control of them.

"It is not the same color as it used to be." V'Alen angled his head.

Ajos' frown deepened, his entire being stiffening. "What do you mean?"

"It is turning...red."

Ajos blanched.

Impossible.

"What?" He reached a hand back to touch the soft fin that ran down his back.

It moved against his hand as his fingers brushed against it.

"Your nefre," V'Alen repeated, "is red." His friend blinked. "Are you ill?"

No. No, he was not, but it would be better if that was the case because the alternative was much worse.

"Brother?" V'Alen asked, his eyes flashing. "I will contact Aker. He will—"

"No, that will not be necessary." Ajos gulped. "I just need some fresh air."

Before V'Alen could say another word, Ajos stepped out the door and away from the bunker.

He couldn't tell V'Alen what the change in his nefre meant.

He couldn't tell him because he didn't want to believe it himself.

9

AJOS SHOOK HIS HEAD TO CLEAR IT AS HE WALKED TOWARD THE SUPPLY center.

Maybe he could find some soft bedding there for he was positive Keh-reh-nah could not sleep on his resting slab.

He was used to the hardness, but he doubted she was.

It was clear she was used to soft, comforting things on her planet. Her thin skin would break otherwise.

He kept this in mind as he headed to the supply center. If he could find anything there for her to sleep on, he'd be relieved.

As he walked though, V'Alen's words repeated in his head.

Qef.

He ran his hand over his nefre again.

It didn't feel any different. Maybe V'Alen had been mistaken.

He had to be.

In front of him, light illuminated the supply center, and he knew Hemmil, the Ghanzot who worked there, was probably working overtime managing resources because of the explosions.

The doors to the supply center slid open and Ajos walked in.

Hemmil raised his hand in greeting.

"Ajos, my friend!"

"Hemmil."

Ajos kept walking, and he was sure he saw, from the corner of his eye, that Hemmil's face fell.

He was usually cordial with the Ghanzot, and Hemmil liked the conversation. But tonight he didn't want to hang around and chat. He was too focused on the turmoil in his head.

He moved straight to the back and began going through the shelves there.

As he searched for some sort of bedding, his nefre pulsed annoyingly.

It was hard to focus on the task at hand.

Ajos swallowed hard.

Keh-reh-nah needed the bedding.

Focus.

But thinking of her only seemed to make things worse.

Her touch lingered on his skin and he held back a groan as what felt like a lightning bolt traveled from his nefre straight to his genital pouch.

Minutes passed as he searched, unable to find anything suitable for the female in his quarters...on his rest slab.

Inappropriate images of her stretched out over his rest slab flew to his mind and Ajos squeezed his eyes shut and tried to control his breathing.

In that brief silence in his mind, the voices of two other beings within the supply center caught his ear.

"They are the reason they bombed the base." The voice was hushed, but he could still hear. Ajos cocked his ears.

"The Tasqals have never been successful with bombing us before. Why now?" The male snarled.

"It is those creatures' fault. The *hyoomans*." The word was spat as if it made a sour taste form in the other male's mouth. "We have lived relatively peacefully. Our sky towers have always protected us. But this stasis hold..." the speaker growled, "I knew it would bring us trouble from the first day I set sight on it. And now..."

"They might bomb us again..."

Ajos stiffened as he listened.

"The commanders are bound to the code of protecting all who are vulnerable to the Tasqals...including the cause of this disaster. They will do nothing about these new pests." There was a pause. "We have to do something about it. We have to protect ourselves."

"By any means necessary," the other agreed.

Ajos was no fool.

He knew exactly where their thoughts were going and what their conversation meant.

But to hear such words...

A sudden rage filled Ajos, so much so he was moving before he even realized what he was doing.

Turning the corner, he grabbed the male nearest to him, his hand closing around the male's throat as he slammed him into a shelf.

Supply boxes fell, their contents scattering with a loud crash.

"Do something like *what*?" Ajos growled, his words barely making it through his teeth.

In his grasp was a Krinqrid, and the male's purple skin paled. His four arms were flat against the shelf behind him as he lay plastered against it, his terrified gaze locked on Ajos.

Having not realized Ajos was so close, the friend had stumbled in an effort to escape and now he was trying to regain his footing.

Ajos' gaze didn't even flick to the male scrambling to his feet. His sole focus was the one in his grasp, and his other fist burned with the need to bury it into the male's flesh.

It was the gods' own hands that were holding his fist back from doing what his muscles itched to do most.

The male stuttered, unable to form words, and Ajos' rage only grew.

"Listen to my words," Ajos snarled, "and listen to them carefully." He leaned in close so the male could focus on nothing else but him. "If you even have the *thought* of doing something *stupid* to the humans...*erase it*," he growled, "or I...will...erase...you."

The male gulped and nodded vigorously, his gaze flicking to his friend.

"Ajos?"

Ajos stiffened at the sound of his name, and he looked sideways to see V'Alen and Hemmil standing there.

Hemmil's mouth was wide open in shock while V'Alen's gaze simply flicked over the fallen items, the Krinqrid in his grasp, then back to him.

Ajos let go of the Krinqrid so suddenly, the male fell to the floor in a heap.

He was hardly aware of the male and his friend rushing away with a scramble of limbs.

"Is everything all right, brother?"

"Everything is fine." Ajos squeezed his eyes shut for a second.

What the hell had gotten into him?

Sudden fits of rage were not a character trait of his. That was more like his brother, Akur.

Akur was a ball of Shum'ai rage all-round.

Ajos wasn't.

He was the calm one.

Taking a deep breath, he opened his eyes and glanced around the supply center.

He'd made a mess.

"I apologize, Hemmil"—his gaze flicked to the Ghanzot—"for the mess."

Hemmil's mouth finally closed. "I have never seen you behave in such a—"

"Ajos is ill," V'Alen spoke up, cutting the Ghanzot off and closing the conversation.

Ajos' throat moved. He'd never been more appreciative of his friend's lack of decorum.

Hemmil's mouth opened again slightly. "I don't think I have ever seen Ajos ill either."

"He is ill because of the explosions." V'Alen didn't wait for Hemmil to question that, he simply stepped in front of the male and addressed Ajos instead. "And it would be wise for him to head back home to rest."

Ajos swallowed hard.

V'Alen was right, as usual.

"Yes," he finally managed to say, his gaze flicking over the boxes that had spilled and that's when he saw an inflatable foam. That should work well for Keh-reh-nah.

Her name in his mind made an odd feeling develop within him.

Ignoring it, he grabbed the package and walked toward the door.

"Leave the mess, Hemmil. I will return to clean it up," he said as he passed the male.

He needed some time to think first, and he wanted to be alone.

Hemmil blinked, his singular eye making that one movement look dramatic. "No, you are ill. Please rest, my friend. I will take care of this."

Ajos moved his head in a nod before the doors opened and he walked out.

There was mild discomfort within him from the lie he just told, but he had no other explanation for his behavior.

A commander didn't behave the way he just did. *He* didn't behave the way he just did.

Maybe he *was* ill.

He walked in silence, completely aware of the fact that a few steps behind him, V'Alen followed wordlessly.

He could almost feel his friend's eyes boring into his back.

For the next few moments, he tried to ignore it, but nothing was worse than the silent judgment he felt V'Alen meting out behind him.

Stopping dead in his tracks, Ajos let out a deep breath.

"Say it." He turned.

"You are behaving out of character. I was right to follow you."

Annoyance stirred within him and coming close behind it was that rage he was feeling. Ajos squeezed his eyes tight to hold the feelings back.

"You followed me?" he ground out. "Why?"

V'Alen paused and a growl left Ajos' lips that surprised even him.

"Your nefre is red," V'Alen finally said. "I have known you for many moons and it has *never* been red before. That is a cause for concern." V'Alen studied him. "I took the liberty to investigate on my own."

Oh no.

Ajos turned and began walking again.

He didn't want to hear it.

V'Alen's form of investigation probably involved digesting every archive on the planet about him.

It was a blessing and a curse that he could do that.

V'Alen's footsteps sounded behind him.

"You are Shum'ai. Your species' reproductive cycle is catalyzed when your planet goes through its period of great warmth when it is closest to its star. Because of the strange orbit Tonvuhiri takes, most of the time it is so far away from its star, the planet remains cold. The warm cycle, however..."

Ajos groaned in annoyance at the words but kept walking anyway.

V'Alen continued.

"It is possible the extensive thermal energy from the explosions has catalyzed your reproductive cycle prematurely."

Ajos squeezed his eyes shut and held back the growl that was bubbling in his throat.

"Ajos," V'Alen said, "You are going into heat."

Sometimes, just sometimes, he wished his friend was not as curious as he happened to be.

Qeffing phek.

He couldn't be going into heat.

He was too far away from Tonvuhiri and even then, the warm cycle of the planet wasn't until many, many more moons.

Going into *heat*...and in the middle of a war?

He'd just have to find a way to ignore it.

"Brother, you *cannot ignore it*. It is already clouding your judgment and influencing your behavior. I am concerned about what it may do to your mental state."

"I'm fine."

"You are not."

They were just at their bunker, and Ajos stopped in front of it and turned.

"Drop it."

V'Alen opened his mouth again and Ajos didn't wait.

As the door slid open, he slipped inside and all but fled from his prying friend.

Kerena slipped off the hard bed, her knee-high boots touching the floor.

The room was warm enough now that she wasn't shivering anymore, but the cold had reminded her she didn't have any extra clothes.

That meant she had one dress, one pair of shoes, one bra, and one pair of panties.

Damn.

Glancing at the bathroom, she took a few steps toward it.

There was a stall she assumed was the shower and an oval receptacle that must be the toilet.

It all looked so alien, she wasn't sure she could even make it work.

Still, she was filthy.

There was dust stuck in her hair and on her skin, and even though she was dead tired, there was a good chance she wouldn't be able to get a good night's sleep when she was so icky.

Her gaze moved to the door.

She wasn't sure how to lock it, but after Ajos had left, he hadn't returned and she hadn't heard any sounds on the outside either.

It seemed he had left her alone, or he'd gone to sleep.

That meant she could probably take a quick shower and air dry before morning.

Stripping off her clothes, she let them fall to the floor by the bathroom door and walked into the small space.

Everything was so white, she was impressed at how well the minty-teal alien kept the place clean. But, he was a soldier.

Every military man she'd met had been tidy.

It was like walking into a futuristic hospital.

Even the air smelled super clean and fresh.

Walking over to the stall, she reached forward to touch the door, and it slid open on its own. Inside was...nothing, just plain white walls.

Kerena blinked, her mouth falling open as she looked around. Hugging her naked body, she turned and studied the rest of the room.

Was there some sort of button she was supposed to press?

But the walls were bare.

How on earth did he bathe?

She was about to let go of her plans to take a shower when she scratched her head and her matted hair caught in her fingers.

No, she really needed to wash. Regardless of how tired she was, she needed to get clean.

"Ughhhh," she groaned. "This should be simple. All I want is a shower."

Within two seconds, that female voice spoke. "Shower, activated."

In the roof above the stall, the ceiling opened, and a rectangular pole descended.

Kerena could only stare at it wide-eyed and wide-mouthed before it started spraying water into the stall.

Blinking at it, her mouth formed into an "O."

"So that's how you do it."

Eyebrows high on her forehead, she stepped into the stall and the door slid shut, but as soon as the water hit her, she screamed.

It was freezing cold.

"Fuck!" She jumped back. "Goddamnit!"

Fanning her hand in front of the door, she tried to get it to open but it wouldn't budge.

"Um, um," goodness gracious, it was cold, "computer, make it hotter!"

The temperature of the water changed almost immediately, and Kerena grinned, her shoulders rising and falling with relief.

However, she realized quickly that it was getting much too hot for her to shower comfortably.

"Goddamnit," she murmured. "Computer! Make the water warm enough for me, a human, but not too hot!"

"Confirmed."

Kerena's lips formed a thin line, but the water changed to a comfortable and even relaxing temperature.

Glancing around the stall, she realized something else though. There was no soap.

"Um, computer? Soap?"

"Do you wish to add cleansing products to the spray?" the computer asked.

"Um, yes?" Kerena looked up into the ceiling, her eyes moving over the whiteness. "Yes."

"There are three cleansing products loaded. Which one would you like to use?"

Kerena bit her lip. Why was this so complicated?

"Can I see a sample?"

It seemed the computer obliged because a slot in the wall beside her slid forward with three small teardrop packets on a tray.

The first one smelled like coconut, and she found she quite liked it.

The second one made her close her eyes and she inhaled it twice. Fresh winter air.

She was about to inhale the scent again when she caught herself.

Her cheeks burned with realization immediately.

Ajos.

This was the scent he liked to use.

It smelled exactly like him.

Clearing her throat, Kerena put down the packet and tried the last one.

It didn't have a scent.

"Computer, is the green one unscented?"

"Affirmative. Would you like to load the unscented cleansing agent?"

"Yes."

The slot slid back into the wall and soon a soft foam was forming on the water as it rained down on her.

As she showered, Kerena smiled.

The water felt good and as the minutes ticked by, she could feel herself slowly relaxing.

This wasn't so bad.

If she wanted, she could pretend she was at some futuristic hotel on Earth on a vacation or something.

Ajos' place was...nice.

And the computer. Wow.

It was some high-tech shit.

If the bad guys had technology that was even better than this, then what the fuck did they have?

A thought crossed her mind.

"Computer, tell me about this place."

Kerena bit her lip as she waited for a reply. It was just a hunch, but she hoped the computer was a bit like Siri and she could "alien-Google" things.

"These quarters belong to Ajos Khattull. Species: Shum'ai."

Oh...

Kerena paused and froze. She hadn't intended to ask about Ajos, she was asking about the Restitution as a whole, but now that the computer was talking, she couldn't help the fact that she wanted to know more.

The way he'd frozen up when she'd asked why he'd left his planet was still on her mind and she knew she was prying, but her survival was at the forefront of her mind.

What if she was mindlessly trusting him and it would lead to her demise?

Clearing her throat, she asked, "Was there some kind of disaster on the Shum'ai home world? Like something that forced them to leave."

There was a pause and for a moment, she thought she had probably asked the computer too much.

"No such disaster is on the record."

Wiping the water from her face, Kerena frowned.

"Then why did he leave?" she murmured to herself. "He said he 'had to go.'"

"That part of the commander's records is classified," the computer said.

Kerena felt a surge or slight shock. "Oh, I didn't mean to ask—" Letting out a breath, she shook her head. "Nevermind."

She was just about finished showering anyway.

Telling the computer she was finished, she watched as the water shut off. The pole disappeared into the ceiling, and the water at her feet seemed to seep into the floor itself.

The door to the stall slid open and Kerena stepped out, hugging herself.

Shaking as much of the water as she could from herself, she headed back to the bedroom only to realize she was no longer alone. Kerena yelped, one arm covering her breasts as the other flew to cover her crotch.

Ajos turned at the sound, and his eyes visibly widened.

"Um, I—" Kerena stuttered.

Fuck. It.

This was the second time she'd shown him her nakedness without intending to.

"I didn't know you were in here."

He was crouching over the bed and she realized he'd been setting something on it that looked like a mattress.

Something inside her melted a little.

He'd gone to look for bedding for her? He'd even placed a blanket on top.

It was obvious he didn't sleep with those things, so he'd gone out of his way without her asking.

"A mattress?" She smiled. "Thank you. You didn't have to." Just looking at it, she knew she was going to sleep like a log and God knew she needed the rest.

These past few days had just been *mad*.

That's when she realized that he wasn't saying anything.

And, when her eyes fell on him again, she became aware he was simply staring at her.

And...he looked different.

Something about him was different, and she couldn't quite tell what that thing was.

For what felt like long seconds, he just stared at her, and he was looking at her as if he was some wild thing that was about to pounce.

Shit.

She could almost feel herself go pale as she took a step backward.

Had he heard her? Had he heard her asking about him in the bathroom?

Shiiiiiiit.

Kerena blinked, trying to find the right words.

What should she say?

She'd been a horrible guest by being so nosy, but she'd done it because she also didn't want to be that idiot who got killed because of their own ignorance.

Before she could even think though, Ajos moved toward her, and with her stupid ass, she couldn't move.

She was frozen like a deer in headlights.

He stooped when he was almost upon her, so close she could smell that fresh winter scent of his, and reached forward.

His arm brushed her naked leg as he took hold of her dirty clothes, his large hand fisting the fabric in such a way that made her gulp, her mind moving to some dirty, dirty thoughts that had nothing to do with laundry.

He paused there, so close to her body, and the entire thing was suddenly so intense, she didn't know what to do.

What's worse, there was a tingle—a tingle deep inside of her that wasn't supposed to be there.

She opened her mouth to speak, but Ajos spoke before she could.

"I will clean these for you," he said, slowly rising to his full height.

The air stirred and every hair on her body stood on end, her skin tingling as if there was unseen energy charging the space between them.

When his eyes met hers, they looked feral and even his voice had come out like a growl.

Still, she wasn't afraid.

She fucking should be. Some long-lost instinct was telling her that. But it seemed it was being trampled by something more powerful.

"Sleep well, Keh-reh-nah." Ajos jerked as he moved away from her, almost as if he was forcing his limbs to move. Even the tendons in his neck looked taut.

What was happening?

"Ajos, I..."

At the sound of his name, Ajos blinked and his throat moved.

Without another word, he moved toward the door and stepped out.

Kerena's mouth remained open, even though she didn't know what she'd been about to say.

He left her staring at the closed door and it took her a few moments to realize the last image she saw was Ajos' hands grasping her clothes—her dirty clothes, filthy drawers included.

Fuck. Her.

10

Sleep was eventful.

The nightmares that had her waking every other hour ranged from images of being taken to images of Cindy Clawford meeting an untimely demise in her apartment.

The cat was all alone and she really could only hope and pray her neighbor visited and took Cindy home.

As she opened her eyes for probably the seven hundredth time, Kerena stared up into the white ceiling.

The bed was comfortable, but despite her exhaustion, she wouldn't be able to sleep properly.

This was probably how her mind was sorting through this life-changing experience—with nightmares. She probably just needed time for everything to settle.

Releasing a breath, she stretched underneath the blanket Ajos had provided her.

What now?

What would today bring?

She guessed she was going to head back to the hospital and offer any help she could.

Damn, if she'd known she'd have been placed in this situation, she wouldn't have specialized in botany, she'd have become a medical doctor like her father had wanted her to.

It's not like she even had any plants here that she could study. She wasn't in the pharmaceutical business anymore.

But there must be some way she could help.

Easing up on her elbows, she yawned. The light had been dim, but now that she'd moved, it brightened, illuminating the room.

Her gaze fell immediately on the clothes placed at the foot of the bed.

Her dress was spread out and her bra and panties were placed to the side of it.

Kerena blinked before moving fast to grab the items.

He'd come in here while she was sleeping?

Not only that, but the clothes were clean.

Sniffing the dress, she couldn't get any sense of sweat or dirt from the fibers. It was the same for her panties and bra.

Kerena squeezed her eyes tight, a cringe and a giggle developing within her.

Of all the things to allow her host to do, washing her intimates hadn't ever been on the list.

Anyway, she shrugged and slipped the clothes on.

Raking her hands through her hair, she hoped she looked presentable enough.

She moved to slip on her boots when she noticed that they looked clean too.

He must have come in and done them while she was sleeping.

She wasn't sure how to feel about that—the fact that he'd been around her while she'd been unconscious—but it seemed he really had come in just to complete her laundry.

Straightening her dress, she moved toward the door and slipped out of the room and into the corridor.

She could hear voices coming from down the hall, so she headed that way.

As she reached the room, she saw the source of the voices.

Ajos sat with V'Alen at a counter, facing away from her.

With their backs turned, they didn't see her approach, but she was sure V'Alen was aware of her presence.

He didn't turn to look at her, but as soon as she came to the room, his head angled a bit in her direction, as if he knew she was there.

"You are awake, Kerena," V'Alen said.

At the sound of her name, Ajos noticeably stiffened and whatever he was eating paused halfway in his hand on the way to his lips.

"I am," she answered. "Good morning." She stepped into the room, her eyes on the minty-teal alien.

He was still pissed. He'd definitely heard her asking the computer about him then.

V'Alen slipped off a seat. "Sit here," he said before brushing past her to move to the other side of the counter.

Her eyes remained on Ajos as she moved forward and took a seat.

As she sat, Ajos slipped the food he was eating into his mouth, but he still didn't look her way. She could hardly see his face under the hood he wore.

It didn't seem as if he was chewing either.

Maybe he was upset with her, but he also wasn't a morning person.

Still, his whole demeanor seemed strange.

Different.

This wasn't the same alien who had helped her yesterday. This wasn't the same alien who had saved her life.

"Is everything all right?"

Ajos seemed to stiffen even more, and he even adjusted the hood he was wearing.

"Ajos is...ill," V'Alen said.

Kerena's eyes widened a little.

Was that what it was?

"You are?"

"I'm *fine*." It was a growl, but Ajos was glaring in V'Alen's direction and not at her.

"He—"

"*Drop it.*" Those words also came out as a growl, and Kerena felt the vibration down her spine.

V'Alen seemed to drop the argument, Ajos obviously didn't want anyone worrying over him, and slid something toward her in a bowl.

It looked like a bowl of couscous with some kind of sauce on top.

Her stomach growled.

"What is this?"

"Your fellow humans prepared it. It is rai cooked strangely with alae sauce."

V'Alen passed her a curved utensil that could work as a spoon, and she dipped it in the food and brought it to her lips.

The food had a strange texture but not strange enough that she wanted to spit it out and the sauce...the sauce had a sort of lemony taste.

Chewing quickly, she took another spoonful.

"This is," she chewed, "this is good."

As she dipped the spoon again, she paused and glanced at Ajos, only to find that he was looking at her with the same intensity with which he'd been looking at her the night before.

For a moment, she forgot what she was doing, but as she brought the spoon to her lips, his gaze followed her movement and held there.

He watched as the spoon slid into her mouth and she suddenly felt self-conscious as she chewed.

She didn't know what to think of the way he was looking at her.

Did aliens not eat the way humans did?

Was the way she was using the spoon strange to him?

The way she chewed?

Ajos groaned—she was sure of it—and turned away from her a little, adjusting the hood of his clothing some more.

He must be in pain.

"Is... I don't know if I'm crossing any cultural boundaries here. I mean, a few days ago, I was just a regular girl on Earth and today I'm eating breakfast with aliens, but...you sound like you're in pain." She studied Ajos. She could hardly see his face because of the hood of his clothing. "Is there anything I can do to help?"

She reached toward him, touching him lightly, and Ajos hissed. Kerena's eyes widened, her hand jerking away at the speed of light.

Ajos groaned and stretched the muscles in his neck as a deep rumble left his throat.

"Actually, Ajos, the female could help with your—"

"Qef, V'Alen! *Drop it!*" Ajos slammed his fist into the counter and the thing must be made from the strongest material on that planet because it didn't crack from the pressure.

Kerena was surprised she, herself, didn't jerk and fall off the seat in shock at the sudden outburst. V'Alen didn't budge.

Seconds that felt like minutes dragged by.

"As you wish," the robot man finally said. "Should we continue our conversation later, brother?"

Ajos loosened his fist, but he didn't answer his friend.

Kerena cleared her throat. She'd made him furious. It was evident.

"Did I interrupt something?"

V'Alen studied her. "No, but what we were discussing is classified."

Ajos let out a breath. "Classified, yes, but the entire base is probably discussing it already." His voice sounded different. Deeper. Raspier. "It doesn't matter if she hears it now or later, the worry will reach the humans soon."

"What worry?" Her spoon balanced in her fingers as her gaze moved from one alien to the next.

Ajos seemed to sigh and set down what he was eating—something that looked like a wonton.

"We do not know how the sky towers didn't alert us of the fighter ships approaching. Almost four days and they still have not figured it out." He took a breath. "The sky towers are there for this purpose. They monitor everything that comes into orbit close to us. It's how we've kept safe all these years or the Tasqals would have bombed us to the ground already." His eyes finally met hers. "Now we know they can. But we do not know how."

Kerena blinked a few times and put down her spoon.

"So..." she began. "The Tasqals. You're saying they managed to just...turn up? The sky towers didn't pick them up at all?"

V'Alen spoke. "Correct."

She must be dumb or something because it seemed obvious to her.

"Stealth? Could they have used some sort of stealth?"

V'Alen spoke again. "That would be the first assumption, but it is not that simple. The ships that attacked..."

"They jumped into the troposphere, then exited the same way."

Kerena frowned before her eyes bugged out. "What?"

She glanced from Ajos to V'Alen then back.

"They entered from hyperspace so close to the surface, then exited the same way," Ajos murmured, turning over another maybe-wonton between his fingers.

She was no rocket scientist, but she'd watched enough sci-fi movies to know that the discharge from doing that would have caused major damage.

Had that been what had happened?

Had it been the result of the enemies' ships entering hyperspace and not the effect of bombs that had killed so many and destroyed so much?

"No," Ajos answered, and she realized she'd asked the questions out loud. "But you are right, Keh-reh-nah. What they have done... what they did is theoretically impossible. They entered, bombed us, and left. They jumped into hyperspace right on top of us, but it had no effect. The bombs did."

For a few moments, no one said anything.

"What does this mean?" she finally asked.

"It means," Ajos answered, "the Restitution and all that it protects is in grave danger." He paused. "We are all in grave danger."

"And all vulnerable worlds within the Tasqals' reach," V'Alen answered.

Kerena stared at her bowl.

She didn't feel like eating anymore.

Back on Earth, when she'd wished for a great new year with new horizons, she hadn't been speaking literally. She certainly hadn't been asking the universe to place her in the middle of an intergalactic war.

This is why you have to be specific with your manifestations, Kerena, because apparently, that shit works.

The silence between them continued even as Ajos popped the food into his mouth and continued eating. Taking up her spoon, Kerena ate more slowly than she had started, a bunch of thoughts swirling in her head.

This wasn't a war the humans could escape from. They were in this now, and it was something they were going to have to face.

"How do we help?" She chewed the last spoonful and put down the utensil. "How can *I* help?"

"What?" Ajos turned, his words a growl and his eyes flashing what she was sure was liquid fire.

That made her lean away from him a little.

Gathering her wits, she continued. "I want to help. I can't fight. I don't know how to use a gun. But there must be some way I can help." Those golden eyes of his studied her with an intensity that almost made her squirm.

"I'm a botanist. That might mean nothing in this world, but on Earth, it meant that I had at least something going on up here to have passed those exams." She pointed to her head. "I want to help in any way I can."

Ajos glanced at V'Alen before his gaze settled back on her. "We did not expect any of you humans to wish to join the fight so quickly."

"Well, it beats sitting on my ass doing nothing when we all are in danger of being killed."

Neither he nor V'Alen said anything.

Instead, Ajos' golden gaze held hers in its grasp for such a long moment, she forgot to breathe.

There was that tingle again—a tingle like something was fluttering deep, deep within her because of the intensity of that gaze, and she wasn't sure what it was...

It felt like, if she allowed it to grow, it would consume her.

Just then, there was a sound from what she'd thought was a watch on Ajos' hand.

"Commander, do you read?"

Ajos pressed something on the "watch."

"Speak, Iceon."

"Please come to Sky Tower 2," the transmission crackled. "There is something I wish for you to see."

Ajos was still holding her gaze, and Kerena licked her lips as she waited for his decision.

Would he let her help or what?

Slipping off the seat in a movement that was much too graceful for such a large man, Ajos adjusted his hood over his head.

"Okay," he said. "Keh-reh-nah..."

A moment passed before he continued.

"Welcome to the Restitution. Let's go."

11

IT TURNED OUT THAT ALTHOUGH SHE'D HAVE TO ATTAIN SOME MORE clothing, the dress that she wore was perfectly suited to Murn GZ.

It was a favorable temperature outside. Not hot but not cold and the air was dry but not uncomfortably so.

The whiteness of the sun still rubbed against her senses, that and the hardened dirt everywhere. Back on Earth, she'd spent so much time indoors, so much time at work, she'd hardly gone outside just for the sake of it.

She'd been missing out.

There was so much more than sterile laboratories and white walls.

She glanced around as they walked, trying to familiarize herself with where she was.

It had been dark when Ajos had taken her to his home the night before, and along with her tiredness, she hadn't been able to see much around her.

Now, though, she could see everything.

The first thing she tried to pinpoint was the blast zone, but they were either too far away from it or the rebels had done a good job of cleaning everything up.

As far as she could see, the buildings looked intact.

"I must know," V'Alen suddenly spoke. "How is it that you know of hyperspace—of jumping?"

She was walking between them, him and Ajos, and she turned her head to glance up at the robot by her side.

"Your planet is...a Class Four planet," V'Alen continued. "You have not yet discovered such technology, neither have you created it. Records concerning your planet state you have not yet fully discovered your planetary system. Even the closest body to you, the satellite, you have yet to explore one side of it—the side you call the dark side."

Kerena's eyebrows rose and she smiled. It surprised her that he knew so much about Earth.

"How is it that a civilization that is so...primitive...knows of such advanced science?" He tilted his head as he spoke as if he was trying to figure out some difficult puzzle.

"We have sci-fi movies. There's Star Trek, Star Wars, and a host of others. That's where I learned about hyperspace jumps from. Like, in Star Wars: The Last Jedi, they had to save the Resistance by jumping to hyperspace straight through..." Kerena caught herself and a sheepish smile came over her features but V'Alen only cocked his head some more.

He didn't frown, she noticed. His facial muscles seemed mostly unaffected by emotion, but the way he cocked his head said he was still confused.

"It was just a movie." She couldn't help but chuckle.

"A movie?"

"You know, *movies*. Like...wait, you don't have movies?"

He blinked at her but didn't answer.

Kerena gawked at him. "You know, like imaginary worlds that people create and turn into moving pictures for entertainment?"

V'Alen blinked again and Ajos grumbled something.

"What was that?" She turned her attention to the tall alien.

"V'Alen does not imagine. He cannot understand the concept."

Her mouth formed an 'O'.

That was something she couldn't wrap her mind around.

"Oh. Well..." she glanced at the robot man, "that's how I know about that stuff. But I don't know how to explain it to you now that I know you have no idea what I mean."

V'Alen jerked his head almost imperceptibly and she assumed the conversation was finished.

They were walking for maybe five minutes now and the farther they walked, the more aliens she saw.

Most were going about their daily lives, walking down the streets pushing carts or carrying loads in their arms. Some were walking in groups and were heavily kitted out with weapons.

There were so many types of aliens, she couldn't keep track.

There were tall man-beasts that looked like yetis...small beings dressed in little brown robes who didn't even pass her knee in height...she was sure she saw an octopus man and there was even an alien that had hard scales like chitin all over his body.

It felt like walking down any street, except she was walking among beings that were so different from her in many ways.

However, despite that the beings around them were so different, she noticed one distinct similarity—most, if not all of them, were looking directly at her.

At first, she thought they were looking at the three of them collectively.

They were quite the trio—a robot, a human, and a tall minty-teal guy—only, it soon became clear that the onlookers were paying no attention to Ajos and V'Alen.

They were looking at *her*...and she knew she wasn't imagining this second part, but the looks there were giving her sent distinct shivers down her spine.

It made the hairs at the back of her neck stand on end as if there was some kind of threat in her midst and when Ajos brushed against her, she was sure it was because he sensed it too and had moved closer to her.

There was a growl in his throat again, one that made his body vibrate and she could feel that vibration each time he brushed against her bare arm.

Just what the hell was going on?

"We're here," he said, breaking the musings in her head and she realized they were walking up to a strangely shaped building.

It looked like a brown cone with the top chopped off.

The door slid open and an armed alien was standing there. He was purple with four arms and as soon as Ajos saw the alien, a rumbling sound began in his throat.

"Krinnnnnqrid." The word came from Ajos' lips in a drawn-out growl.

"Com-Commander." She was sure the alien lost some of his color. He looked utterly terrified and when his eyes settled on her, they widened even more.

V'Alen moved forward, blocking them both from the quivering alien's view. "We are heading to Sky Tower 2."

"Y-yes," the male said, inching backward a little. "Iceon already sent the approval." His eyes were on Ajos. "Please board."

V'Alen moved forward and Kerena followed him, her brows furrowing.

A lot was happening that she didn't understand, and that was to be expected. She'd just arrived. But the strange woman in the hospital, the strange looks she'd gotten as they'd walked down the street, and Ajos' change in attitude were making her feel unsettled.

V'Alen walked toward a set of four seats with the backs facing each other in a circle. As he sat, he secured the seatbelts around himself and Kerena attempted to do the same. Only, she couldn't figure out how to do it.

It wasn't like the seatbelts on Earth that had a simple clasp that you could slip in and hear it click. This one didn't have any connections that looked like they went together.

Minty-teal hands grasped hers and for a second, both of them paused.

She was sure she heard Ajos inhale sharply but as soon as the moment came, it went. Ajos secured the restraints before sitting on her other side.

He refused to meet her gaze.

Instead, he pulled the hooded garment he wore even farther over himself, almost obscuring his face completely.

Kerena pursed her lips.

Men.

There were two types: the ones who got sick and behaved like the world was ending and those who could walk through a minefield and pretend that losing an arm was just a regular occurrence.

She didn't have to guess which one Ajos was.

"Pod launching," the purple alien said, and a metallic cover came over the three of them.

The top of it was see-through, and it took her a moment to realize what was about to happen.

"Launching?"

There was no other indication that she was going to be shot upward with a force that made it feel like her brain was trying to escape from the top of her skull.

A scream lodged in her throat as she gripped the seat beneath her and watched, wide-eyed, as everything on the ground below quickly became smaller.

When they'd said "sky tower", she'd been thinking something like a huge radio tower. She hadn't thought it was actually *in the sky*.

God help her, it seemed to be even farther than that, for the pod slowed down and something that sounded like thrusters began working as it spun about ten degrees and began heading into SPACE.

"I apologize," Ajos said. "We should have warned you. I forgot what it was like my first time."

Kerena stared at him wide-eyed.

Ya think?

But her initial fear soon gave way to the wonder that was before her.

For the next few minutes, she tried to keep her entrails within her as she gripped the seat. The transport changed trajectory once more, spinning a little as it headed to a structure floating above the planet.

It was like a small disk with a series of antennae above it.

The sky tower.

And space...space was beautiful!

It was black, empty, vast, but oh so beautiful.

Below them, the planet they'd just left came into view and it was the most wondrous thing she'd ever seen in her life.

It looked nothing like Earth.

From above, it looked like a brownish-red ball, like pictures she'd seen of Mars.

There was no green for foliage and no blue for oceans.

Kerena leaned forward as her eyes widened, taking in the sight.

This was the type of view the astronauts on the International Space Station saw every day.

How did they ever return to their lives on the surface after witnessing something so profound?

Her awe must have been present on her face because she noticed Ajos was watching her with interest.

"I've never seen anything like this before," she whispered.

He averted his gaze to the outside of the pod before looking back at her.

His gaze traveled over her face so slowly, it felt as if he was memorizing the moment.

"I think," her gaze moved over the planet below, "I think it's one of the most beautiful things I have ever seen."

There was a pause, and she thought he wasn't going to respond, before he said, "I am beginning to think so too."

There was a note in his voice that made her gaze snap to his and her breath stopped in her nostrils at that one look.

As she blinked, he seemed to snap out of whatever trance was holding them in stasis and his throat moved. The moment was gone, and he bent just enough that she couldn't see his face underneath the hooded clothing anymore.

AJOS ADJUSTED the hood he was wearing as soon as the small pod landed.

His skin felt warm underneath the thing, uncomfortable, but he had to wear it for as long as they were on the base.

He couldn't allow anyone else seeing the blatant redness of his nefre and figuring out what was happening.

Slipping out of the seat, he moved over to Keh-reh-nah, steeling himself on this occasion in case their skin touched again.

The last time he'd helped her with the restraints, he'd touched her and it had caused his nefre to pulse so hard, he was sure it had sent all his life blood straight to his genital pouch.

And then he'd had to sit with his seed sack aching for the entire flight.

He was beginning to think him being this close to her might not have been the best idea.

Whatever was happening to him, this *heat*, was escalating too quickly.

Taking a deep breath, he grit his teeth as he disengaged the female's seat restraints.

Bad. Qeffing. Idea.

Leaning over her like this, her scent floated upward toward his nostrils.

She hadn't used any fragrances to wash last night.

He could tell because he could scent her—fresh... natural...earthly...

She smelled good.

So good.

His throat moved as he tried to control the sudden groan that developed within him, and he thought he'd done a good job of hiding it too, but when he looked at her, those brown eyes were searching his gaze.

Ajos turned away.

He was a commander and *she* was a refugee—someone he'd sworn to protect, if even from himself.

He needed to control this...problem he was having, but his will was as weak as V'Alen's ability to control his mouth.

His friend could not keep his mouth shut, and the last thing he wanted was for this small human to find out she had a male in her presence that was having trouble controlling his *urges*.

She'd just been rescued from sick beasts that had wanted her solely for her body.

He did not want to remind her of that.

Further, he was nothing like the sick beasts called the Tasqals.

He shot a glare at V'Alen, willing his friend to keep his mouth shut.

He knew the cyborg could hear every groan he made when he tried to keep himself in check.

He had to push through it.

At least, until he could find a way to fix the problem.

But qef...she smelled good.

Inhaling one last time, Ajos held his breath and eased back to allow Keh-reh-nah to exit her seat.

"This way," he mumbled. It was his best effort at keeping his voice sounding normal.

As they walked from the dock into the Sky Tower, Keh-reh-nah's steps were confident alongside his and V'Alen's.

He was a little impressed that she'd even considered offering assistance in this fight.

She'd just survived a bombing recently. He'd thought she'd be cowering in his bed.

A pulse in his nefre went right to his cock at that thought.

His bed.

She'd been sleeping in his bed.

When he'd brought in her clothes the night before, she'd laid curled up in his space, her strange filaments covering most of her face, and the strangest sound coming from her nostrils as she slept.

It had sounded like a baby pherzah. It should have been a horrible sound, but he'd found himself pausing a little too long as he'd listened to it.

It had sounded...cute.

Endearing.

The qef was wrong with him?

The doors that led from the dock into the sky tower slid open and Ajos led them down the corridor to the control room.

There was hardly anyone working in the Sky Tower, most of the refugees and rebels wanted to live on the surface, so those that volunteered to do the job of guarding the planet often led a lonely life.

Only those who didn't have any family or much of anything to look forward to on the surface took such jobs.

He wondered briefly which category their host belonged to.

As the door to the control room slid open, Iceon turned from the many screens in front of him to glance their way.

"Commander," he said before turning back to his instruments. Then he spun around again and did a double-take.

Ajos grunted.

He guessed it was the hooded garment he wore.

"Commander?" Iceon asked.

Ajos moved the hood back enough for the male to see it was him, and Iceon jerked his head in confirmation before his eyes wandered and suddenly focused.

For a moment, Ajos thought the male was looking at V'Alen but when he followed the Ochair's line of sight, he realized the male was looking at Keh-reh-nah.

She was looking at him too, her eyes filled with awe. Then she smiled slightly and waved her hand in the air at Iceon.

Ajos growled.

He hoped that wasn't some sort of invitation in her culture.

He didn't want Iceon getting any ideas.

Keh-reh-nah's gaze flashed his way and this time she frowned, those brown eyes of hers studying him again.

Better to get this meeting over with, and fast.

"You said you had something to show me, Iceon."

Iceon jerked his head in a nod, his eyes still on Keh-reh-nah, and Ajos held back another growl.

Moving so he stepped a little in front of her, Ajos broke Iceon's line of sight.

"What is it?" he pressed, agitation riding on the edge of his nefre like an annoying wave.

Iceon blinked and ran a hand through his strange fur.

"The ships that attacked a few days ago," he began. "We had intercepted a signal some time before they came."

"I picked up on that signal," V'Alen said. "It started broadcasting as soon as we breached the stasis hold."

"Right." Iceon ran his hand through the fur on his crown again. "We believe the Tasqals will return. The explosions were just a warning. I think," his gaze slipped from Ajos and fell on—Keh-reh-nah... and it seemed the Ochair forgot his line of thought, for he stopped speaking.

Ajos frowned, his gaze falling to the movement by his side.

She'd stepped from behind his body shield and was in view of the male again.

Ajos stretched the muscles in his neck.

Annoyance grew and the urge to punch Iceon in the face, if only to set his gaze in another direction, was almost overwhelming. So overwhelming, he had to clench his fists at his side.

It was just the need.

He had no claim on this female.

He had to remind himself of that.

Still, Iceon was phekking him off with the way he couldn't stop looking in Keh-reh-nah's direction.

"You think *what*?" he growled, a little harsher than he'd intended. It was enough to bring Iceon back to the present, but it also caused Keh-reh-nah to frown at him once more.

"The Tasqals want the humans back. I'm afraid they will come again and we don't nearly have enough ships to patrol our borders. Even then, they might do what they did the other day and bypass all our defenses, exiting hyperspace in the midst of the city...we still don't know how they managed to do that."

"Has this ever happened before?" Keh-reh-nah's voice cut in, and Ajos closed his eyes for a second. She moved to stand beside him, so close, he could feel the warmth of her skin.

And it was so, qeffing, inviting.

If he pressed himself against her, melded their warmth together, the combined heat would consume them both.

Great going with that thought. His seed sack was aching even more now.

Ajos crossed his arms over his chest as he shifted on his feet, just enough to move away from her a little without making it look obvious.

She shouldn't be affecting him so much. No one affected him this much, heat or not.

With a few steps, he moved to lean against the control panel and faced the three beings in his presence.

"Have these guys, the Tasqals, ever tried to destroy the base to get refugees back before?" Keh-reh-nah continued and Ajos watched her mouth move, barely hearing what she'd said.

She had intelligent eyes, asked valid questions...from the very first moment he'd met her, she hadn't behaved the way he'd expected her to.

She wasn't cowering and hoping for this nightmare to end. She was already facing reality and was even active in the fight.

Unlike those cowardly Krinqrids he'd found in the supply center the other night, she was putting herself in the position to fight their common enemy—not wasting her energy planning rebellions within their ranks.

Memory of the gutless males made him even more agitated.

He should have broken their necks.

But there were laws, codes of conduct, at least, that he as a commander had to follow.

"No," V'Alen said, pulling Ajos back to the present. "They have never outright attacked us like this. At least, we didn't know they could...and possibly, they didn't because they only discovered the technology to do so recently."

Ajos glanced at his friend. "Do you really believe that?"

"No," V'Alen admitted. "Such technology...it is not something one just happens to discover."

"So they've been working on it..." Ajos murmured, "and used it because we found the stasis hold."

Keh-reh-nah's eyes widened a little. "You think they bombed the base because of us, humans, *specifically*?" Her brows furrowed a little. "Why? What do we have that they want so badly?"

That was a good question, and one none of them could answer.

Ajos' gaze narrowed as he looked at Keh-reh-nah.

What made the humans so special that the Tasqals were so upset over losing them?

It went much further than simply losing precious cargo.

"There's something else," Iceon said, breaking the silence. "We hit one of their ships before it jumped. Hit it with a magnetic charge."

Ajos eased up a little off the control panel, becoming instantly alert.

"We didn't manage to bring down the vessel before it left, but it seems the charge did something at least." Iceon paused.

"Go on," Ajos urged.

"Look at this," Iceon said before turning back to his screens and pulling up a diagram.

It was one that showed Murn GZ's planetary system.

Iceon zoomed in on a section past the asteroid zone.

"We believe the magnetic charge disrupted the ship's navigation. It dropped out of hyperspace just outside of the asteroid zone and it seems it crashed on Choria G622."

"Why is this of note?" Ajos asked, leaning forward to study the diagram.

Iceon let out a breath. "Because," he said. "It is emitting a signal."

"Another beacon?" V'Alen stepped forward.

"No," Iceon said, and his gaze once again fell on Keh-reh-nah as she came between him and Ajos to look at the diagram too. "It's not a beacon, but it's a signal nonetheless," he said. "It's not transmitting anything, more like...interfering. I only noticed it because it is affecting the tracker in the charge we hit the ship with."

V'Alen leaned forward. "Let me hear it."

As Iceon pulled up the data so they could investigate further, Ajos' eyes moved down the female by his side.

Was she oblivious to the fact that she was affecting the technician?

The closer she leaned to study the diagram, the more Iceon's vibrissae seemed to shiver.

Ajos held back another growl, his brow knitting into a frown.

The silence was suddenly broken with a crackle as Iceon played the signal in the room.

V'Alen stood up straight. "This is not like anything I have ever heard before."

"Can you decode it?"

"No," V'Alen said. "It is...ancient. I cannot determine what it is... only that it is from another time." He looked at Iceon. "Are you sure it is coming from the ship?"

"Positive." Iceon nodded, and his vibrissae shivered again.

Movement caught Ajos' eye, and he noticed that Iceon's furry tail was curling upward toward Keh-reh-nah.

He couldn't hold back his growl this time, and everyone in the room looked at him.

"We should investigate it." He ignored that the sound he'd just made was threatening.

Hopefully, they would think it was because he was angry about the whole bombing situation.

"Yes," V'Alen agreed. "I will get the ship ready."

"Oh," Keh-reh-nah's eyes lit up. "You're going off-world?"

"Yes," he answered, noting the sudden glee mixed with mild trepidation in her eyes.

"Ok. I guess since this is a military thing, I might not be cleared for that." She glanced around the room. "I could maybe stay here and help Iceon brainstorm why the Tasqals want us humans so badly," she offered.

Iceon's eyes lit up and his vibrissae flexed again.

Ajos grit his teeth.

Qeffing trusting this human was. Her planet must hold little danger.

She didn't even know Iceon.

His frown deepened. She trusted him, too.

"You are not afraid of me?" Iceon asked.

Keh-reh-nah looked at the male and smiled a little.

"I wasn't sure at first, to be honest." She eyed Iceon. "You look like a tiger almost, and I should be afraid, but...you can talk. It takes the fear away, a little." She shrugged. "I guess I have a thing for cats."

A spike of rage shot through Ajos, so much so, he could hardly see. In one movement, he moved to stand between the two, not caring that what he was doing was obvious at this point.

"No," he said. "You are under my care. You are coming with me."

There was a pause and Keh-reh-nah's eyebrows lifted a little. Excitement filled those brown pools of hers even more and Ajos felt something tingle within him that dissipated the rage simmering at his core.

She'd rather come with him than stay with Iceon, even though Iceon's appearance pleased her.

Ajos' fists unclenched somewhat. He hadn't expected that.

"Do you think that's a wise idea?" V'Alen piped up. "Especially since you are going through—"

"It's *fine*," he cut his friend off before V'Alen could tell the world he was in heat.

It *was* fine.

He could deal with it.

He could deal with his *urges*.

All he had to do was keep his distance away from the female. Keh-reh-nah.

That shouldn't be too hard.

Should it?

12

"ARE YOU SURE IT'S OKAY FOR ME TO COME?" KERENA GLANCED UP AT the tall alien as they walked into what seemed to be a shipyard.

"Are you worried?" Ajos asked, glancing down at her. "I wouldn't take you if it wasn't a relatively straightforward mission. We will go, retrieve whatever is giving off that signal, and return. Choria G622 is untouched and we'll scan the area before landing."

They ducked under the hull of a massive vessel and Ajos studied her some more. "V'Alen, can you calculate the chances of encountering difficulties on this mission?"

V'Alen answered immediately. "I have already calculated it. Kerena should be safe unless something random occurs."

"Oh, I'm not worried about that," Kerena spoke up. "I'm asking because I want to know if—"

The truth was, she didn't want Ajos to feel like he had to babysit her or anything.

"I would rather you come with me than stay with that Ochair."

"Ochair?"

"Iceon," Ajos growled out the name as they came to stand in front of a ship, and Kerena had to look up at him with puzzled eyes.

The way he acted was as if he was...*jealous.*

Of what, though?

"This is ours," he said, pulling her gaze away from him to the ship now in front of them.

The door to the shuttle slid open and Ajos hopped in.

Shaped like a fish, the ship had a sort of tapered front and a flared tail with three big pipe-like things sticking out.

"It looks like a fish."

She had no idea why those words left her lips because both aliens were now looking at her as if they had no idea what she was talking about.

It was then that she suddenly felt as if *she* was the alien.

Ajos stretched a hand toward her and she grasped it.

His skin felt warm, hot actually, hotter than the last time she'd touched him at least, and that hadn't been too long ago.

When he didn't immediately pull her up, she rose her gaze to his face only to find him focused on the contact of their hands. There was a grimace on his face.

Was he in pain?

It felt like he was running a fever.

He was still acting strange, different, and she was beginning to think it was because of whatever illness he was experiencing.

It didn't seem to be anything life-threatening, but he *had* hurt his back while protecting her.

And now he was burning up.

She couldn't help but wonder if he had some sort of infection and this was his body's way of fighting it off.

As he helped her into the shuttle, he let go of her hand as if her touch was the thing causing him pain.

"Ajos, are you okay? I—"

"I'm fine," he grunted, turning away quickly. Then, as if realizing how angry he sounded, he added. "You shouldn't worry about me."

She frowned at his back as he took a seat at the front of the shuttle and began punching buttons in front of him.

They'd stopped by the hospital before they headed to the shuttle, just to check in on the other humans there. He'd spoken to the doctor guy, Aker, and she was sure she saw the doctor hand him some vials of something.

It must have been medicine of some kind, so she shouldn't worry about him. Yet...

The doctor seemed to know what he was doing, and she'd been happy to see that most of the humans in the clinic looked well.

Some still had the devices that were repairing the eye damage from the light exposure and some were still nursing more severe injuries but, largely, the entire group seemed to be more tolerant of the aliens that were helping.

Alaina had been up and about and Constance too. The cut on Alaina's head had completely healed, and Constance's broken arm was on its way to recovery.

It seemed the aliens had some super medicine that she couldn't wait to study herself.

As V'Alen hopped into the shuttle next and took the second seat in front of the controls, Kerena settled into the one behind him just so she could freely look at Ajos without it being obvious she was staring.

He was still wearing the hooded shirt and his face was hidden. But, from the rigid set of his shoulders, she knew that despite that he was pretending everything was okay, something was very wrong.

She'd only known him a few days and God knew it felt like it was longer than that, but she could tell, alien or not, that he was hiding the extent of his pain.

Clenching her teeth, she frowned at his back, his advice about not worrying echoing in her head.

He knew what was medically best for himself, more than she would.

She'd give it a rest and not push it further, but if it looked like he was killing himself, she sure as hell was going to say something about it.

The finality of those words settling in her head, she began looking around.

The spaceship was smaller than she'd thought it was going to be. It had four seats set up in two rows—two seats in front and two in back.

Behind her, there was a space with what looked like a hatch on the ship's floor.

On either side of that, she could see four suits standing in cases.

As the door to the ship slid shut, the seat restraints tightened around her automatically.

Kerena took a deep breath.

She still couldn't believe she was about to do this. As if the short trip up to the space station hadn't been enough, she was going to go to a whole other planet.

"Systems ready?" Ajos asked.

"Systems ready," V'Alen confirmed.

"Thrusters engaged?"

"Thrusters engaged."

Ajos turned to look at her, and once again she was surprised at how huge he was.

Unlike her, dwarfed by her seat, Ajos looked almost too big, too tall, to be sitting in such a small space.

"Ready, Keh-reh-nah?" It felt like his gaze was molten gold, burning her skin as he stared at her, his voice caressing every syllable of her name.

Why was it that every time he looked at her, it felt as if he wasn't *just* looking at her?

"Ready." That breathless voice was hers. She only realized that after she heard the words and realized they'd left her mouth.

Ajos heard it too because his gaze lingered a little too long.

Jerking his head in what she assumed was a nod, Ajos pulled his gaze away.

As the lights in the shuttle dimmed and the aliens in front of her initialized the lift-off sequence, she couldn't help but stare at him.

The night before, after she'd exited the shower and he'd brushed against her...

She shouldn't be thinking this but...

What would a relationship with a being like him be like?

Athena and the other three women who'd been rescued first had formed relationships with the aliens. Close relationships.

It felt wrong to be thinking about something so trivial now, in the middle of a war, and when the lives of not only everyone in this shuttle but everyone on the base hung in the balance.

But...

Still...

The thought lingered.

And she supposed it had a strong basis to stay.

There weren't any human men to form relationships with. If this was her life now, was she going to spend the rest of it alone?

Ajos wasn't human...

But he was handsome in a sort of way that had her staring and admiring from afar. His bone structure alone...

He looked like he was carved from something else—some other material that she wasn't made of.

He wasn't just carbon, oxygen, and the other nine elements essential for life.

He was *other*.

He was something *else*.

Ajos glanced back at her and she blinked rapidly before looking away.

What was she thinking?

She didn't know how it worked with Athena and the other women, but she doubted such a thing would work for her.

What if he found her strange-looking?

Her skin was pale; his was rich in color.

His body was strong and hard. Hers, in comparison, was weak and soft.

They were opposites.

Yet, the way he looked at her...

"Here we go," V'Alen said, cutting through her thoughts.

The shuttle lifted off the ground and shot into the air so fast, she hardly had time to register what was happening.

It didn't feel as if they were going fast, but based on the blur that was the outside, she could tell they were going much faster than any craft she'd ever been in before, even faster than the transport up to the sky tower.

It didn't take long before they were in space again above the planet, and V'Alen spoke once more.

"Get ready for the jump."

She knew he was saying it for her benefit, since both he and Ajos knew exactly what they were doing and what to expect from the journey.

But jump?

"We have to jump?"

"Choria G622 would take three day and night cycles to get to if we use this shuttle. It is easier if we jump," Ajos answered.

"Okay." Kerena nodded.

"Engaging hyperdrive..." V'Alen murmured.

Nothing happened for a split second and then, the ship shot forward and they were there.

Hyperspace was strange.

It felt as if they'd brought the shuttle into a strange other dimension full of colorful, parallel lines.

It was like having a weird dream where she was in a car that was going so fast, she couldn't see anything outside.

Just as she thought that, the ship began shaking.

"The signal Iceon mentioned," V'Alen said. "It's interfering with our instruments."

"Qef," Ajos uttered. "Take us out before we get lost and end up somewhere we don't want to be."

"Noted."

It lasted for what could only be a few more seconds before the lines suddenly disappeared and a huge sea of asteroids appeared in front of them.

The change was so sudden, her sharp intake of air into her lungs was audible.

Actually, the asteroids were all around them.

They were in the middle of an asteroid belt.

"Engaging autopilot," V'Alen said.

The thrusters fired up, and the ship began weaving around the asteroids.

It was so quiet out there, and inside the ship too, and Kerena couldn't help but wonder if both Ajos and V'Alen were as awed as she was by the magnificence before them.

Huge asteroids moved as if floating on an invisible ocean. There was a gentle sway to the rocks, as if they were all moving in harmony and Kerena could only stare in wonder.

Their ship came close to many of the giant masses of stone—close enough for her to see the details on some of them.

They looked like giant, jagged brown boulders floating.

"We're almost out of it," Ajos murmured, glancing her way, and she knew he spoke for her benefit.

She gave him a small smile and was looking out the large transparent shield at the front of the shuttle when her heart suddenly stopped.

It came out of nowhere.

A dark ship. One so dark it seemed as if it sucked in and destroyed the light of the star within itself.

The ship just appeared and then, boom, it was gone, colliding with an asteroid and erupting into a giant fireball.

It all happened so quickly, she didn't have time to process it before another dark ship appeared.

This one wasn't as unlucky as the first.

One of its wings skirted an asteroid as if whoever was controlling the vessel had lost control, but they managed to not suffer the same demise as their companions.

There was something ominous about the second ship, just as the first, for as soon as she saw it, there was a deep dread within her.

Evil emanated through the strange ship's metallic hull.

"Hedgeruds!" That was all she heard Ajos shout before their shuttle was hit.

The vessel shook and Kerena bit back a scream as she held on to V'Alen's seat in front.

It was an enemy ship, and they were firing at them even as their own ship spun out of control.

"Disengaging autopilot," V'Alen spoke as he took hold of the controls.

Kerena watched in horror as the enemy seemed to regain control of their ship and shot towards them, firing what looked like green laser beams.

Their shuttle banked hard to the right, barely missing an asteroid. It shuddered and Kerena knew they were hit.

"We've taken damage!"

"Employing evasive maneuvers."

The ship sped up but the enemy ship swerved and, for a moment, she didn't see it.

Tension rose.

"They are heading to Choria G622," Ajos said.

"Yes, and that signal that's coming from the planet interrupted their navigation. It pulled them from hyperspace like it almost did us."

Kerena's eyes widened.

The first ship had crashed within a second of exiting hyperspace.

That could have been them too.

Between the many asteroids and the speed at which they were going, her heart lodged in her throat every time they had a near miss.

God knew, she didn't want to become mere splatter against one of the same rocks that she'd been admiring earlier.

But the asteroid belt was thinning out. She could see ahead, and she breathed a breath of relief while still holding on to her seat.

Kerena bit her lip, feeling helpless in the situation.

But she had to trust that Ajos and V'Alen could get them to safety. She had no other choice.

Both males both were pressing buttons like crazy and the ship shook once more.

They were hit again.

"Shields at fifty percent."

"Qef," Ajos cursed.

V'Alen looked at his friend. "We have two options, Commander. Divert all power to the beam array and hit them with all we've got or divert all power to the thrusters and shoot ourselves toward the surface of Choria G622."

"Chances of survival if we hit them with the beam array?"

V'Alen blinked, but his answer came one second later. "Chances of survival are at fifty percent."

Ajos glanced back at her, and their eyes held.

What she saw there was fear.

Regret and fear.

At first, she thought he was reconsidering coming on this journey as he saw his life flashing before his eyes, but something in his gaze told her differently.

He wasn't scared for himself.

He was scared...*for her.*

"If we divert the power, we'll be left open. Not even the shields will work anymore." Ajos delivered the news as he held her gaze and she respected the fact that he was telling her this even though he didn't have to.

"Do it," she said as she caught sight of the enemy ship once more. "Hit them with all you've got. If we run for it, they might follow us to the surface. Don't worry about me."

Ajos blinked and paused, his hesitation clear.

"Do it!" Her voice surprised her.

She sounded a helluva lot stronger and composed than she felt inside.

Inside, she was a withering fool who might piss herself.

Their ship shook again.

"Shields at ten percent," V'Alen announced.

"You put your life in my hands once again," Ajos said with a note of something she could not read, too busy freaking out about the fact that THEY WERE BEING BOMBED BY AN ENEMY SHIP while in an asteroid field and she didn't want to die in space!

"Because *I trust you.*" Now it was her words that surprised her.

She was sure color drained from his face a little before he jerked his head and turned back around.

"Get ready to divert all power to the beam array," he said.

V'Alen punched some buttons. "Ready, Commander." There was no fear in the robot man's voice and she didn't know if that was because he didn't feel any emotions or because he was so used to this shit, he wasn't fazed.

The enemy ship swooped again.

This time, it was coming at them from the front, guns blasting.

She couldn't see who was piloting the ship, it was just all black, and she was happy about that.

She didn't need to see who it was to know that it was the same beings that had taken her from Earth—the same beings who'd bombed the base and killed so many innocents—the same beings that the Restitution was fighting to bring to justice.

Ajos gripped the controls, his face grim as he stared ahead.

Nothing seemed to shake him, not even as the enemy ship came closer.

Their ship shuddered with each hit it sustained and an alarm began blaring, but Ajos held fast.

The black ship was coming straight at them, obviously sure that this last pass was going to take them out—and she hoped they weren't right.

"Shields at one percent."

"Now!" Ajos shouted, and V'Alen engaged something.

She literally heard the power go down; it sounded like a battery draining. The ship sounded like it died, and they were suddenly enveloped in darkness.

Only dim light strips that ran along the floor lit up the interior along with the buttons on the control panel.

There was a rumble that turned into a growl as Ajos began snarling, his gaze focused on the approaching enemy ship. And as his growl turned into a roar, he pulled back on his controls.

Then, it happened.

A bright light erupted in front of them, so bright she was momentarily shaken, not realizing what it was.

It took her a second to register that the light was coming from their ship.

The light shot forward and the other ship couldn't have seen it coming until it was too late. The enemy ship couldn't change course, and Ajos' plan became clear.

He'd waited till the last moment to fire just so he wouldn't miss and boy oh boy did his shot hit its mark.

The ship in front of them fractured and split right through the middle, breaking apart.

Ajos roared, the deafening sound echoing through the shuttle as the enemy ship disintegrated in front of their eyes.

Nothing could have survived that. Nothing.

V'Alen hit something to shut the weapon off, and what was left of the power returned to the ship.

Kerena breathed, her chest heaving, anxiety still flooding through her veins.

All she could do was stare at the wreckage.

There was hardly any space debris.

The enemy ship had blown apart in less than a second.

There was silence now, and she realized it was because the roar was no more. Ajos was silent, his face hard.

"Nice work, Commander," V'Alen said, as their ship turned and began moving through what was left of the asteroid belt. "Diverting the remaining power to the thrusters."

"Can we make it?" she asked.

"It will be a rough landing, but nothing I can't handle," V'Alen answered. "I will have to land by sight. That signal grows stronger the closer we get. No doubt the Hedgeruds were heading to retrieve whatever device is causing it when they came upon us."

Kerena finally found her voice. "Hedgeruds? I thought you said the enemies were the Tasqals."

"They are. The Hedgeruds are the mercenaries they use as muscle," V'Alen answered. "Soldiers."

Kerena let that settle in her mind as her gaze flicked back to Ajos.

He still had not said a word and he still wore that hard mask over his face as he stared ahead.

This was serious business. Not that she'd thought the opposite.

This was what these rebels did every day. This was their life.

And now it was hers.

Looking out the screen in front of them, to the fast-approaching planet, Kerena felt a change within her.

This was no longer only their fight—it was no longer their war.

It was *her* fight now too.

Her war.

She'd never met her enemy face to face, but she already knew they were scum.

Scum should be eradicated, and she was going to do everything she could to contribute to making that happen—not only for herself but for all those people left on Earth...Cindy Clawford...her parents... her coworkers...her friends and for every single being whose lives had been made into a nightmare because of the terror known as the Tasqals.

Her face hardened too as she looked ahead.

This was now her oath.

13

A HUGE DARK-GREEN PLANET WITH MASSIVE OCEANS APPEARED IN FRONT of them.

Kerena's mouth opened, her eyes widening as she looked at the planet they were approaching.

It reminded her of Earth.

"This looks like my planet," she whispered, her eyes traveling over the surface of the strange world. "What are the people that live there like?"

"The planet is uninhabited," Ajos answered. "Engaging thrusters. We will navigate the rest of the way by sight."

Kerena frowned.

A planet with so much vegetation that was uninhabited?

Even in some of the harshest places on Earth, life managed to thrive. She found it hard to believe the planet only had plant life.

"You're telling me that this huge planet only has…plants?"

"Affirmative," V'Alen said. "It is mostly untouched." An untouched planet with some of the rarest plants she would ever see in her life. This was like every botanist's dream. A feeling settled through her—one of mild trepidation mixed with excitement for the unknown. It couldn't be a coincidence. There must be a reason she was sent to this exact spot at this exact moment.

She was sure of it.

This was probably going to be the most important trip she'd ever taken in her life.

It made her lean forward in her seat, her gaze locked on the dark-green sphere they went towards.

The closer they went, the more Choria G622 seemed like Earth.

The water was blue...the trees were green...

It looked all so familiar, yet not at the same time.

"I cannot determine the exact location of the signal," V'Alen spoke. "It is scrambling my instruments."

He turned his head and stared out the screen to the surface below. "I will try to land as close to where I think it is as possible."

They were close enough now that she could see more definition of the surface, and it looked like a dense jungle.

It seemed illogical that nothing lived there. How?

"We will have to find the source of the signal on foot," V'Alen said.

In silence, the ship swerved as he took them closer.

"Going in," he said. It felt like the engines suddenly shut off and their ship was falling through the planet's atmosphere without their control, but when the trajectory changed from vertical to horizontal, she knew V'Alen still had full control of the vessel.

Choria G622 looked like Earth from above, but as soon as they landed, the difference in the plant life was evident.

The tree trunks looked a little too thick, the leaves a little too big.

As soon as the ship settled and the engine powered off, her seating restraints released, and curiosity pulled her to the front of the shuttle to stare out of the huge screen.

Despite the larger size, the density of the plant life was rich, and nothing looked overly alien, but Kerena knew that was simply outward appearances.

If she could get some samples into a lab to investigate, she was sure the differences would jump out at her immediately.

It had been some time since she'd done any field work, having spent most of the last few years in different labs she'd worked for, and just looking outside now caused a thrilling feeling she'd long forgotten.

She'd always been more interested in the medicinal and chemical properties of plants more than anything, and what she was looking at now looked like a botanist's gold mine to her.

"The ship has been compromised." V'Alen suddenly broke the silence. "They damaged the mechanism that engages the hyperdrive. I will have to stay back to repair it."

"Keh-reh-nah can stay with you, if she prefers," Ajos said, drawing her attention to him for the first time in a while. "I do not wish to put her into more danger."

He removed something from his pocket, a vial of ice-blue fluid, and without warning, he jammed it into his leg like one would do with an EpiPen.

Kerena grimaced but, alas, he didn't appear to mind the attack he'd inflicted on himself.

As the blue fluid left the vial and disappeared into his body, Ajos' eyes closed for a few moments and his jaw clenched.

Medicine.

That must be medicine.

"Keh-reh-nah, you stay here. It will be safer for you if you do," he spoke through gritted teeth.

"And miss going out there? No, thank you," she answered, studying him as she did.

When he finally opened his eyes, he didn't seem in pain so much anymore, and he finally pulled the hood from over his head.

Stretching his arms, he pulled the entire garment off, leaving his undershirt behind, and Kerena was treated to a view of thick, muscly arms.

He seemed happy to be without it now, and when he turned and found her looking at him, she was sure she saw him smile a little.

"If you're going," V'Alen interrupted, "you need this commu-nicator."

He slipped the communication device that looked like a large watch over her wrist.

"Navigation may not work," he said, before glancing at Ajos. "You will have to do things the old way, brother. Use markers to mark your path. The signal," he glanced toward the screen, "it's interfering with our instruments too much. I do not wish for you to lose your way."

Ajos stood as the ship's door swung open. "Keep watch, brother."

Hopping out, he turned his head to the skies. "They will send more fighters once they realize they've lost contact with their comrades. I am sure of it."

"Noted," V'Alen said, rising as well.

Ajos glanced up at her, his eyes finding her effortlessly in the ship.

In one of his hands was that wicked spear of his, and the other was outstretched for her to take it.

She expected him to help her down when she grasped his hand. Instead, as soon as their fingers touched, he took hold of her hand and pulled her against him.

Kerena fell forward and the only place to land was on his chest.

Her body pressed against his as she slid down to stand on her own two feet, and a deep blush filled her cheeks immediately.

He was so hard, she could feel every single corded muscle underneath his clothing.

"Are you ready, Keh-reh-nah?"

Kerena nodded as he released her.

With one glance back at V'Alen, they began walking through undergrowth.

AJOS WATCHED the human without disturbance.

Walking behind her, he could best protect them from any threats coming from the front or the back—not that there should be any but he'd learned a long time ago that he couldn't ever be too careful.

Not only that, with her walking ahead, he could stare at her for as long as he wanted without her knowing. Creepy? Maybe. Did he care? Nope. At his height, he couldn't see her face fully, but he could see the perky little nose she had jutting from her face. She seemed to scrunch it up a lot—a strange characteristic, if any.

She walked just in front of him, her eyes round pools as she stared into the forest.

Reaching over her, he slashed a vine out of their way. The edge of his spear cut through the thing quickly and cleared the path for them, making walking easier.

Absentmindedly, he rubbed his leg with his other hand.

The site where he'd administered the metcer cells ached a little, but he could already feel them working.

The little bio-organisms would cool him down and, hopefully, delay the heat.

That didn't mean he was immune to everything, though.

He knew this for a fact because the memory of Keh-reh-nah's body sliding down his was vivid in his mind.

She was so soft.

It felt as if her body could be molded against his, where he could keep her permanently pressed flush against him as his cock extruded, his seed sack bunched at his base as he thrust into her, ready to release his seed deep within her.

He wanted to see that pretty mouth of hers twist in pleasure as she called his name.

He wanted—

"Ajos?"

Ajos jerked a little as he focused on Keh-reh-nah. She'd stopped walking and was looking right at him, and he wasn't sure how long she'd been doing so.

"Are you okay? You were..." she frowned a little, "...rumbling."

Ajos cleared his throat.

"The rumbling..." he glanced around the forest, "it helps me to..." —now what silly lie could he come up with? He'd been rumbling at the thought of her beneath him, but he couldn't tell her that—"...it helps me to concentrate."

Keh-reh-nah looked at him funny, her eyes narrowing a little.

"O...kay," she said, before she continued walking.

She knew he was lying.

Qef him.

His body wasn't burning up so much, but his mind was, apparently.

The metcer cells couldn't enter his brain to help him there. He'd have to control that himself.

Frowning at his lack of control, he checked his communicator as he tracked the source of the signal.

V'Alen was right. The thing kept cutting out, the direction changing now and then, but he was hoping they were heading in the right direction.

His gaze moved to Keh-reh-nah once more.

She still walked ahead, but close enough for him to reach out and touch her with one simple movement.

His gaze moved down her back.

The garment that she wore swayed as she walked.

It was short, showing her long pale legs and ending not far below what he could already tell was a shapely behind.

His gaze lingered on her skin.

In contrast to him and his people, she was so noticeably pale.

Granted, Shum'ai females tended to be paler than the rich minty-teal of the males, but he'd never seen one that had Keh-reh-nah's ultimate lack of pigment.

And that's because she wasn't Shum'ai.

Not that it made a difference.

He was suitable for no female—Shum'ai or otherwise.

"These look so much like aloe vera, the resemblance is uncanny," Keh-reh-nah muttered, pausing to look at a particularly fleshy plant.

She reached out to touch the leaves before pulling her hand back.

"I really can't touch it. I don't know if I'm allergic to it or anything like that," she mumbled to herself again.

She stooped closer to the plant and grabbed a fallen branch from the ground to poke it with.

"Aloe vera has thorns on the leaves to protect it—a sort of defense mechanism. This plant is smooth all over," she murmured. "Maybe it evolved like this because it had no threats to his existence." She kept poking the plant before she glanced around them. "Not even insects?"

He realized that was a rhetorical question because she kept murmuring to herself.

"No predators..." She was frowning now. "Not even other predatory plants?" Her frown became almost severe.

She kept the fallen branch in her hand, stood up, and continued walking, her eyes studying the trees.

Watching her, he set a marker so they could find their way back easily, in case the instruments were still going haywire when they retrieved the "source."

"No birds," she muttered. "At least, I can't see any." She continued looking around. "It appears this forest is really wholly plant life. I can't see nor hear any other creatures around us."

A smile split Ajos' face before he even realized he was amused.

She was so caught up in her ruminations, it appeared she didn't even remember he was there.

"Micro-organisms though...surely..." She let out a huff of a breath. "It just doesn't make sense. I'd suppose there are bacteria, single-celled organisms, and the like living here. Have to be."

She was talking to herself like an insane ratgull. Ajos' shoulders shook in a silent chuckle.

"So many vines along the forest floor as well," she mused, poking her stick at the vegetation as she walked.

She did this for the next few minutes, mumbling some things he could not hear, and when he caught a glimpse of her face, there was such concentration there, he was positive he'd been right about her forgetting he was even there.

"So many vines..." she murmured again, "The density is amazing."

She frowned at the ground as she walked. "I've never seen so many vines in one place in my entire life."

For a few more minutes, she walked in silence, but Ajos could tell from the frown on her brow that she was still caught up in her own mind.

She paused at a few husks of a plant on the ground and used her stick to poke it.

"Seeds," she murmured, before she looked above at the tree

towering over them. "The seeds are good. They germinate, replacing the dead underbrush to make the forest healthy."

She continued walking.

"This ecosystem is so rich." She suddenly turned to look at him, and Ajos hid his smile behind a mask of neutrality. So she did remember he was there. "I've counted at least one hundred different species and that's from sight alone."

Her awe was captivating.

Watching her in her element was captivating.

It wasn't hard to imagine what she'd been like on her home planet, before she'd been taken away.

"It's so...wonderful...and strange." She looked around again. "So many plant species have died out on Earth, most of them over the last twenty or so years. It's heartbreaking." She touched a leaf. "When you study them as much as I do, you get to know them, you know. They become your friends."

At that, her cheeks changed to a rosy hue.

"I sound like a proper lone soul, don't I? Here I am with a handsome alien, on an expedition in an alien jungle, and all I'm talking about is that plants are friends."

Wait, she thought he was handsome?

Ajos opened his mouth to ask her to clarify that bit when the comms crackled.

"Ajos, do you read?" V'Alen's voice reached their ears.

Ajos activated the receiver, his eyes still on the female before him. "I am here."

"Damage to the hyperdrive is more extensive than I thought. We might have to spend the night here."

Ajos' gaze moved to the heavens. They would have to make it back to the ship before nightfall, anyway. He didn't want to keep Keh-reh-nah out here in this wilderness.

"Received," he answered.

"I assume you have not located the source of the signal yet."

Ajos continued looking around the undergrowth.

They'd been making good time, but he had yet to see any sign of a fallen ship. He'd been setting markers every few meters though, and regardless that the signal seemed to be growing stronger, he had no way to pinpoint it directly.

The coordinates of the source kept shifting.

"No," he answered. "I will update you in a few hours. We might have to head back and restart our search tomorrow."

As V'Alen clicked off, Ajos noticed Keh-reh-nah was also eyeing the undergrowth.

"We should press on." She checked her comm device. "Maybe we can find the wreckage before nightfall?"

"We could try."

At his reply, she nodded and continued walking.

With her still in front, he once again found himself staring at the sway of her hips.

There was a curve at the junction of her upper and lower body, and he itched to put his hands at that spot.

His nefre pulsed against the back of his neck and his genital pouch bulged so hard, it was painful.

Heat surged through his body—not only the literal heat, but need.

Ajos grimaced, forcing the urges back.

Pulling out another vial of the metcer cells, he stabbed it into his leg, squeezing his eyes shut as the bio-organisms flooded into his system.

This wasn't right.

Aker had promised him that one vial would last him at least three days.

He was already on the second one within one hour.

When he opened his eyes, Keh-reh-nah was frowning at him, a look of concern on her face.

She'd moved close while he'd been distracted, and he'd opened his eyes just as she was about to touch his cheek.

Her hand paused as their gazes locked and Ajos felt his throat move.

His life organ sped up and he wanted to tell her to get away from him.

If she touched him now...while he was weak...before the cells spread through his system...

As her hand settled on his skin, a deep groan rumbled through him.

He didn't know when his hand had let go of the vial still buried in his leg or when he'd gripped her, pulling her against him.

All he knew was that her softness was now pressed against him exactly like he'd imagined. He could feel those round orbs on her chest pressing into him, and he wanted her...

Ajos growled, grimacing as he fought the feelings within himself.

He couldn't lose control. She wouldn't want him to, and the gods of Tonvuhiri knew the last thing he wanted to do was to hurt her.

"Ajos?"

Her voice was breathless, and it only made him wild.

He buried his face against her neck, pulling her tighter against him as he fought to control his need. His chest heaved with the exertion.

A few more seconds, he told himself.

A few more seconds till the metcer cells worked.

As he held her to him, Keh-reh-nah did not protest, even though she had all the right to.

Instead, she nestled against him, allowing him time to fight with the demon that wanted to have her there and then.

"Keh-reh-nah..." he groaned.

"Ajos..."

And that was when he knew—he knew it with a clarity that he'd never had before—he wasn't going to be able to let her go.

Ever.

14

———

They'd been walking for at least two hours or more. Still, they found no evidence of the source of the signal.

It was like air.

They knew it was there; it interacted with their instruments; but they couldn't see it.

Ajos touched the last vial of metcer cells in his pocket.

Only one left to last him through the night.

It was getting dark now, and he had no idea how far away from the ship they were.

"V'Alen, do you read?" He activated his communicator, his eyes on Keh-reh-nah.

She hadn't complained, but it was obvious she was tired.

She'd used the branch she'd picked up as a sort of walking aid, and she hadn't been afraid to get her hands dirty as she climbed over huge roots and boulders within the terrain.

But even *he* was feeling the strain in his back.

It was time to rest.

"I am here, Commander."

"Status?"

"I will be working on the hyperdrive all night. I have many repairs left. Any word on the source of the signal?"

Ajos let out a breath. "None."

"We could keep going..." Kerena said. Her breaths were coming faster now, as she turned to look back at him.

She was tired, but probably ignoring it because she didn't want to seem like a burden. She came off like the type of person to do that.

"No, we will have to take a break," he replied to her. "V'Alen, we have stopped for a rest. If I do not contact you before the middle of the dark cycle..."

"I understand," V'Alen said, and the comms clicked off.

Keh-reh-nah's eyes were slightly wide. "You think we're in danger?"

She glanced around. "Do you think those bad guys survived the crash?"

"No," he said, "it is just a precaution. We scanned the surroundings before we landed. We picked up no lifeforms."

Her shoulders sank a little. "Good."

"We should rest," he repeated.

She looked around before pointing behind him.

There was a section where the vines that crawled over the ground created a sort of flat surface that would do well for that purpose.

Ajos jerked his head in confirmation.

As he took a seat, Keh-reh-nah sat beside him and her skin brushed against his—pale softness that he wasn't supposed to rub himself against.

His throat moved as he clenched his teeth at the thought.

"Do you think we'll find it before it gets dark?" Her voice was soft and in the stillness of the forest around them, it sounded almost intimate, even though her words weren't.

"I do not. We will have to head back and try again in tomorrow's light."

She turned to him then. "But what if we come out again only to make it back to this spot? It would be better if we spent the night out here and continued as soon as the sun rose."

Ajos studied her.

She wasn't afraid of doing such a thing?

She was alone in the middle of an unknown world with an unknown male by her side.

He frowned a little as he studied her.

Maybe he'd been right about her being too trusting.

Memory of how she'd almost stayed with Iceon returned and he had to stifle the urge to growl.

"I thought you'd prefer being in the safety of the ship."

"I feel safe out here," she said, her voice so low, he almost didn't catch her next words. "With you."

Those words only made something stir within him and he knew if he tried to use his vocal cords to reply, he'd probably end up groaning instead.

He was supposed to keep her safe, protect her—not scare her away.

"What do you think it is? The source of this signal?"

She was looking out into the forest and he turned to do the same. The darkness was coming in much quicker than he'd expected it to.

"I don't know," he answered as he lay down his spear. He could only hope it was something the Restitution could use to their advantage.

From his pocket, he pulled out two meal bars and handed her one.

Her eyebrows moved up a little as she took the bar.

"Oh, thanks!" A smile brightened her face and Ajos found himself staring. "I'd resigned myself to not eating till tomorrow when we got back."

He'd never have allowed that, but he hadn't the voice to reply.

They ate in silence and Ajos watched her chew.

She was grimacing as she did and he had to look at the meal bar in his hand.

It was standard sustenance for missions such as this, but she was eating it as if it tasted like the pebbles embedded in the ground beneath their feet.

"It does not please you," he murmured, turning his bar over in his hand.

"No, it—"she took another bite"—it's fine."

She tried to hide her grimace and that small nose of hers wrinkled in a way that had him forgetting that he was eating.

Before long, she was yawning, and her body slumped a little as she tried to make herself more comfortable.

"Keh-reh-nah." He opened his mouth before he could stop himself, but now that he'd spoken and gotten her attention, he had to continue. "You can rest on me."

His genital pouch strained at the thought and his seed sack stiffened within, pulsing and almost forcing his cock to extrude.

Qeffing phek, he was an idiot.

"Are you sure?" she asked. "I'm not small. I might make it uncomfortable for you."

He wanted to scoff at what she said, but he was too caught up in controlling the urge to pull her toward him now that the thought was in his head.

"I'm sure," he managed to get out.

She paused for a moment before she moved to lean against him and rested her head against his shoulder.

For the next few minutes, they lay in silence, and Keh-reh-nah's body slowly relaxed.

Ajos released a slow breath, careful not to move.

It was a mistake offering to let her rest on him.

He was barely in control.

Thank the gods it was dark now—dark enough for shadows to creep among the trees all around them.

If it was the middle of the day cycle, Keh-reh-nah would see his shame.

"You know what I've noticed?" she whispered.

She was oblivious to what was happening to him.

"What?" Good grief, it had taken almost all his energy to make his voice sound relatively normal.

"These plants...the trees above us, even the bushes and plants below them..."

"Hm?"

"Most of this is roots, not vines... There are so many aerial roots... and they seem to be running from one tree to the other."

Her nose scrunched up in a most strange manner. He almost wanted to poke it to see if it would bounce back to its regular form.

"What do you mean?"

"It's like...I know this might be reaching but...it's like this," she motioned around them in a big sweep of her arm, "is all one big tree...one big organism. At more than one point, I even noticed one root connected to two different trees."

Ajos frowned a little, he didn't get what she was saying.

"We have something similar on Earth, called the Pando Aspen. It's in Utah—not that you know where that is—but it's the largest living organism on Earth." She paused. "I can't be positive, this is all just speculative, but I think that this forest is something similar. There are seeds but not many of the trees seem to bear fruit, only a few. Yet, they dominate the land—at least, this section of it. There is no wildlife to spread the seeds either. Wherever they fall, that's where they end up. So for the forest to grow and spread, it's possible it uses its root system. I could be wrong, but the trees look identical too."

She glanced up at him, her filaments brushing against his chin as she did so.

"Sorry, I'm babbling."

Ajos blinked. "Don't stop. I like it."

She smiled and moved into him more, either of her own accord or involuntarily, he didn't know.

All he knew was that the brush of her body against his was making his cock pulse so hard she'd feel it.

Ajos swallowed hard as a cool breeze blew across them and Keh-reh-nah shivered a little.

He shouldn't...

He really shouldn't...

But though his mind was strong, his flesh was weak.

Knowing he was playing a dangerous game, he wrapped his arms around her as he leaned back to lay against the vines with her cradled against his chest.

She went with him without protest, only adjusting herself so she was more comfortable.

In the silence of the forest, a deep peace settled over Ajos. One that felt undeserved but, yet, one that he craved.

This felt...good.

She felt good.

For long minutes, he stared up into the darkness, watching as the stars above them began to appear, and he wondered what the gods were trying to tell him.

She felt warm against him. Warm and soft and it didn't take long before he realized she'd drifted off to sleep.

She snuggled into him, spinning so that her front was turned to him and he could feel every single beat of her life organ.

Did he dare relish in this feeling she was stirring within him?

Ajos swallowed hard as his arms closed around her tighter, pulling her closer to him and when she sighed, he lost all his resolve.

His shoulders shook with the tension of unspent emotion.

He wanted her.

And it was not his body, not the urges, not the heat, that he was feeling.

This was more than the heat.

He wanted her.

For the first time in a long while, someone was evoking feelings in him that he hadn't allowed himself to feel.

The only problem? He wasn't worthy of a female and Keh-reh-nah was too pure to be associated with him.

But could he allow himself this one moment?

Maybe...

Just once, and tomorrow, he would accept the fate the gods had given him.

Pulling her a little closer, Ajos buried his nose into the pale strands on her head.

Tonight he would allow himself to live a little.

Tomorrow, he would forget this ever happened.

15

Kerena woke with a start and strong arms closed around her immediately, preventing her from moving.

Ajos.

She remembered now. They were in the forest.

It was still dark, but she didn't remember falling asleep.

She must have been more tired than she'd thought.

She felt warm, so warm and she soon realized the reason for that.

There was warmth underneath her.

Ajos was burning up.

"Ajos?" She tried to ease up so she could look at him, but his arms tightened around her even more.

"Don't move."

Kerena stilled.

It hardly sounded like Ajos at all.

That voice was hard, rough, strained...

"Are you in pain?" She tried to move again but he only held her tighter.

"Keh-reh-nah," he rasped. "Don't...move."

For a moment, she didn't move, and her eyes widened as she tried to sense if any threat was around them.

But it soon became clear that he wanted her still for some other reason—some reason she did not know.

She lifted her head and looked upward. She couldn't see his face clearly because of the angle at which he held her, and the darkness around them didn't make it any easier.

Reaching upward, she felt for his face and as her hand made contact with his neck, she heard him inhale sharply.

There was a thin layer of perspiration there but just that one touch told her that he was indeed burning up.

A small yelp left her lips when her hand was suddenly snatched as Ajos' palm closed around her wrist. He pulled her intrusive hand from his flesh.

"You're burning up." She searched his face in the darkness. She could barely make out his outline, but she was sure she saw the muscle tick in his cheek.

He was burning up and agitated.

This wasn't the same Ajos she'd fallen asleep on.

She had no idea how long she'd been sleeping for, but it must have been for a few hours at least, judging from how dark it was.

"Ajos—"

"Keh-reh-nah," he rasped again, and his entire body shuddered.

He sounded so strained, panic rose within her.

"Let me go," she ordered. She needed to get a better vantage point so she could help him somehow.

His arms tightened around her, but when she struggled against him, he finally loosened his arms a little. Still, he did not release her.

"No," he said. "Just don't...don't move."

Was she the reason he was in pain?

She could understand that his body must be hurting laying on the hard ground and with her added weight, it must have been agony. Was he cramped?

Plus, she knew he'd hurt his back.

But that didn't explain the heat underneath his skin and her instincts told her something else was amiss.

"Let me go," she repeated and pushed against his arms.

He released her, but it felt as if it was reluctantly done.

She rose over him, moving so she could peer at his face in the darkness.

"Don't come any closer…"

"Ajos, what's happening to you?" She touched his cheek and he hissed as if she'd just branded him with a hot iron.

What the—

She rubbed her hands together. Maybe her skin was cold?

When she had a fever, her skin was sensitive to any slight bit of cold. Cold fingers would feel like daggers poking at her. "You have a fever and it's come on strong. Shit." Her eyes flicked around in the darkness before settling back on Ajos. "We should probably get back to the ship. Maybe V'Alen knows some doctor stuff that could help."

Such high fevers usually meant something very wrong was happening. They were never good—at least, not for humans, and she was going to assume that was the case for him too.

She could even feel the warmth of his body without touching him directly.

"You *definitely* need medical attention."

"That's not what I need," he all but growled and Kerena frowned, refusing to roll her eyes.

He was stubborn.

"This is going to hurt, but I have to check you," she warned him before she pressed her hand against his skin again.

A deep rumble that sounded like it came from the bottom of his chest filled the air around them and Kerena tried not to panic as she felt the temperature of his forehead and then his neck with the back of her hand.

He felt like a real-life hot water bottle filled to the brim with boiling liquid, and she had no idea what she should do.

Fuck.

She'd been the one to suggest they stay in the middle of the forest. If they'd been back at the ship, V'Alen would have known what to do.

If she had access to a lime tree or even some white willow, she'd have been able to do something for him. But in this alien world, she couldn't even go hunt the native bushes for anything because she knew nothing about the plants here.

Then she remembered.

"Your medicine." She brushed her hands against his leg, trying to find his pocket that held the blue vials she'd seen him with.

"No," he groaned. "I can't take it."

"Don't be ridiculous," she snapped. "I don't know about you, but I'm freaking out because I don't want you to die." She continued running her hands over his legs and Ajos groaned some more.

Damn it.

She couldn't find the damn pocket.

"Where is it, Ajos? Tell me." She was getting frantic, but he refused to say anything. Frustration rose within her. "Do you want to die?"

To her horror, the hard-headed male chuckled, his body jerking with his mirth.

"That is not what I want." He chuckled through gritted teeth, then he sobered. "What I want," he growled, "I should not have."

Her eyes adjusted enough for her to see a pained expression cross his face before he tensed once more. "You shouldn't touch me."

Confused, Kerena eased back a little.

He was breathing harder too. She could hear it now. His chest was heaving with each breath he took, and it seemed as if he was groaning with effort to restrain the pain he was feeling.

Good god.

She needed to do something.

V'Alen.

He'd know what to do.

Tapping the watch on her arm, she tried pushing the buttons on the side of it like she'd seen Ajos do to activate the comms. Hopefully, she'd press the right one.

But no crackle of the comms came on. Instead, the watch turned into a torch, beaming a bright light in the area.

Kerena squinted as her gaze got accustomed to the sudden brightness, and when she focused on Ajos, she gasped.

His mouth was slightly open, and his entire body was covered in the sheen of his perspiration.

The muscles in his neck were tense, his chest was tense, and his arms formed fists at his sides.

But it was his head and his eyes that caught her attention.

His head, the fin-like structure that ran on it, was blazing red and his eyes...his eyes looked wild...feral, and dark.

He looked nothing like himself.

For a moment, a jolt of fear shot through her and she froze.

It slammed into her that she knew nothing about the lifeform in front of her—yet, she was all alone with him on a jungle planet in the middle of nowhere.

Very responsible, Kerena.

Still, she couldn't move or run away.

Something wrung deep inside her.

He needed her help.

"Go, Keh-reh-nah," Ajos breathed. "Go. Move away from me. Run if you have to. I will contact V'Alen. He will come for you."

What? He expected her to leave him when he was obviously dying?

"You don't really expect me to leave, do you?" She crawled over to him, not caring that it was inappropriate to straddle him the way she was, and began her searching of his garments again.

"I'm not leaving you here like this. Are you insane?" She just needed to find his medicine then everything would be all right.

"Keh-reh-nah, don't." Ajos' voice shook.

"That medicine thing must be in here somewhere."

"You need to go, I am losing control."

His words didn't even register.

"If I could just find the damn thing—"

"Keh-reh-nah!" He growled so loud she was momentarily taken aback.

Ajos jerked forward and spun.

She didn't know how she ended up on her back so quickly, but she was suddenly staring upward with wide eyes and Ajos was above her.

His hands grasped hers, pinning them above her head as he leaned over her.

He growled again, something feral, something inhuman, and some unknown emotion shot through her.

Ajos dipped his head close to her ear and his breath rumbled from him.

The sound was so raw, so animalistic, that her own breath caught in her throat.

Her heart began doing pushups in her chest, slamming against her ribs and her lungs forgot how to work.

"I told you to run," he growled and Kerena opened her mouth to answer but found the organ she used to speak wasn't working anymore.

She couldn't find words as she stared up into his eyes.

Maybe she should have run—she was really considering her wisdom on that particular advice right now—but, alas, said advice didn't mean jack shit now that he had her pinned down.

"Ajos?" Maybe she could talk reason into him. It was obvious the fever was getting to his head.

That's all this was.

Kerena swallowed hard, trying to wet the desert that was her throat, but fear was building within her, mixing with adrenaline and excitement, and flooding through her veins like a deadly concoction.

Her heart was still slamming against her chest, and as she tried to release herself, it felt as if Ajos only held her tighter.

His grip on her wasn't painful and she took comfort in that fact. He seemed to only want to prevent her from wriggling.

The only problem with that was...well...she obviously had some trauma she needed to work through because instead of turning her off...terrifying her...she was being...turned on?

Ajos buried his head into her neck and inhaled deeply.

Another growl rumbled from his chest even as he twisted his hips so he settled between her legs.

She felt it then, the hardness between his legs, and it made her eyes widen.

She'd seen him naked.

She hadn't seen a cock but there was obviously something there for he was hard.

So hard.

Shock made her freeze.

She should push him away, fight for him to release her, but there was something preventing her from doing so. A deep tingle started in her stomach and found its way to the bud nestled between her thighs.

Fuck.

She couldn't help the sharp rise of her chest as she pulled air into her lungs.

Ajos groaned at the movement, opening his lips to trail his teeth over her skin.

Good God...if he bit her now, she'd probably enjoy it.

The thought confused her. She didn't want this...did she?

"Keh-reh-nah," he growled her name as he inhaled her scent again. "I don't want medical attention," he rasped. "I want you."

Kerena blinked and when he moved against her again, that hardness hiding underneath his garments rubbed against the thin material of her panties.

Kerena stifled a moan.

He was...

He was turned on by this.

She was turned on by this.

Ajos opened his mouth, his hot breath brushing over her skin before something wet and thick ran from her collarbone right up to her ear.

Kerena inhaled, her back arching with the movement of his tongue.

It was slick and warm and her eyes rolled back in her head a little at the unexpected feel of it against her skin.

It shouldn't feel that good.

Ajos licked her again, following the path of her collarbone to the other side of her face, and this time, she couldn't help but moan out loud.

She felt a burst of pleasure at his touch, pleasure that seemed to swell directly from the path his tongue took, and her eyelids fluttered as she tried to focus on him.

Suddenly, her nipples were hard and aching for his mouth to close over them, her breath quickened in her chest, and her clit throbbed, pressing against her thin cotton panties, begging to be touched.

She didn't understand it and she didn't care.

It was nonsensical...but there was no denying that her body was screaming for more.

Suddenly, there was no more fear. All was replaced by ecstasy, and Ajos must have felt this change in her too, because he growled again.

"This is..." she didn't know how to describe what was happening because her mind couldn't understand it. It felt as if she was being overtaken by a vehicle on the way to the most unexpected orgasm she'd ever have in her life.

She whimpered shamelessly as his kiss went lower toward the V in her dress.

She knew where she wanted his mouth, knew his hot tongue should go where she needed it most.

Ajos released her wrists, his arms sliding down her body as if tracing her every curve before landing on the juncture of her hips and he groaned again.

One hand slipped underneath her dress to caress the soft flesh of her thigh, and his hand pressed gently into her skin.

The raw power she felt underneath his palm, she knew if he wanted to, he could do anything right then and there, without regard for her feelings.

Yet, he didn't.

Emotion caused his body to shake as he withheld himself, choosing instead to grind his pelvis into hers again—and fuck her if her clit didn't respond.

This was better than the last time she used her magic wand.

Kerena panted as she raised her arm to rest it on his shoulder.

That movement caused the light from the watch she was wearing to fall on her directly, leaving Ajos' face in shadow.

She felt him freeze, the movement of his hips halting as his body went rigid, and as quickly as how he'd flipped her underneath him, he let her go.

His weight disappeared from above her and she felt a sudden chill as he disappeared.

Somewhere close by, the bushes rustled as Ajos moved into the undergrowth.

Shocked and puzzled couldn't begin to describe the way she felt.

What the hell?

It took her just a few seconds to respond, and Kerena eased up on her elbow to shine the light in the direction he'd gone.

She didn't expect to see him there, about a foot or two away. She'd thought he'd gone farther, or worse, ran off completely, but there he was.

He was crouching, staring in her direction, and the image of him made her breath catch in her throat once again.

He didn't look like a man.

He looked like an animal.

His teeth were bared, his face twisted into a snarl, and he was crouched as if he was some predator about to pounce on its prey.

"Ajos?" Kerena fought to control the pleasure still coursing through her veins.

Never before had she been this turned on to the point of her having trouble controlling it.

Her clit pulsed and begged for his touch. It wanted his mouth, or his hand...fuck, it wanted him grinding against it again. It had no shame.

Ajos' throat moved.

"You need to get away from me." His voice sounded strange coming from his lips.

"Why?"

Because he's feral. Are you blind? her mind answered for her.

"I am not myself. I could have hurt you. I *will* hurt you. I will take from you what you do not want to give. I almost—" He stopped speaking.

It sure felt as if she wanted to give him exactly what he was saying he wanted to take.

Her body was still begging for him—and even though the craving confused her somewhat, she couldn't deny that it was there.

"You're reacting to my saliva. I should be able to control this better." That sounded more like a murmur to himself. "I have to control this better."

As he spoke, something on the ground caught her eye.

It was the vial she'd been searching for. The one with the medicine that he needed.

She reached for it and grabbed it with her free hand as she kept the light trained on Ajos.

He was looking at her so intently that she wasn't even sure he saw that she'd found the thing.

His eyes, such a brilliant gold, shone with the light reflecting off his irises.

His gaze slipped over her, moving down her face, to fall on her shoulder. She was surprised he could see her at all with the light in his eyes, but it was clear that he could.

His gaze lingered and a glance told her that her dress had slipped down her shoulder, exposing her skin and the brown lace bra she wore underneath.

Her gaze fell to her half-exposed breast and she stared at it for a moment.

She was shameless, for she felt no urge to cover herself.

Her breath was still coming in short gasps but that feeling of absolute ecstasy that had hardened her nipples and caused the bud between her legs to swell was slowly ebbing.

She could think clearer now, but when she looked back at Ajos, it didn't seem like it was the same for him.

His chest heaved as he fought to control his breathing, and his throat kept moving as another rumble began deep inside him.

His growl had scared her at first...now, not so much.

Now, that same sound was making her excited again.

"Ajos?"

His gaze seemed to focus at the sound of his name, and he shook his head as if to clear it.

Kerena felt the vial in her hand. Her fingertips moved over the thing, and now that she was thinking more with her head and not her body, it was all becoming clear.

It was his sickness...

He'd come on to her because of his sickness.

Kerena blinked as she sat up slowly and kept the light on him.

Shame filled her.

How could she have, for even a second, considered otherwise?

As she eased into a sitting position, Ajos watched her move; he watched her fingers grab the dress and pull it back over her skin and she was sure he moved toward her before he stopped himself.

His muscles strained against his will to do what some part of his mind was stopping him from completing.

Moving on all fours, she crawled toward him slowly.

The vial was still hidden in her hand, but that didn't matter.

He was solely focused on her.

His eyes held hers and he growled low once more, before his gaze moved over her head.

A thrill went through her and she had the distinct sense that he was staring at her ass as she came forward.

He made an appreciative sound in his throat once more and in another situation, she'd have probably blushed.

It's the fever, Kerena, she berated herself. *It was always the fever.*

"Stay away," he growled, but his words held no threat as he moved to meet her. It sounded more like a plea.

She didn't wait.

The vial had a flat end like a normal syringe did and she'd seen him stab himself with it before.

As soon as she was close enough, she stabbed the vial into his leg and Ajos frowned.

His muscles tensed as his gaze fell to his leg.

Fuck.

She didn't expect it to feel like that. Burying the vial into his leg had felt like she had stabbed him with a dagger.

It left a horrible feeling in her chest, feeling the sharp end go through his flesh, and she found that in the few moments that ticked by, she was holding her breath, waiting for his response.

A harsh growl left his lips as his teeth bared.

She should have been scared, but it seemed that once fear had left the room, it never returned.

Instead of jumping back and away from him like evolution intended her to do, she pressed herself against him and wrapped her arms around his neck.

"It's okay," she cooed, and she noticed immediately that her voice seemed to help. His snarl lessened and he hesitated.

"It's okay," she whispered again, pushing back the anxiety that was rising within her. "It's just the fever. You'll be okay."

Guilt gripped her.

He was probably sick because he'd hurt himself the other day trying to protect her.

That injury in his back...it could be infected.

"What have you done?" Each word came out with much difficulty, she could hear. He sounded angry and pained at the same time and, for a moment, she wondered if she'd made the right decision.

Ajos' shoulders sagged a little and it must be her, but she was sure his temperature was already going down.

"Keh-reh-nah," Ajos groaned. "I am ashamed. I could have... I almost... I would never hurt you that way."

He eased up so he could look her in the eyes.

It was clear the medicine was working but there was still some strain there, as if he was still fighting a mental battle.

"No matter what, I would never have forced you to..." He gulped and searched her gaze. "I would have stopped."

"You did stop."

"Not soon enough."

Not soon enough.

Despite the situation, his words hurt a little.

Maybe she wasn't his type.

"To take you by force would have been the ultimate dishonor to my lineage, my bloodline, and I have already done enough to destroy that." His arms encircled her, and he pulled her into him. "Forgive me."

"I'm not upset." Lies. All that just happened confused her more than anything. Her body still ached a little from his touch, yearned for him in a way that she had never yearned for anyone before.

Back on Earth, she'd never been one to connect with men quickly—sexually or otherwise.

That's probably why she'd never had any man turn her on as easily as Ajos just did. At least, not when they tried.

Yet, Ajos had just managed to...

"I fell asleep and you almost..." she whispered. "I could have helped you sooner if I didn't fall asleep."

He shuddered and pulled her closer.

"It is not your fault. I was saving the vial," he said. "It's the last one I have." Ajos paused. "I do not know how I will fare tomorrow. I thought..."

Kerena waited for him to continue.

"I thought I could control myself."

Ajos released her, eased up, and took a step away.

The light from her watch cast shadows that made him look even taller than he was.

He didn't say anything more, and she didn't have the guts to ask what he meant.

She felt confused, more than anything else.

Settling back on her haunches, she released a slow breath.

It didn't matter, did it?

She knew nothing about Ajos. It was probably best whatever had just transpired between them had ended before it got too far.

If she'd been like most of the other human women who'd been taken, she'd have been safe now on the base—at least, relatively safe.

She wouldn't be in the middle of a jungle with an alien she hardly knew, dry humping in the bushes.

The shame burned against her cheeks.

Ugh. What was her purpose for being here? Back when the shuttle had been coming in, she'd thought there was something, that the universe had led her to this planet for a reason...but what?

She hadn't discovered anything of note, and they'd been walking most of the day.

All she'd discovered was that her magic wand *hadn't* been all she'd needed. Her body yearned for more.

Taking another breath, she tried to ground herself and think of something else.

It the next few moments of silence, she made a pact with herself.

She could never allow herself to be so weak again.

Never.

She repeated this in her mind, forcing the thought to her prefrontal cortex...yet there was a nagging feeling that she was surely going to disappoint herself.

The comm on Ajos' arm crackled in the night, stirring them both.

"Commander," V'Alen spoke, his voice breaking the silence between them. "Do you read?"

Ajos activated the device and she moved so she was sitting on the nest of roots again.

"Report, V'Alen."

"I am almost halfway done with the repairs to the ship. I should finish by daylight."

Ajos paused before he replied. "Good. I will update you if anything changes here."

He was standing somewhere behind her and she wasn't brave enough to look at him.

It was best they ignored what had transpired between them.

The comms crackled off and she could almost feel him studying her.

Kerena cleared her throat.

There was tension between them now, tension that hadn't been there before, and she didn't like it. She had at least another day out here in the wilderness with him.

She wished it would go back to how it was before.

16

———

The star was rising, spreading brightness through the vegetation and bringing light to his eyes.

Ajos turned his head to look toward where Keh-reh-nah slept.

He'd taken off as soon as she'd drifted off to sleep, expelling his energy as he sprinted in a wide circle around where she slept.

It helped a little, slowed down his body's use of the metcer cells, and he had lasted through the night without attacking her again.

He hung his head in shame as he came to a stop, leaning against one of the huge trees.

He was revolting.

To think he'd lost control...

Memory of her beneath him filled his mind and, as if on cue, his genital pouch swelled in anticipation, his cock pulsing.

Qef.

He shook his head.

He had to think of other things.

He had to think of death and destruction, of all the beings who were depending on him back on the base, of his people, the Shum'ai who would shout in horror at the way he had behaved.

Anger filled his veins—anger and hatred for himself—and he landed his fist into the trunk of the tree.

163

Wood split but so did the skin on his hand.

He watched his blood drip, the droplets marring the leaves beneath him, and snarled.

Back on Tonvuhiri, during the heat, he'd have been fighting other males for the chance to mate with a female.

It would have been an honor.

He would have been challenged for the right to release his seed in a fertile female. And then, when he'd won, a female could choose him if she so desired.

Shum'ai females were smaller, weaker, and rarer than Shum'ai males. In his bloodline, only one in ten births resulted in a female—in some others, the incidence was none. Males of his species often lived twice as long as the females, too, and these reasons made Shum'ai females his culture's greatest treasure.

All females were a treasure and he'd almost...he'd almost forced Keh-reh-nah...

Qef.

How far would he have gone before he caught himself?

Ajos slammed his fist into the tree again, enjoying the burn the action produced in his fist.

His anger was building and the pain from his fist hitting the wood seemed to quell the emotion somewhat.

He'd never thought this would have happened to him, being away from Tonvuhuri.

He'd particularly checked Murn GZ's climate before joining the Restitution, and he'd never gone on missions to extremely hot planets.

Not to mention, the heat had been one reason he'd left Tonvuhiri. Without the warm cycle, his heat would not have been activated.

And then there was the other reason why he'd left...

The memory of Nama's pleas lit up in his mind's eye and he punched the tree once more.

The deep pain of old simmered within him, mixing with his growing rage.

He did not deserve to mate.

Not after what he'd done.

His life organ wrung and he planted his other fist into the tree. More wood split and broke away.

He had watched his sister die, and he hadn't been able to save her.

It was something he could never be forgiven for.

Not only had he lost his family's treasure, but he'd inadvertently lessened the bloodline of his people.

That's why he'd joined the Restitution to fight. But no matter how many beings he saved, how many females he helped rescue from the Tasqal's clutches, it didn't lessen the guilt he lived with every day.

And now this...

The gods must be punishing him even more.

Memory of Keh-reh-nah would haunt him now forever.

He'd tasted her...

His cock pulsed again and there was pain in his seed sack, but it was a pain he'd have to endure.

He'd gone too far...now there was no going back. There was no way he could control himself around her now that he knew what her skin tasted like...what she felt like whimpering beneath him...

Qef.

He'd have to stay away from her.

As Ajos hit the tree one last time, the trunk snapped.

The sound of wood splitting apart filled the forest followed by that of the huge tree crashing down.

Ajos watched it fall, feeling nothing.

His rage was still simmering, an effect of the heat, of not finding release, and his bloodied hands itched for something else to punch.

He could use his fists...pleasure himself...but that would only make things worse.

As soon as he touched himself, he would cross a barrier that he wouldn't be able to uncross. It would open the gates of his need and he still needed to try to hold it together, at least till he got Keh-reh-nah back on the base.

How he was going to do that?

Only the gods knew.

As he turned to begin running again, a high-pitched sound echoed in the direction in which Keh-ren-nah rested.

He'd heard a similar sound before, when he'd helped his brothers open the stasis hold.

The sound was human. A sound of fear.

A chill down his spine immediately.

Keh-reh-nah.

He was shooting through the bushes so fast, it felt like he was moving faster than light.

His feet were made for running and he knew he was fast, but his body pushed even harder as another scream echoed through the forest.

As Ajos broke through the bushes and came upon her, he stopped dead in his tracks, unable to process what he was seeing.

One of the roots she'd been observing yesterday was wrapped around her leg and she was trying unsuccessfully to use his spear to pry it off.

His heart was finally allowed to beat—he hadn't even realized it had stopped—and Ajos took a breath.

She was okay.

"Ajos!" she screamed, "Help me!"

He moved, grasping his spear and prying it from her fingers. With one swift downward movement, he slammed the sharp part into the vine by her leg, slicing the plant in two.

It almost seemed as if the thing retreated somewhat and the part that was still wrapped around her leg loosened a little.

Her fingers were frantic as she tried to pry the vegetation off.

"Let me," he growled before clearing his throat.

He still sounded angry and he needed to hide it.

Taking her leg in his hand, he fought back his feelings and grit his teeth as he pried the vegetation from her leg.

As soon as it was removed, Keh-reh-nah pulled her leg toward her and rubbed the area.

Her movements were still frantic as she rubbed her ankle. It was as if she wanted to remove her actual skin with how hard she rubbed and he had to swallow his feelings as he reached forward and touched her once more, placing his hand over hers.

"Keh-reh-nah?"

She sobbed a little and that's when she glanced at him.

Her eyes were wet.

She was hurting and he didn't know exactly why.

He had never felt so helpless in his life. "Keh-reh-nah?"

"It wrapped itself around me," she met his gaze and blinked back the wetness, "I swear. It wrapped itself around me while I was sleeping. I felt it tighten. I felt it pull me." She scrubbed her skin again. "I mean, I work with plants but that just...it creeped me the fuck out and you weren't here. I thought you'd left me and—"

She stopped and took a deep breath.

Her throat moved as she swallowed hard and then she was standing.

Her back was turned to him as she wiped her eyes and then her shoulders stiffened and she took a deep breath.

"I freaked out," she said. "It won't happen again."

He could see her throat move the more she tried to hide her true emotions.

"Maybe these plants just grow ridiculously quickly and the root thought I was something to climb over. Climbing plants can curl or cling to other plants." She looked up into the trees. "That can make them dangerous in some cases..."

Her gaze scanned the vegetation and Ajos got the distinct impression that she was talking to herself again.

She seemed to do this whenever she was talking about plants and he found his anger and rage quelling a little as he watched her.

Keh-reh-nah spun, her gaze still moving around them. "But these are roots, not vines..."

Her fingers were working in a strange pattern as another breath shuddered through her and she caught hold of her emotions. It was as if she was weaving invisible thread with her fingers and his eyes locked onto her movements, mesmerized.

"They're roots but they act like vines and vines that grow that quickly could choke the plants they grow on..." Her eyes held no wetness anymore and she frowned. "...because they'd deprive the other plant of light to the point they'd kill it."

Her gaze finally landed on him, the frown still on her face.

"Ajos," she said. "I don't see any roots climbing on the trees or even the plants around us."

She looked down and he followed her gaze.

There were roots all below them and Keh-reh-nah crouched.

He watched her work, his own urges halted momentarily in awe of the female before him.

He'd expected her to shout or scream at him. He'd expected her to send him from her presence.

He hadn't expected *this*.

Though...there was still time for her to proclaim that he shouldn't come anywhere near her again.

It could still happen.

"I don't think these are completely roots," she finally said.

Ajos' gaze fell to where she poked with one hand.

"What?"

"I don't think these are fully roots," she repeated. "But I don't think they're vines either..."

Ajos looked around them.

He didn't know about that. There were so many.

He'd never seen so many roots above ground before, except in places where the ground was too soft to hold them. They looked more like vines to him, but she was the expert at this on her planet. She'd know more than he did.

"I don't see any root caps, no root hairs, and these motherfuckers are thick, thicker than any vines I've ever seen before, but," she took a breath, "a vine is a plant on its own. These things...they're connected to the trees..."

Keh-reh-nah rose and rubbed her hands over her shoulders. "We should go," she said. "I'm suddenly creeped out."

Ajos jerked his head in confirmation. "Do you wish for me to escort you back to the ship?"

He was reining in himself but who knew how long he could keep it up. She'd probably feel better being around V'Alen anyway.

V'Alen had the advantage of not having any urges at all.

Keh-reh-nah's frown was suddenly directed his way. "No. We have to find the source of that signal. I'm not going through all this to just return empty-handed."

For a beat, he studied her, but her shoulders were set and, somehow, he knew if he pressed, it was an argument he was going to lose.

"Let's go," he finally said, rising to his full height.

Keh-reh-nah averted her gaze, looking off into the distance.

He could cut the tension between them with his spear.

"Let's."

17

—————

THIS TIME, AJOS WALKED IN FRONT. HE KEPT HIS PACE A GOOD FEW meters ahead of her and she wasn't sure if that was because he didn't want to be close to her or if there was some other reason.

It didn't matter.

She had bigger things on her mind.

There was a niggling feeling at the back of her mind as they trekked through the undergrowth and Kerena frowned.

She could be paranoid, but since she'd woken that morning to find the vine wrapped around her leg, she couldn't relax.

She was missing something.

Something important.

Coupled with the fact that the alien she was with was confusing her to bits, she just had a lot to think about.

Releasing a breath, she let her gaze roam over the vegetation.

What was it?

What was she missing?

Ajos stopped for a moment to check his communicator before glancing back at her.

He was turning red again, she could see, and she knew he was out of medicine.

Well, that explained why he was walking so far ahead. He didn't want to touch her.

"The signal is still scrambled," she heard him say, and that prompted her to look at her own device.

There was a little dot on the screen that kept lighting up now and then, and she assumed that was where the source of the signal they were searching for was.

However, the dot kept disappearing and appearing. They'd be walking straight toward it at one point and the next time it appeared on the screen, it was in another direction.

That and the unsure feeling at the back of her mind had her on high alert as she looked around them.

Kerena eyed the roots along the ground as they continued walking, and the more she studied them, the more she felt disturbed.

They didn't burrow into the earth, as she'd noted before.

They crept like vines. Kerena frowned, her gaze focused on the vegetation, and she almost bumped into Ajos.

She hadn't realized he'd stopped walking.

She opened her mouth to ask him if the signal was scrambled again but he was standing so rigidly, she realized there must be something ahead of him that she couldn't see.

Glancing around him, she decided to take a look for herself.

The first thing she noticed was the fallen trees, snapped in two like a great hand had come down upon them.

But off in the distance was the dark metal hull of a spaceship.

Kerena's breath caught in her throat.

The enemy ship.

It was mangled, as if something had ripped through it, but even with the damage done to it, it looked huge...menacing.

Ajos blocked her with his arm.

"You should wait here," he said.

Kerena's gaze darted to him. "You think they're alive?"

He stared at the wreckage. "No, but it might still be safer if you stayed here and out of sight."

Kerena nodded. She understood that.

Only, even though she and Ajos weren't on the best of terms, staying by herself all alone made her anxiety rise a little—and that's thanks to the vegetation introducing itself to her leg earlier.

Something creeped her out about this place, and the presence of the enemy ship so close only freaked her out some more.

She'd known what they'd been heading toward, but seeing it big and menacing, the dark metal sticking out against the green vegetation like a bad omen, was something else.

It made alarm bells ring in her head.

Nevertheless, she nodded to Ajos.

"I'll wait here."

He glanced down at her and hesitated.

"Keep your comms on." He turned to her and put a finger over one of the buttons. "Press this one if you need to talk to me."

He glanced back at the ship. "I won't be long."

As Ajos moved off, Kerena settled behind some bushes, her eyes on him as he headed toward the huge ship.

He had his spear poised as if he would attack anything that moved near that ship, and Kerena watched him nervously.

As he neared the vessel, the mere size of it made Ajos look small, and seeing the large alien dwarfed was alarming in itself.

Kerena bit her bottom lip as she cracked the bones in her fingers.

This was what he did for a living. This was his job, something he did every other day.

So why was she so scared?

As Ajos disappeared into the vessel, her anxiety only rose.

Minutes ticked by and the silence in the forest became ominous.

How long should she wait before she assumed the worst?

"Keh-reh-nah?"

Kerena jumped before she realized the sound had come from the watch on her hand.

She fumbled to press the button.

"Ajos? Did you find anything?"

For a few moments, there was no response and it sounded as if the connection had cut out.

"Yes." His voice came back in.

He sounded so strained, Kerena felt an icicle begin to form at the base of her spine.

Something was wrong.

She could feel it.

"I can't be certain—" His voice cut out again. "—sure I have the right thing. It is scrambling my comms."

"Is everything all right in there?"

Kerena bit her lip again as she waited for a reply.

"Yes..." he grunted. "...and no."

Fear spiked within her.

"Wh—what's wrong?" She lowered her voice to a whisper. "Are there bad guys in there?"

Ajos grunted again but didn't answer.

She could hear him breathing hard through the receiver.

Kerena gulped as she crouched some more in the bushes, her eyes wide as she stared at the enemy ship.

"Tell me what to do," she whispered, glancing around her for anything she could use to defend herself should she need to.

"There are no Hedgeruds," Ajos rasped. "But you need to do something for me."

"What?" she whispered. She was prepared to do anything.

"I need you to..." His breath came hard and the beginning of a rumble changed his voice to something feral.

"...run."

His words pushed fear deep inside her.

But he'd said there were no enemies.

Why would she need to run?

Ajos made a tortured sound and then there was a loud crash as if he had fallen.

"Ajos?!"

"Go!" he growled. "Get away from here. Head back toward the ship. Contact V'Alen. He will find you and get the qef out of—"

The transmission crackled and his voice cut off.

Kerena rose slowly, her heart beating hard as she stared at the huge enemy vessel.

"Run, Keh-reh-nah." His voice was beginning to sound like he was possessed by something, and there was another loud crash.

Her heart was slamming so hard against her chest now, she could hardly think.

He'd said there were no enemies in there with him. Yet, it sounded as if he was in combat with someone.

It hit her then.

That was right because he was in combat.

He was fighting with himself.

"Ajos—"

"Go!" he snarled. "Do not let V'Alen return for me till you are safe on the base."

Fuck.

This was just like last night.

His fever was overwhelming him again.

Kerena stood, her fists clenching and unclenching.

She needed to make a decision.

She could either run as he said and use those markers he'd set down to help find her way back...

Or she could put on her brave hat and head into the enemy space-ship to find and help him.

Kerena began running.

Someone wise once said, "You are only one decision away from a totally different life," and somehow, as she ran, that thought echoed in her head.

The enemy ship grew even larger the closer she went toward it and, in any other situation, she'd be terrified of it.

Heck, she was terrified of it now, but that wasn't going to stop her.

"Keh-reh-nah." The voice that said her name sounded livid. "My comms must be really qeffing scrambled because—" his voice cut out "—that you're coming toward me."

Something else crashed.

"Tell me you are not so stupid."

"I am," was all she said, and a vicious snarl sounded over the comms.

"Don't..."

"Why not? I told you last night, I can't let you die on me."

"You don't understand..."

"You're ill. I understand that."

The connection cut out.

She was out in the open now and the wind pressed against her face as she ran toward the huge structure.

She was doing this. She was heading in there to help him.

Something sliced her leg and she hissed in pain, only glancing down to look at the thin line of her blood.

It was only a thin cut caused by a jutting piece of bark she'd ran too close to.

It hurt like the dickens, but she didn't stop. She'd just have to be more careful.

"—stubborn female. You don't understand."

Anger filled her.

Why was he resisting her assistance so much?

"I don't understand what?!"

The line cut out again and she didn't think she was going to get an answer.

"All I want to do..." whatever had possessed him took complete control of his voice "...is qef and kill."

Kerena's mouth fell open a little and her steps slowed.

"I want to qef you..." it wasn't possible for his voice to get harder, lower...yet it fell even more decibels "...and I want to kill anyone who even looks your way."

Kerena skidded to a halt not far from the huge alien ship.

She'd heard those words right, she was sure, but she was having a hard time believing he'd actually said them.

"If you come in here..."

He left the words unsaid and Kerena gulped.

Her body heaved with the exertion of running and she took in deep breaths as she tried to calm the burn in her lungs.

"Ajos, I—"

The words stopped in her throat.

Even if she wanted to complete them, she wouldn't have been able to.

One moment, she was standing and the next she was pulled to the ground as someone attacked her from low on the ground.

No...it wasn't someone...it was something.

Something firm, sinewy, and strong wrapped around her leg and brought her down.

A scream barreled from her breast as she hit the ground hard.

Pain rocketed into her back as her body kept colliding with the rough earth beneath her.

She was moving.

It was pulling her.

She was moving so fast, she could hear the vegetation around her swish by, and the last thing she was able to shout, before something sealed her mouth shut, was his name.

It pierced the air as her singular plea.

"Ajos!"

18

She was being pulled across the terrain fast. So fast, she could hardly see where she was going.

Whatever had gripped her had wrapped itself around her almost completely.

Her arms were wrapped within it, her legs…it had even wrapped itself around her neck and mouth, sealing her lips shut.

It felt as if she was within the clutches of a giant serpent and even though she was trying to scream, her sounds were quieted by the sheer speed of the force taking her away.

She could see it, her foe, but she couldn't comprehend it.

Around her, vegetation continued rushing by as the thing carried her away.

The *things*, rather.

Roots.

Many, many roots.

Large, sinewy, black roots.

They'd wrapped around her completely, and with amazing speed.

She could see it, but her mind refused to acknowledge it—because it was impossible.

Heck, the fastest growing plant on Earth was bamboo, but

compared to bamboo, these roots...these roots were like putting Usain Bolt against a toddler in a race.

Even as she struggled and fear made her heart hammer against her chest, she knew she wasn't getting out of the plant's grasp.

Her life flashed before her eyes.

This was how it was going to end?

Of all the ways to die?

She had no idea how long she'd been moving or how far she'd been pulled away.

It felt like ages but it could be less than a minute. She couldn't know for sure. The terror of the situation alone had distorted time.

Kerena gulped as she attempted to control her breathing.

She could only assume that she'd tripped some kind of mechanism that made the plant latch on to her—kind of like tickling the hairs on a sundew or Venus flytrap—and that thought only made her freak out even more.

She could only hope the plant would release her soon, but there was a sick feeling in the pit of her stomach.

It wasn't acting like any plant she'd ever encountered...it seemed sentient—as if it was taking her to a specific location—and that thought chilled her to the bone.

The light of the sun seemed to dim as the movement of the roots slowed down and Kerena realized it was taking her to a dense area where the vegetation was a lot thicker.

She could hear her pulse in her ears as her breaths came ragged through her nostrils.

Please, God, don't make this be some sort of carnivorous plant.

Please.

Gravity suddenly tilted and she was going down, down, then all movements stopped.

Kerena's heart hammered against her chest.

Nothing happened.

There was no sound, no movement, nothing.

If she wasn't still caught in the grasp of the plant, she'd have thought she'd imagined it pulling her across the terrain.

"—reh-nah!" The sound came from the device on her wrist.

It was still there and her heart rate picked up when she realized that it hadn't fallen off during the journey.

Ajos.

He was still out there somewhere.

A glimmer of hope made her heart flutter but there was no way for her to access the device so she could answer him.

She couldn't move.

"Keh—" The signal cut out. "—nah!"

Tears formed in her eyes.

She was on her back and she could barely see the sky above through the canopy.

It was so dim where she was, she could hardly see and that only made her anxiety rise.

Her only consolation was that there seemed to be no movement from the plant and, for now, she was going to look at that as a good thing.

Moments passed with no other sound. Minutes went by.

And then there was movement.

It started with the roots around her neck loosening and she only noticed this because she was suddenly able to breathe easier.

Then, the root covering her mouth loosened too.

Kerena held her breath, not daring to move lest the roots tighten around her again.

"Keh-reh—" Ajos' voice cut in again and hope flared within her once more. "—please, say some—"

His voice still sounded strained and she wasn't sure if it was his fever or because he was freaking out that she'd been taken away.

More of the roots loosened, slipping away from her body and Kerena's pulse quickened.

If just a few more loosened, she could probably wriggle away.

The next few minutes of waiting felt like whole eons, but as soon as she felt the roots loosen from around her, Kerena pressed her hands down, spinning slowly so she could position herself to scramble backward.

She bit her lip hard, her breath making her nose burn with the pressure of her breathing, as she prayed that the roots didn't latch on to her once more.

They were so thick and fibrous underneath her, it made her skin crawl.

With one heave, she pushed away using her hands. The movement launched her forward like a dive and she scrambled out of the plant's grasp.

But she didn't make it far.

As soon as she managed to leave the nestle of roots, she went down again.

Her breath caught in her throat as she realized one of her legs was still caught in the plant's grasp.

In horror, she looked back, her gaze darting over the roots for any movement. But there was none.

It was like she was staring at any regular plant and the eeriness only made her more frantic inside.

Her gaze fell to the leg that was still caught within the plant's grasp and that's when she noticed something.

The roots surrounding her leg were different from the others—a difference that would have been hard to miss.

All along her leg, growing from the root itself, were a set of gorgeous purple flowers—the likes of which she'd never seen before.

"KEH-REH-NAH!" Ajos shouted once more. He was running so fast, the vegetation around him moved like a blur.

"Keh-reh-nah!"

Qef it.

Either his comms weren't working, hers weren't, or the "source" he was carrying was interfering with the signal.

He glanced down at it—a glowing white orb. He had no idea what it was.

The orb glistened along his side, shining a light from its strange surface. It was so small, it fit in his palm.

The size had surprised him, but he was sure it was the thing they sought.

When he'd found it in the engine room of the ship, it had been encased in a sort of metallic shield that fell away as soon as he'd touched it.

His nefre had been burning and he'd found a satchel and slipped the thing inside just before he'd communicated with Keh-reh-nah.

The strange orb rested in the satchel hung over his shoulder now, bouncing against his side as he ran.

He was seeing red and he wasn't sure if it was his heat or the rage surging within him.

Keh-reh-nah was in danger...and he hadn't been lying. All he wanted to do right now was kill—the urge burned within him now even more than before.

He'd told her to run, but he was sure that's not what she'd done.

She'd made that high-pitched sound of fear that humans did, right before she'd gone silent.

She had been taken.

"V'Alen." He spoke through his comms, but there was no answer.

Another growl ripped through him, this one louder than the last.

He was running but he didn't even know where he was running to, and that made fear play a ballad on his spine.

They must have made a mistake.

Somehow, the Hedgeruds must have survived.

They had hidden in the forest, hidden their biosignature from scans of the planet's surface, and had ambushed Keh-reh-nah.

This was his fault.

He shouldn't have allowed her to be alone.

Qef. He shouldn't have brought her on the mission in the first place. That was painfully clear now, but hindsight was a jekin.

What's worse, he had no idea which direction they'd taken her.

He'd exited the ship as quickly as his body had allowed him to, the heat surging through his muscles making him faster, more deadly...yet, there had been no trace of her.

It was like she hadn't been there.

"—jos."

Ajos stopped dead in his tracks, his gaze scanning the forest.

"Keh-reh-nah?" Hope flared within him.

She was alive but that didn't lessen the fear now surging or the rage riding the lifeblood in his veins.

If there were Hedgeruds around her, there was a reason they were keeping her alive and he was sure it had something to do with him.

"It is not safe." He lowered his voice. "How many of them are there with you?"

For a few moments, there was no sound, only the crackling of the comms, and Ajos resumed running, albeit slower, his eyes peeled as he scanned the bushes around him for any sign of life.

"—lone but the roots are —" She cut off. "—a hole I think. I'm not—"

Ajos growled. This wasn't going to work.

He could hardly understand what she was saying.

She was risking her life trying to communicate with him and he couldn't qeffing hear her.

It sounded as if she said she was alone but that didn't make sense. Unless...

Unless the fighters had taken her and locked her up somewhere.

That might make things easier. He could—he *would*—take them out before they returned to where they'd hid her.

He glanced down at the orb he was carrying once more and growled again.

Was it the reason the comms were giving trouble?

He stared at the thing for a few seconds and it glowed as if it was aware it was being watched.

It took two seconds to make a decision.

He couldn't allow another female to die under his watch.

He was responsible for keeping Keh-reh-nah safe, and she was more important than the stupid orb.

He'd just have to leave the device and the Restitution would simply have to send another team to retrieve it.

As he slipped his arms from under the strap of the satchel, his communication device crackled.

"Commander."

V'Alen.

"Commander," V'Alen repeated. "I have repaired the comms. I had to fix a component that caused a magnetic disturbance that affected all instruments. The comms are operational now."

"There is no time." Ajos didn't bother with a greeting. "Keh-reh-nah was taken. I have to get to her before the Hedgeruds..."

He couldn't say it.

"The human...she was taken?" V'Alen asked. "There was no sign of life on the scans."

"I know, yet, here we are," Ajos growled. "I will find her." It was an oath. "Make sure the ship is repaired in short order. We might need a quick escape."

"Understood."

Ajos let out a breath as he resettled the satchel over his shoulder and began running again.

His eyes scanned everything as he moved.

He would find her.

He had to.

"Keh-reh-nah, do you read?"

There was no response.

A chill ran down Ajos' nefre, hardly cooling the heat emanating through him.

"Keh-reh-nah—"

"Ajos—" Keh-reh-nah gasped and Ajos swallowed hard, his life organ felt like it suddenly started beating again.

Never before had he felt so relieved hearing a female's voice.

"Speak quickly but quietly." He kept his voice low. "Try not to let them hear you if they are close." He was still looking around him as he ran, his eyes peeled for anything out of the ordinary. "How many of them are there with you?"

"Like," Keh-reh-nah paused, "a lot."

Qeffing qrak.

He'd been expecting two Hedgerud fighters at most.

"More than I originally thought," she whispered, and he heard a shuffle as if she moved. "They're not moving anymore though, so that's good."

Ajos almost stumbled. "What do you mean they are not moving?"

"They stopped. As soon as they brought me here." Another shuffle. "They all stopped then I was released. Only—" she paused and made a sound as if she was struggling.

"Keh-reh-nah?!" Ajos hissed.

"It's just," she grunted, "one of them is wrapped around my leg and I can't seem to get it off."

She wasn't making any sense.

"Keh-reh-nah..." He had to press through the strain against his own mind. Not only was this a bad time for his heat to be fighting his sanity, but someone's life depended on him and he was having such a hard time focusing, dread filled him that he wouldn't be able enough to save her at all. "Tell me how many fighters are around you. Can you see anything that would give away your location?"

He glanced around as he spoke, blinking to clear his blurred vision.

He wouldn't say he was the greatest tracker, but it bothered him that there was no trace of her.

No trampled grass, no broken branches, no ripped garments caught in the vegetation...nothing.

Also, the Hedgeruds weren't the type to play hide and seek. They were a race that thought of themselves as highly competent fighters. It was unlike them to hide.

"Fighters?" He could hear the fear in her voice. "There are no fighters here. I am alone."

Now, she really wasn't making any sense.

"Where are the Hedgeruds that took you away?" Another pulse run down his nefre, causing his entire body to quake, and Ajos felt shame at the fact that he was so weak.

He looked to the heavens, knowing the gods were watching him.

They were doing it to him again.

How much more did he need to suffer?

What lesson must he learn?

Surely, there was something he was missing.

He could not let another female die under his care.

He could not...

"You mean the bad guys? There are no bad guys here, Ajos."

He didn't understand.

"What?" He had to inhale hard as he stopped for a moment to lean against a tree.

The heat was overwhelming him.

Every muscle in his body felt strained.

Every fiber in his being pulsed with need.

And he knew...

He knew that when he did rescue her, she wouldn't be safe from him either.

But that was something he'd have to deal with when he got there.

"It's the roots, Ajos."

Glancing down at his communicator, he frowned.

Maybe the heat was affecting his grasp on reality as well.

"The roots?"

"The roots." She took a breath. "They wrapped around me. Pulled me away." She paused and he could hear her panting a little. "I'm in some kind of hole or cave, I think. I'm not sure."

The roots.

Ajos looked around him, trying to understand.

"There's still one hooked around my leg and I'm trying to get it off now." She panted. "If I can, I'll try to climb out of here."

Just as she said that, a fat drop of water landed smack on his face.

Ajos turned his face to the heavens.

Another drop landed on his cheek and a crack of thunder sounded above as the skies grew gray.

"Ajos?" There was a note of fear in her voice. "What's that? It sounded like..."

Rain.

It was going to rain and Keh-reh-nah was stuck in a hole somewhere.

Pushing himself forward, Ajos took off on a run once more.

"Ajos?" He could hear her breaths. They were coming fast and hard. "I know this isn't helping, but I'm kind of starting to freak out here."

"I will find you, Keh-reh-nah."

He knew this as sure as he knew his own name.

He was Ajos of the bloodline Khattull.

He would find her, if it was the last thing he did.

19

―――――

THE ROOT WRAPPED AROUND HER LEG WAS HARD TO DISLODGE.

Kerena strained against the thing till her fingernails cracked and the tips broke, but she finally managed to pry her leg from its clutches.

Heart beating like it was pumped with drugs, she scrambled even farther away from the nestle in which she'd been a prisoner.

Her gaze moved around the strange place.

There were dark roots everywhere, and it did seem as if she was in a hole.

Why had the plants brought her here?

Standing on shaky legs, she glanced around as she spun in a slow circle.

She could hardly see the sky above and it had gotten darker.

Another crack of thunder echoed in the heavens and the faint sound of heavy rainfall reached her ears, but where she was, the rain didn't hit her.

Kerena clenched and unclenched her fists.

She had to find a way out.

The roots were long, spilling over the top of the hole and hanging down to where she could reach them. They hadn't moved since they'd deposited her there.

Staring at them, she exhaled through her mouth. She was no gymnast or rock climber, but she would just have to climb out by hanging on to one—regardless that the last thing she wanted to do was to touch them again.

She could still feel them wrapped around her and the thought made her skin shiver.

Gripping on to one root, Kerena tried to pull herself toward the opening above, only for her to lose her grip and fall back onto her tailbone.

Pain rocketed up her spine and she hissed, squeezing her eyes tight as she breathed through the pain.

But she had to try again.

Still breathing through the pain, she attempted to climb up once more only to slip again. This time, she managed to land on her feet.

The roots were too slippery.

It wouldn't work.

If she could find a way to increase the friction...

Frantic eyes glanced around the hole.

She didn't know what she'd expected to see.

There was nothing but more roots there. She couldn't even see the ground.

She could have probably used the dry earth to "chalk" her hands but that wasn't an option.

Swallowing hard, a shiver went through her.

The plant had brought her here for a reason and she didn't want to wait around to find out what that was.

It was obviously nothing good.

As she bit her lip and paced a little, she heard a faint drip of water.

Kerena's eyes fastened in the direction of the sound.

There, running down one of the roots hanging from the top of the hole, was a thin line of water.

Somehow, that bit of fluid sent a shot of fear straight through her and as she turned in a slow circle, there were more and more little streams running from the roots down into the hole.

Droplets from the leaves of the canopy above started dropping down too, and one fell smack onto the bridge of her nose.

"Shit."

She needed to do something, and fast.

She could get out of the hole. She was sure of it.

Think, Kerena. Think!

Her eyes were darting around as she worried her lip between her teeth and that's when her gaze fell on her dress.

There was only one thing she could do.

Slipping the dress over her head, she stood in her underwear and shivered again. It was getting cold. Possibly, the change in atmosphere because of the rain was causing that.

Also, she was wet.

Enough raindrops had fallen on her that her hair was getting damp and the roots beneath her were wet.

"You can do this," she whispered to herself.

Slipping one hand in the dress, she twined the clothing enough so it didn't slip off before placing her free hand into the other side and doing the same thing.

She now had a sort of cloth handcuff, but she hoped it provided just enough friction for her to climb out.

Moving toward the hanging root once more, she grasped it and tugged.

Rainwater flashed into her face, but the root felt secure.

Heaving upward, she grasped the root and lifted herself off the ground.

Her hands slipped a little, but she held tight.

The rain was making the roots even more slippery and her core muscles strained and protested as she raised one hand to grasp and pull herself higher.

Her muscles strained as her outstretched hand fought to grasp higher on the root.

Gravity was pulling in the opposite direction and her body obeyed, sliding down the slippery root so quickly, she only got the sense that she was falling—the thought didn't come till after.

Pain rocketed in her buttocks as she landed hard.

"Fuck!"

She swallowed hard and got up, wrapping her hands again.

A second attempt ended up the same way.

"Goddamnit."

Her body heaved with the heavy breaths she took.

"Keh-reh-nah, do you read?"

Kerena swallowed hard, her fingers trembling as she unwrapped them from her dress and activated the communicator.

"Ajos." She could hardly catch her breath and she shivered again.

The hole was really cold now, and she was half-naked and wet.

Fuck, this was a bad situation.

"Keh-reh-nah, you are hurt." Ajos' breaths were coming hard too, and she remembered immediately that he was ill. Ill, yet he was pushing himself to find her.

"I'm not. Just got the wind knocked out of me. I was trying to climb out. I can't—" She took that back.

She could.

She would.

"V'Alen has sent me the coordinates of your communicator," he said, and hope rose within her. "But..." He trailed off.

"But what?"

"The device I retrieved from the Tasqal ship is still messing with the navigation. Even if I leave it behind...it would still..."

Kerena took a breath. She understood.

"It's okay. I'll wait. The plants haven't moved again."

And she hoped to hell that they wouldn't.

Her shoulders sagged as she took a step back, looking up at the mouth of the hole.

There must be a better way to attempt escape, but she could think of none.

Her body ached, she was low on energy, and her palm burned something vicious.

Switching on the light on her communicator, she turned the light to her palm.

There was a cut there, probably from when she'd been trying to climb on the vine.

She watched the rain hit her palm, mixing with her blood, and the mixture ran to fall on the root directly below her.

"I'm sorry, Ker-reh-nah. I should never have taken you to this place."

She watched the blood drip as she pressed the button to talk to him.

"I wanted to come."

"If you didn't come, you would be safe on the base."

She held back a sad laugh.

"I don't think I'm really safe anywhere...not even on my own planet. I was taken—"

Her words died on her lips as she froze.

There was movement.

"Keh-reh-nah?"

"It's moving," she whispered.

Even to her, fear laced her voice.

"Qef," Ajos cursed. "Move away from it, slowly."

"I—" Her eyes widened as she watched what was happening before her. "Ajos...it's..."

Kerena blinked, not believing what she was seeing.

"Keh-reh-nah, talk, please. Let me know what's happening." Ajos sounded tortured.

"It's making a flower," she whispered.

KEH-REH-NAH WENT silent again and Ajos collapsed against a tree, leaning his shoulder against it as he took a breath.

The rain was helping.

It was cooling his body but not his need.

Still, he had to push forward.

As soon as he got her out and back to the ship, then he could deal with his problem.

"Ajos," her voice came over his communicator and he released a breath. "Ajos, I—"

"Keh-reh-nah," he leaned off the tree and staggered forward, "don't go near the things."

She chuckled a little and the sound of her laughter surprised him.

"You have no idea how many of them are around me. There's no way I can avoid them all but..." she paused, "I think I know why they pulled me away."

Ajos checked the communicator's nav function as she spoke. It said she was to the west just a few minutes ago and he'd been heading that way. Now it said she was north-west.

Switching his trajectory, he kept searching, slowing down so he could search more effectively.

She said she was in a hole of some sort and he was sure he hadn't passed her by accident before.

Glancing behind him, he frowned. She'd been pulled much farther away than he'd expected or realized.

"It's my blood," she said. "Wherever my blood falls, strange flowers bloom."

A growl erupted from within him and Ajos staggered a little more before taking a moment to lean against a tree to regain his strength.

"You're bleeding?"

"It's okay. I'm okay. It was just a scratch. It's stopped bleeding now but not before some of the blood caught the root and...well, it grew a flower." She paused. "I should be terrified but...this is the strangest plant I have ever witnessed in my life."

Ajos growled again. "It doesn't explain why the plant pulled you away in the first place."

He checked his navigator once more.

Qeffing qrak. The direction changed again.

Hauling himself forward, he continued forward.

"It does," Keh-reh-nah said after a while. "I cut myself while I was running. I guess my blood caught one of the roots or something. Though..." she trailed off, "this doesn't explain why it had climbed over me while I was sleeping. I wasn't bleeding."

"The forest wants your blood?" He didn't mean to growl but at this point, he couldn't help it.

"I don't know. I can't understand it. I assume something in my blood is a catalyst for this plant, causing some reaction that makes it bloom."

"Well, I need to get you the qef out of there," he growled again and winced at the sound of his own voice.

There was silence in his communicator as he stumbled through the forest.

He checked the navigation again and realized the dot on his screen that told him where she was had shifted again. Though not considerably so.

He could only hope it meant he was heading in the right direction this time.

"Ajos…" Her voice sounded soft. So soft and delicate.

Qef him.

He was cursed.

Ajos gulped. "Keh-reh-nah…"

"You don't have a fever, do you."

Ajos swallowed hard and continued forcing himself forward. He could hardly see with the downpour around him but that wasn't the main thing that was hindering his vision.

His lifeblood was hammering so hard in his skull that it was blurring his vision.

He was denying his body of a natural process. It was only logical that he could hardly keep sane.

But he needed to.

Not only for his sake, but for hers as well.

"Don't worry about me," he growled. "I am fine."

"Bullshit."

He paused at that.

"What?"

"You're talking b-bullshit." It sounded like she was shivering.

Cold.

Of course, she was.

If the rain was helping him to cool down then she, with her thin skin, would positively be freezing.

He needed to hurry if not for that reason alone.

"What's happening to you? Tell me," she pressed.

Ajos gulped again.

He didn't want to tell her.

He didn't even want to think about it. Thoughts only made the surges worse.

"I know you don't kn-know me. I know we don't know each other, but I also think that these aren't r-regular circumstances that brought us together." She took a breath and it sounded as if she shivered again. "For some reason, and h-hear me out, I trust you." She paused. "Y-you can trust m-me too."

Ajos' throat worked as he collapsed against another tree, breathing hard.

He looked up into the gray sky of Choria G622 and searched the nothingness as if for an answer.

"It's the heat," he finally said, sinking down into a sitting position as his chest heaved. "I am consumed by it. Completely." He paused. "I am afraid...you are not safe from me."

He waited for her to say something, but nothing came across the line.

"When I get you out of that hole, Keh-reh-nah...you need to run... and try not to bleed again." He gulped. "Take my spear with you and if I..."

A few moments passed and he struggled with himself.

"If you what?" her voice prompted.

Ajos took another breath and spoke the next words as fast as he could.

"If I attack you, you need to use the spear. Do what it takes to protect yourself."

A few more moments passed and Ajos rose to his feet, staggering once more as he continued on his search.

"Ajos?" Keh-reh-nah's voice sounded like sweet surca juice, like the taste of her skin. "Why would you attack me?"

Ajos had to stop at those words, the images in his mind too strong.

Images of her pale, naked skin...of his hands on her body...of her writhing beneath him...

"Because I want you, Keh-reh-nah..."

A soft sound left her lips. "Yes...you said."

There was no other sound for a few moments, only her breathing.

"Because you're horny and I'm the only female around." She paused. "That's all this is...isn't it?"

He stumbled, the question catching him off guard.

And his answer?

No.

No, it wasn't as simple as that.

He wanted her now and he wanted her tomorrow.

He wanted her the next day and the next after that...

Ajos' eyes widened as the reality hit him.

His nefre pulsed with confirmation.

It wasn't just the heat...

This burning desire to consume her wasn't just a result of his biological processes.

Somewhere, somehow, he'd done something he never thought was ever a possibility in his future.

It was something that happened to only the luckiest of the Shum'ai. Something others prayed to the gods for and never received. Yet, somehow, they'd bestowed the gift on *him*.

A life bond.

Ajos stopped running completely, his chest heaving with the huge breaths he was taking.

Rain poured down over his skin, the thick raindrops running off the leaves above to drench him with the shower of the heavens.

Keh-reh-nah...

Keh-reh-nah was his life mate.

20

Kerena hugged herself.

It might have been a mistake to take off her dress, but she hadn't had a choice.

It had been hours since she'd been stuck in the hole, so long now that night had come again and still, she hadn't found a way out.

Well, at least it had stopped raining.

Water was still trickling down the roots, though. She was lucky it hadn't created a pool in the hole itself.

That would have been another problem she was glad she didn't have to face.

She shivered in the darkness and adjusted her feet on the roots on which she stood.

She didn't dare sit down or even relax for a moment.

Who knew? The plants might just start moving again.

So far, they'd kept still since depositing her to this place.

Using the light on her communicator, she shone it around the dark hole.

There were flowers in a few spots that she'd tested her blood on.

Call her a mad scientist or something, testing her blood on what was obviously not a normal plant, but the curiosity within her had been pressing.

There were several blooms around her now, and despite that this was creepy as hell, she marveled at the size of the flowers.

They were about as big as a dinner plate, the purple petals spreading away from what looked like a pollinated center.

They reminded her of giant hibiscuses in the way the petals were arranged.

Now and then, the pollen-filled bulbs within the center of the plants would pop—the yellow specks of pollen floating into the air.

"I think I am close." Ajos' strained voice came over the communicator and Kerena tilted her head upward. "Your signal isn't moving so much anymore."

He sounded tormented, as if he was about to collapse when she saw him next, and Kerena worried her lip between her teeth as she searched the darkness above.

Activating the device so she could speak, she shone the light above her as she did.

"I'm shining my light out of the hole. I don't know if you can see it, but maybe it will help."

There was a grunt. "I think I see you."

Relief shot through her, but at the same time, anxiety did as well.

She hadn't forgotten what he'd said.

He'd told her to take his spear and run.

He'd said she should use his own weapon to defend herself against *him*.

There was a sound above her and Kerena tensed, shining her light so she could see.

There was a grunt and the sound of boots hitting the leaves.

Her heart rate sped up a little more.

"Ajos? Is that you?"

A figure leaned over the hole, directly in her light and Kerena gasped, stumbling back a little as she did.

It was Ajos all right, but he looked...he looked like he'd been through hell and back.

His skin was damp, but something told her it was his own perspiration and not just the rain that had caused that.

Not only that, but the protrusions on the side of his head were completely red.

He looked like he was in pain but there was such intense focus in his eyes, it was like looking into the eyes of a tiger.

"Ajos?"

His gaze found hers and Kerena's mouth opened in shock.

Completely black. Not even one gold fleck was in that darkness.

"I'll get you out," he said, before his head disappeared and she heard some shuffling above.

Kerena paced a little.

A part of her was scared to be close to him again and another part of her…

That other part of her was…excited.

Memory of the contact of his pelvis against hers…the feel of his tongue against her skin…Ajos appeared again and lowered himself over the edge of the hole, almost so his entire upper body was hanging down. He was upside down, his back to the roots, and one of his legs was secured by something she couldn't see.

He stretched his spear toward her with the dangerous end facing his way.

"Can you reach it?"

Kerena gulped. She wasn't even sure if she should touch him.

His warning kept repeating in her mind.

She had no choice, though, so she eyed the distance.

She'd have to jump, but she could definitely reach.

"I can," she said, tying her dress around her waist. She was moving toward the handle of the spear when her gaze landed on one of the strange flowers.

She hesitated for a second before she plucked the thing and stuffed it into the band her dress had created.

"Ready?" Flattening her feet, she crouched to give herself more upward momentum and pushed off the ground with her legs.

Up she went and she almost missed the spear but managed to grab on to it with one hand.

The muscles in that arm began screaming immediately and she

flailed a little, stretching hard with the other hand to grab hold of the stick.

"You can do it, Keh-reh-nah."

She appreciated the confidence, but her entire body begged to differ. She began to slip, unable to hold her weight with the one hand, and with a loud cry, she made one last effort to grab hold of the stick with the other hand.

She did it. Her palm closed around the wood and she held on tight, taking a second to let the jittery feeling of relief flood through her.

"Can you climb up?"

"Not sure, but I have to try." Now it was her voice that sounded strained. Her arms felt like string cheese. There was absolutely no strength in them. But as she said to him, she had to try. Glancing upward, she met Ajos' dark gaze, and another shiver went through her, this time not because of the cold, but because of what she saw in his eyes. One thing at a time, Kerena. Deal with one thing at a time. "I will help you." Ajos grimaced and began pulling the spear toward him.

Slowly but surely, she was lifted and Kerena forced the muscles in her arms to keep steady.

With much effort, she lifted one hand to grasp farther along the spear. Together, they could do this.

She was looking down as she was pulled up and only when the spear stopped moving did she look up again.

Air went into her nose in a sharp intake. Her face dangerously close to his.

Ajos seemed frozen as he stared down at her, and this close, his eyes were utterly terrifying.

"Ajos?"

Her voice must have lit something in his mind because, for just a moment, his pupils contracted a little so she could see a ring of gold at the edges.

"Keh-reh-nah," he said in that way that seemed to caress every syllable. "Your garments..."

"Oh...about that..." She'd forgotten she was only in her underwear. Her only thought had been about getting out of her plant prison.

A growl rumbled from within him and now it was her time to freeze, her gaze moving over his face.

The sound made another shiver go through her.

But she wasn't terrified.

She should be.

He himself had warned her that she'd need to run.

"You will have to climb over me," he growled before squeezing his eyes shut. When he looked back at her, they'd gone even darker, if that was even possible. "You must do it quickly."

Noted.

Grasping his shirt, she pulled herself upward.

It was much easier to do since he wasn't as slippery as the roots and was easier to hold on to than his spear. Soon her upper body was almost aligned with his and she smiled.

She could almost see over the edge of the hole now. Just a little more...

That's when a groan so strong it made his entire body shudder vibrated through him. It was so powerful, she swayed a little on his chest.

Looking down, her eyes widened as she realized just why he'd reacted that way.

Her crotch was right over his head and, not realizing it, she'd cause him to bury his nose right in the center of her panties.

Ajos groaned again as he inhaled deeply.

He shuddered so hard, she almost slipped, and she realized that if she didn't hurry, they both risked ending up in the hole.

Pushing forward, she grasped whatever she could, and something pulsed underneath her hand.

Oh shit.

Ajos groaned again and Kerena's hand flew off him so fast, she almost fell backward.

That hadn't been his leg she'd grabbed. "Hurry," Ajos groaned. Shaking her head to clear her thoughts, she pushed forward, closing the distance between her and the edge, and climbed out of the hole.

She took a moment to release a triumphant breath before she turned and shone the light down into the hole.

Ajos swung hard and slammed his spear into the wall. Using the weapon as leverage, he hoisted himself on it as he folded his body and reached for the top of the hole.

He did it with such ease, she was impressed, but as soon as he looked her way he froze again.

Those dark eyes were on her again.

"Keh-reh-nah." He twisted his leg from the clasp of a satchel he'd tied around a nearby tree and swung his lower body into the hole.

The only thing holding him up now was that one hand buried into the ground at the top of the hole.

"I am going to give you my spear," he said through gritted teeth. "Take it. Run. Do not fall or cut yourself. I'll contact V'Alen. He will find you."

He was warning her again, and as the spear landed at her feet, she stared at it.

He really expected her to go off on her own after what she'd discovered about the forest?

Could he be that bad? That indisposed?

"Run, Keh-reh-nah." His voice was so deep now, he sounded like a demon rising from the depths of hell and with dark eyes like his, he fit the image in her head. But his growl only made her freeze even more.

A roar left his lips that finally kicked her head into gear.

"Run!"

As Ajos hoisted himself from the hole, Kerena felt fear shoot through her bones.

Her body reacted before her mind caught up and she was dashing through the night, with only the light from her communicator as her guide.

Somewhere behind her, she heard another roar, and it made fear go deep into her bones.

Ajos sounded like an animal, like something she'd read about in a fairytale—not at all like the gentle alien who'd held her when she'd passed out from lack of oxygen.

Not at all like the alien who'd brought her a mattress and a blanket...

Not like the alien who'd given her his bed to sleep in.

Those thoughts made her pause and Kerena stopped running.

Her heart hammered into her chest as she turned to look back in the direction of the hole.

She could hear the faint sound of vegetation crashing down and she blinked rapidly at the darkness.

She was pretty sure that had been the sound of a tree falling.

Kerena swallowed hard.

Ajos was in trouble.

She couldn't leave him like that.

She knew what he was telling her to run from...she knew what he wanted to do...

Yet, her feet turned, and she began moving once more—toward the alien that had said that he wanted to bury his alien cock deep inside her...

For a moment, she paused again at that thought, her fists clenching and unclenching as she fought with herself.

She was crazy...but a part of her still pushed forward.

A part of her was a crazy botanist whose best friends were plants and whose curiosity ruled her mind.

Another part of her was just a lonely chick who couldn't deny that she was interested in this tall, minty-teal alien.

And, well, another part of her couldn't deny that deep down...she *wanted* this.

21

Ajos struggled against the tree trunk, perspiration dampening his skin.

His fists clenched and unclenched behind him.

He'd used the only thing he could find to tie his arms together behind his back—the bands of the satchel. But even though they held his arms fast, that didn't stop the heat from making his body pressed with tension.

All he wanted to do was to go after her.

His body was straining, his muscles bunching as he pulled against the tree.

He knew she was running—away from him—but everything in his being wanted him to break free and give chase.

He could only hope that she got far enough away before the tree trunk, or the straps that held him, broke and he was released.

He could only hope...

Ajos turned his face upward, his eyes on the starry sky as another loud roar left his lips.

He was being tormented.

Every bone in his body, every fiber, called out for Keh-reh-nah.

He finally understood now what the gods had been doing.

They'd cursed him.

They'd cursed him with a bond he'd never be able to fulfill.

He wasn't meant to be a mate. Not after failing his basic duty.

Not after Nama had died in his care.

Ajos groaned, a tortured sound coming from his lips.

His nefre pulsed and he closed his eyes as another surge went through him.

He could still smell Keh-reh-nah's sweet, sweet scent. A smell he'd never scented before—and one he'd never forget.

And...he wanted more.

More than anything, he wanted to bury his face deeper into her sweet softness.

Without knowing what she'd been doing, she'd rubbed herself over his face and it had taken all he had to not tighten his arms across her waist and hold her there so he could delve deep into her slit with his tongue.

Another tortured groan ripped through him at the thought and his muscles bunched and flexed.

Qef.

Qef!

"Ajos?"

Time stood still.

No.

Ajos froze, not daring to open his eyes.

"Ajos." He heard her move closer and the light was suddenly shone in his face. She gasped a little and that made him stiffen even more.

For her to see him like this...in this state...what would she think?

But worse than that...what the qef was she doing here?!

"Keh-reh-nah," he growled.

He'd told her to run.

He'd told her to get away.

He couldn't...*control* himself. Especially not with her this close.

He struggled against the tree. Against his will, his body trying to free itself.

He could scent her, even from the distance away from him, he could scent her again.

"Keh-reh-nah," he begged, the last of his sanity pleading with her, "run. Go away from here."

"No."

Her voice sounded closer.

She wasn't listening.

She *was* stubborn.

"You don't know the danger—"

"Let me help you."

Ajos froze again, his throat working as he opened his eyes to look at her.

She was cast in the shadows, but he could still see enough to tell that her skin was still mostly bare, the paleness displayed for him to see.

"Let me help you," she repeated.

"You don't know what you're asking for. You don't want this..." Was all he could say because his breath hitched in his throat.

She was moving forward now, closer, and he could see more of her.

She was doing something.

She was taking something from her waist, a flower and what looked like her clothing, and she rested them to the side.

"I think I do..."

No, she didn't.

She didn't understand.

"I don't have a fever, Keh-reh-nah. I told you I—"

Another groan erupted from him as she stepped even closer.

He could hardly concentrate, and it took everything in him to not let the thoughts overtake him.

He had to remain in control.

He couldn't turn into the animal the heat wanted him to become.

"You want to have sex with me," she paused. "And I want to have sex with you."

The words dropped in the air and he could only stare at her as she moved closer.

"I want you too..." Her words stunned him.

He didn't know what to say.

She didn't understand.

If he even tasted her once, he wasn't sure he was going to be able to let her go—EVER.

But she was upon him now, and all thoughts left his head.

All he could see was her strangely beautiful face and all he could smell was her sweet, sweet essence.

She climbed onto his lap, straddling him, and that one movement, the feel of her against him, almost had him spilling his seed.

She leaned into him then, and closed her mouth over his. The groan that rumbled from him could have shaken the ground around them.

Keh-reh-nahhhhh.

He struggled to wrap his hands around her, to pull her closer so he could taste her some more, but he'd tied his hands too well.

Another groan rumbled from him and he twisted his hands, desperate to pull her closer.

The feel of her against his thighs, the taste of her on his lips, the scent of her in his nostrils...his nefre pulsed with jubilation and his cock surged.

She felt so good...too good. He felt himself surge again only to grind against her center.

A whimper left her lips.

She was soft there, so soft. So different from Shum'ai females who had a cartilage casing within their genital pouch. That casing only disappeared when the female was in heat.

But Keh-reh-nah was just pure softness. He could feel it even through his garments.

Her hands clasped either side of his cheeks as her smooth tongue flicked over his lips and Ajos groaned again.

He'd never experienced anything like this before, this strange movement of the lips in harmony, but it was so qeffing good. Such a simple touch, yet it sent such strong shock waves through him.

"Keh-reh-nah," he managed to say against her lips. "What are you doing? You don't want this."

He didn't know what he would do if she agreed that he was right.

Not now. Not after tasting her. If she suddenly released herself from him and walked away, he would go insane.

Her breath came out in a pant as she pulled her head away and looked him in the eyes. Ajos studied her in the darkness.

He couldn't quite understand the expression on her face.

"I want it. I'm sure," she said, as her gaze fell to his lips once more before slipping farther down his body.

Her gaze stopped only when it landed at the junction of her thighs with his.

She was looking at him and he felt his cock pulse at the attention, partially extruding in anticipation, preseed seeping from his tip.

Keh-reh-nah licked her lips as she slipped her hands in the waist of his trousers and as he eased up his hips and allowed her to pull them down, she paused.

"Ajos..." she breathed, and as if hypnotized, she reached forward and brushed her finger over the tip of his cock.

Preseed seeped from the tip immediately as a groan shuddered through him.

He was glad he'd tied himself down.

If not, she'd be on her back and he'd be pounding her into the ground beneath them.

A feral growl left him, his need moving past that line of control he'd fought so hard to keep it behind.

He didn't want to scare Keh-reh-nah, especially not now, but when her eyes met his, there wasn't fear there.

What he saw was anticipation.

She caressed his entire genital pouch and another groan rumbled through him as his hips bucked toward her touch. As she ran her finger up the slit in his pouch, his cock extruded fully to meet her, eager for her touch.

She gasped a little, her throat moving at the sight of him, and his cock pulsed again.

Was she scared of it?

He knew he must be different from human males...but Keh-reh-nah took him in her hand, her fingers running up the length of him.

It was too much. The heat too strong.

He bucked against her, a climax catching him unexpectedly, and with a roar that would have scared the night creatures, had there been any around them, he spilled in her hand.

Emotion surged through him, but that one release felt like the tip of the iceberg.

He wanted more.

He *needed* more.

Keh-reh-nah's eyes widened as she watched the streams of his seed run down her hand.

"You're still hard," she whispered, "*harder* even."

He pulsed in her hand again and she raised her eyes to look at him.

"Keh-reh-nah," he groaned. "Come to me."

To his surprise, she released him and rose over him again.

Looking up at her, she looked like a goddess come down to meet him, and his cock jerked to slap against his stomach as she settled over him once more.

She was panting, her breaths coming hard, and with one hand, she slipped her strange undergarment to the side.

He saw her genital pouch then. There was a slit in the middle, soft lips to the sides, and a strange bud within.

Her fingers spread those lips, exposing the little bud even further and Ajos watched, transfixed, as she lowered herself.

That deep sound must be him rumbling, but it was at the back of his mind. He couldn't take his eyes off her.

Softness and a deep warmth filled the base of his cock as she settled her heat over the backside of his length.

Ajos' eyes rolled back in his head and he heard her moan at the contact of their sexes.

How the qef did she feel so good when he wasn't even inside her yet?

Grasping his shoulders, Keh-reh-nah brought her head forward, sealing her mouth over his as she began grinding against him, running her soft heat over the entirety of his length and back.

Qef.

His cock pulsed again as he watched her. He couldn't take his eyes away.

Keh-reh-nah moaned as she picked up the pace, rubbing herself against his hardness, and the hitch in her breath as she joined mouths with his once again was almost too much.

She was getting pleasure from this, so much pleasure, he could see it on her face for, unlike her, he was unable to close his eyes.

Never had he seen or heard of a Shum'ai female doing this, taking charge of her own pleasure, and just watching Keh-reh-nah use his body, riding that wave to ecstasy, made his cock pulse so hard there was a chance he would black out.

Her brow was twisted in a frown as she gripped him tighter, her tongue flicking against his as her heat cloaked his own.

She was making soft whimpering sounds against his lips as she began to grind harder, her hips bucking as she rubbed her soft bud up and down his length.

"Keh-reh-nah," he rasped.

She pulled away from his lips, her eyes finally opening to meet his, and she whimpered again, her mouth falling open into an O as she looked down at her softness gliding over him.

There was moisture there, a slick wetness that filled the air with her scent.

Her face twisted some more, as she screamed his name.

"Ajos, I'm coming!" She gripped him tight as her body jerked, and stiffened, her entire form trembling.

His own climax crashed through him, depositing seed between them.

"Fuck," he heard her murmur as her head fell against his shoulder. "Fuck," she panted again.

"Keh-reh-nah?"

"You came?" she whispered.

She seemed surprised, as if it was something to wonder about.

Of course, he came, how could he not have?

"But you're still hard." Yes, because he wanted more.

She was still panting and a few shudders went through her.

She grasped his shaft then, her fingers wrapping around him, and he pulsed underneath her hand.

"You're still burning up..."

Yes, with a fire that could consume her. Only now, he was afraid for her to leave.

He wanted her too much.

Rising over him, she positioned his cock beneath her as she lowered herself, grimacing a little as his head met her entrance.

So warm and inviting. The muscles in his arms bunched as he tried to release himself so he could reach for her.

There was resistance. Her softness did not want to let him in, and he brought his worried gaze to her face.

She was still lowering slowly, her bottom lip bitten between her small teeth as she stared down at him, and when the head of his shaft popped past that resistance, she threw her head back with a moan. "Oh God..." she whispered. Thank the gods indeed. He would suffer for eternity, if only to relive this moment over and over again. She settled over him slowly, allowing herself to adjust to his size. Inch by inch, she slid his shaft within her, and it took everything in him not to push along with her movement. Only the fear of somehow harming her kept the need to surge forward in check.

The softness of her buttocks settled against his thighs, and only then did she open her eyes again.

"Fuck me, Ajos."

A roar left him as he reached for her and was surprised when his hands settled around her waist.

Realization hit that somehow, as she'd taken him, he'd strained against the straps so much that he'd broken them apart.

Mild surprise passed over her features as he gripped her but that look soon changed to pure ecstasy.

His hands found the curve of her hips easily and he held her steady.

"Hold on, little one."

A whimper left her as she complied just before he surged forward, burying himself to the hilt and Keh-reh-nah cried out above him.

Her body jerked with each thrust, the mounds on her chest bouncing as he exited and entered her once, twice, three times until he didn't know where she ended and where he began.

There was a slick wetness running down his shaft and he didn't know if it was from him or her, and he didn't care.

Wet squelching sounds filled the air and his cock slid in her channel and he moved one of his hands so he could touch her there, on that soft little bud within her sex.

She cried out when his fingers made contact and that sound alone made his seed sack swell. Another climax was coming, one that shot through him with such intensity that he was momentarily blinded.

Qef. It was a double climax.

He could feel his cock swell, the first globule moving from his seed sack and moving upward. As his seed pod traveled up his shaft and burst at his tip, filling her with his seed, Keh-reh-nah cried out above him once more, her head falling back as her body shuddered.

She was shaking so hard, if he was not holding her, she'd have fallen off him, but he gripped her to him, pulling her toward his chest.

"What—" she breathed, "—what was that?"

But before he could reply, his own body shuddered as another seed pod traveled upward through his shaft.

Kerena screamed, her fingers digging into his shoulder, and for a moment, panic filled him.

She was still shuddering and her eyes rolled back one more time as her body stiffened and she cried out again.

Qeffing qrak. He'd never heard of a female reacting in such a manner to the seed pods.

What if Kerena was allergic to them...to *him.*

He hadn't even considered that.

Ajos' gaze traveled over her face as he waited for her tremors to subside.

He knew his seed pods held a stimulant. That stimulant was supposed to soften the opening to the female's reproductive channel by making the mating act even more pleasurable. It was a sort of mating hormone, evolved to increase the chances of conceiving.

His saliva held it, his perspiration had it, but the greatest concentration was in his seed pods.

Keh-reh-nah screamed again, her body jerking uncontrollably, and he felt her grip his shaft with her sex.

Qef. His sack pulsed again and he was sure he was about to orgasm one more time.

Hold it, you qeffer! She can't handle more than you've already given her, idiot.

Fear struck him as he watched Kerena shudder. He could only see the whites of her eyes, and she stiffened once more as another climax hit her hard.

A Shum'ai female was made for exposure to his mating hormones, but Keh-reh-nah...

...Keh-reh-nah was human.

22

KERENA TOOK A DEEP BREATH AS HER FOREHEAD RESTED AGAINST AJOS'.

It felt like she'd just experienced one whole month of sex all at once.

As she clung to him, small shivers still traveling through her, her breathing finally slowed down enough for her to think.

Now in the afterglow, her thoughts were coming fast and worry found itself within.

She'd never been one to have casual sex, and this was the reason. When she'd only just met him, she'd felt a strange connection to the minty-teal guy. Now that he'd been inside her, that connection had grown.

It felt like they'd shared something, something more than just sex, and she forced herself to not think about it at that moment.

He only wanted release this once and she'd offered.

That's all this was.

She opened her eyes and looked at him only to find his worried gaze on her.

Now, his eyes were gold in most parts and she smiled.

She'd been right, sex was his cure.

But goddamn, she let out a breath, never had she experienced sex like *that* before.

Her body was still shuddering at intervals and, as she gripped his shoulders, she realized that he was still tense.

That's when she felt him pulse within her.

Hard.

He was still hard.

"You're still hard," she whispered, and it felt like she'd said that before.

She'd felt him come. She'd felt the sperm rise within his shaft like a corded ring and when it had reached his tip, the most intense feeling of pleasure had spread through her from within.

It was unbelievable to her that he was still firm and at that thought, she felt him pulse within her once more.

She didn't think it was possible, but desire was rising inside her again and she moved her hips a little.

Ajos' eyes flickered shut as he groaned.

He stiffened and stretched his neck a little and it was clear to her that he was still holding back.

She joined their mouths once more, flicking her tongue over his lips and Ajos groaned again and pulled her closer.

"We should stop, Keh-reh-nah," he groaned. "I am afraid you will die."

Kerena giggled against his lips. She couldn't help it.

This was what he had been afraid of?

This was what he'd been telling her to run from? Selfish motherfucker.

He was dangerous?

Well, she'd never been more attracted to danger.

At this point, she was dedicated to being a rebel for the rest of her life.

Even kissing him made her throb and her entire pussy became engorged with need.

Before she even realized it, she was grinding against him again, her moans filling the air.

Ajos grasped her hips again, his three-fingered hands slipping underneath her ass as he rose to stand.

He held her fast as he stepped away from the tree and she wrapped her legs around his waist.

He still seemed to be holding back though, afraid for her.

"I'm tougher than you think," she whispered against him. "I'm not afraid."

Ajos growled before he thrust upward, burying himself deep inside her.

Pleasure cut off her thoughts and she could only gasp.

"You should be," he said and their eyes locked.

As he pulled out only to delve deeper inside her once more, Kerena's lips trembled. It felt like she was losing control of her body.

Her entire frame shook as Ajos retreated only to slam home again but he held her tight and she knew she wouldn't fall.

"You feel good," she whispered. "How can I be afraid?"

"It's too much for you," he growled. "I don't want to hurt you."

Kerena giggled again. It must be the intense pleasure making her a giddy fool. "Do what you need to, Ajos. I am ready."

Ajos growled again as he surged into her.

She didn't know for how long he thrust into her or how many times his seed filled her, all she knew was that it felt like she was on a train of ecstasy.

The forest around them disappeared and all she could do was feel and hear.

Her entire groin was burning with pleasure, her nipples hardened by the chill of the night, and all she could hear were the pants and grunts of the male holding her as he thrust in and out of her.

So this was what ecstasy felt like...

One climax followed the next until she felt like a noodle hanging on to him—or was she even holding on to him anymore? She wasn't sure of even that.

Her sex ached a good ache, like a warm honeypot was running between her legs and all she could feel was pleasure.

Ajos grunted and groaned, his cock pulsing as he thrust into her. She wasn't sure how many times he thrusted, or how many times he came and brought her to climax, all she knew was that her soul had left her body.

Her body was no longer a vessel in which it could be held. It was now a vessel of pleasure—sweet pleasure, evidenced by the slickness running from her center down her buttocks to drip against the forest floor with each climax.

She was vaguely aware of the world going dim.

Words slipped from her lips before she lost consciousness.

"Ajos…" she murmured.

"Keh-reh-nah?"

"I don't know how I'm going to forget about you after this."

AJOS FROZE, a climax shuddering through him even as he stiffened at her words.

Forget about him?

Chest heaving, he looked down at the limp female in his arms and slowly fell to his knees.

"Keh-reh-nah?"

She wasn't moving and panic gripped him again.

He'd been right.

She couldn't handle the intensity of the mating fever. Still, in his own need he'd pushed forward, selfishly taking too much from her.

"Keh-reh-nah?" His hand moved over her chest as he supported her back with his other arm.

Now on his knees, he stared at her limp form in the darkness.

In his panic, it took him more than a few moments to realize that her chest was rising and falling almost imperceptibly.

She lived.

He released a breath of relief as he fell to his knees, staring at the bundle in his arms.

And, as if to add to the shame of his loss of control, his semi-hard cock fell from within her in a wet slop.

He kneeled there, a mixture of feelings going through him as he looked at Keh-reh-nah's face, and only when his cock went back into his genital pouch did he allow himself to analyze his thoughts.

Forget him…

She wanted to forget him after this.

After what they'd just shared.

His life organ ached, and he swallowed hard as he pulled her even closer.

His eyes searched the dark sky again and a feeling of dread filled him.

She was his.

He knew that.

There was no way he could let her go after this.

But did he deserve her?

No.

Did she want him?

His life organ ached again.

Didn't seem like it.

He didn't have the right to expect more, to *want* more.

Most Shum'ai females had many males during the time of great heat. It was the only way to survive the mating fever because males outnumbered females three to one.

It was the way.

Only... His gaze moved back to Keh-reh-nah...he didn't want it to be the way with her.

The thought of another male touching her, making her moan their name the way she had done his...the thought almost gave him a stroke.

"Commander," V'Alen's voice interrupted the silence and Ajos glanced at his communicator.

"What?" he growled, his voice much harsher than he'd intended it to be.

This wasn't anger and pain because of the mating heat any more. For now, he was sated till later.

This was anger at the thought that Keh-reh-nah was going to leave him as soon as they returned to the base.

"The ship is repaired."

"Noted." He paused, looking at the female in his arms. "We are heading back."

"Commander, there is something else."

Ajos growled again.

"Patrol ships have notified of Hedgeruds heading this way. They did not use hyperspace, instead traveling the long way. Estimated time of arrival is by the rise of the next star."

Qef.

Their ship wouldn't survive another direct attack like the last one. They needed to get the qef out of there.

Ajos rose, still cradling Keh-reh-nah.

She was almost bare; the thin garment she'd worn around her center had ripped in his passion and he knew not where it had fallen.

There wasn't time to search for it now.

Grabbing the satchel, he checked if the strange device they'd come for was still nestled within it.

It glowed back at him in the darkness.

Slipping the satchel over his shoulder, Ajos reached for his spear and his hand brushed against the flower Keh-reh-nah had been carrying.

Her garment was beside it, and he grabbed it and the flower too.

He had no idea why she'd been taking the plant with her but, just in case she needed it, she'd find it when she woke up.

And he hoped she woke up soon.

He'd hate to have to bring her to Aker and be questioned why she was unconscious.

Because I qeffed her almost to death...

Yea...not a conversation he wanted to have with anyone.

Aker wasn't one to gossip but he was sure the humans at the med bay would be interested to hear what had happened. He'd seen them whispering to each other about almost everything over the past few days.

Maybe Keh-reh-nah wouldn't want word to get out too...

If she wanted to forget about him—something within him wrung —then he could keep quiet about what happened this night.

"V'Alen," Ajos activated his communicator, "send a signal above so I can make haste in the right direction."

The markers he'd set would be no use in the night when he had to hurry, and with the strange device by his side, he already knew the navigation wouldn't be working.

"Signal going out."

Within a few moments, a bright light shot into the sky somewhere to his right and Ajos began moving.

He'd take Keh-reh-nah home and then she'd forget about him.

This was about to be the longest journey of his life.

23

———————

Keh-reh-nah was still unconscious.

Ajos looked back at her as the ship headed back to the Restitution. With the ship's navigation being unreliable, V'Alen was using some strange calculations to get them on the right path.

They'd had to travel the long way because of the strange device on board, and he was praying they didn't encounter any Hedgerud fighters on the way.

He was sure their ship couldn't take a second battle, but more than that, he didn't want to put Keh-reh-nah in danger any more than he already had.

His eyes moved over her as she lay on her back on the now-reclined seat.

To his right, V'Alen remained silent.

For once, his comrade didn't make any comments, though Ajos was sure the cyborg knew exactly what happened between him and Keh-reh-nah in that forest.

Even if the cyborg asked, though, he wouldn't answer.

But, he was beginning to get worried.

He'd stopped to slip her tunic over her before he'd reached the ship and her skin had felt warm, unnaturally so.

He didn't know much about humans, but he didn't think she had a mating heat and he was sure his couldn't have catalyzed one in her.

Possibly, she had a fever.

A very high one.

She wasn't moving either and her breaths were beginning to come rapidly.

"Push the engine to the max," he said to V'Alen. "I think something is wrong with Keh-reh-nah."

V'Alen glanced behind him and jerked his head in a nod.

For the next three day and night cycles, Ajos did what he could to tend to Keh-reh-nah in the back of the ship.

He tried to cool her down with damp cloths, but nothing seemed to be working.

Nothing within the first aid kit seemed to be having an effect either.

She wasn't waking up, she was burning up, breathing strangely...it all sent fear deep down within him.

He'd been too rough, taken too much from her.

In his need, he'd gone too far.

He'd known her body couldn't take it.

He'd known it.

As soon as the ship landed, he grasped her against his and hopped from the vessel.

He was vaguely aware of V'Alen watching him as he rushed toward the med bay, hardly seeing the beings on the streets stop to watch him hurry with the human clutched against his chest.

The med bay felt like it was farther than it used to be, his feet too slow, time moving sluggishly as he pushed forward, and when he burst into the medical facility, all eyes turned to look at him.

He must have made some entrance, because the humans still getting treatment gasped, some of them covering their mouths, their eyes wide.

Xul's mate rushed toward him, her eyes wide.

"Ajos! What the fuck happened? What's wrong with her? Is she all right?"

His throat moved. He didn't know.

He'd done this to her.

He didn't know if she was all right.

Aker exited a room, pausing mid-movement.

The medic rushed toward an empty gurney. "Bring her here."

Ajos took two long strides toward the gurney and stood there, his arms trembling as he looked down at Keh-reh-nah's face.

She was flushed.

"Put her down, Ajos."

Ajos did what he was told, his eyes still on Keh-reh-nah.

Only when it hit him that nothing was happening did he raise his eyes to Aker.

"Well, what are you waiting for?" he growled, unable to hold back his fear, his anger, the strain.

The medic was looking at him strangely. "You have to let her go if I have any chance of figuring out what's wrong with her," Aker said, reaching forward to pry away his arm from Keh-reh-nah.

A snarl left his lips that he could not control, and Aker jumped back.

"Easy there, Ajos," someone said from behind him and the voice made him stiffen.

Akur.

His brother.

What was he doing back so soon from his mission off-world?

His brother reached forward and touched him on the shoulder. He was looking at him strangely too.

"You need to release the human so Aker can heal her," Akur pressed.

His brother actually sounded reasonable, for once, and Ajos slowly released Keh-reh-nah till her body lay limp against the white surface of the gurney.

Before he knew it, he was being pushed backward and into an empty room.

The door shut behind them with a click, and Ajos rushed toward it but he was pulled back again.

A roar left his lips as his fist surged forward.

Akur ducked his punch and shot out with one of his own, grazing Ajos on the cheek and he could feel the burn of broken skin.

"The qef is wrong with you?!" Akur shouted his question, making it sound like a demand more than a request.

Ajos growled, stalking away from his brother, but Akur moved to block the door.

Ajos narrowed his eyes at his brother.

He hated the qeffer.

"Move."

Akur crossed his arms over his chest. "No. Not until you tell me why you're acting like this and why there was a half-dead human in your arms."

Akur's voice held such strong accusation that Ajos felt it deep, deep within him.

It was the same voice his brother had used with him many, many times before, ever since that day when Nama had died.

Ajos turned away and ran a hand down his nefre before he spun back around and punched the door beside his brother's head.

Akur didn't flinch.

He was like that.

Nothing ever seemed to faze him.

Akur's gaze studied him, and Ajos bit back another snarl.

Akur was keeping him from seeing Keh-reh-nah.

He needed to be there.

He needed to make sure she was all right.

Akur's eyes widened slowly, his golden irises becoming larger.

"Your nefre."

Ajos swallowed hard.

He hadn't covered his head when he'd returned. He'd forgotten, too concerned about Keh-reh-nah to think about anything else.

His nefre was still red with the mating heat, only now that he'd sated himself in his mate, he could control himself more.

"What about it?"

"That's impossible..." Akur murmured, horror in his eyes.

Ajos released a breath, his shoulders slumping a little. "Aker thinks it's the energy fallout from the explosion. He thinks it triggered the mating heat because it mimicked the warm period of Tonvuhiri."

Akur's eyes widened some more and he leaned off the door.

"The human..."

Ajos' throat moved as he turned away.

He didn't need his brother to see his shame.

This was too much like when Nama died, when he'd had to return home without her.

Akur already had that over him, and he couldn't look in his brother's eyes to see the accusation of yet another female's life being lost because of his own actions.

"You *mated* with her?"

When he didn't answer, Akur let out a sound of disbelief.

"Are you qeffing insane?!"

Ajos' shoulders stiffened as his brother continued.

"Metcer cells. Metcer, qeffing, cells, Ajos. Didn't you use any?! How could you be so reckless?"

"Of course, I used them!" Ajos bit back the urge to punch something else. "It didn't work," he uttered. "The metcer cells didn't work."

"What?" Akur moved to grasp his arm and Ajos had no option but to look at his brother. "The only way that could happen is if the heat is too strong. Only if there is a Shum'ai bond...and there is no way..."

Akur stopped, horror in his eyes. "Impossible," he uttered.

"I thought so too," Ajos said, pulling his arm from his brother's as he headed toward the door.

This time, he exited without Akur trying to interfere.

His brother understood now.

No one stood between a Shum'ai and his mate.

By the time he exited the room, Keh-reh-nah was surrounded by more humans and Aker seemed busy trying his best to do what he could to save her.

"Can you save her?"

His voice made some of the humans by the gurney scatter as he came close.

He gripped Keh-reh-nah's small hand in his as Aker ran tests.

"There is an infection in her life blood. It is increasing rapidly and if I don't administer the medication now, her organs will begin to fail." Aker moved quickly, mixing potions together as he spoke.

"Septic shock, maybe..." one of the humans said.

"Was she introduced to anything that could have caused the infection?" Aker asked.

Ajos swallowed, his gaze moving back to his female.

"Like a wound, per say?" Aker continued. "The faster I can identify what caused the infection, the higher the likelihood of saving her."

"She was cut in the forest," Ajos murmured as he moved some of Keh-reh-nah's filaments from her face. Her face was flushed and even a little swollen. Still, she was the most beautiful thing he had ever laid eyes on.

"Hmm," Aker said. "Possibly contamination with some form of bacteria." He motioned to one of his interns. "Make capsules to fight infections from every known bacteria found on...Choria G622?"

Ajos nodded.

"Choria G622," Aker confirmed, and the intern hurried away to do his bidding.

Meanwhile, Aker injected Keh-reh-nah with a vial as he pressed his fingers at the side of her neck.

"What the hell happened out there?" Xul's mate, Athena, turned to him.

Ajos' throat moved.

"A lot."

Behind him, he heard the door close and he could feel his brother's stare on his back.

"Do you think she'll be all right?" Ajos addressed the medic.

Aker shrugged, his fleshy nose twitching a little. "I cannot be positive." He gave Ajos a sideways glance. "She is near death."

Something wrung inside Ajos.

That wasn't what he wanted to hear.

His eyes refused to see that reality; his life organ refused to believe it...

"She needs a private room, and I will do everything I can to revive her."

With that, Aker and the interns around him began pushing the gurney toward an empty room.

Ajos followed behind when he felt someone grasp his arm.

It was Akur.

His brother opened his mouth to say something and then stopped. Releasing him, Akur shook his head before storming out of the med bay.

It felt like ages before the interns brought the medication and Aker administered it.

Grasping her hand, Ajos brought it to his lips and held it there.

She was still hot, burning up.

An infection that could kill her...

He felt so guilty, he didn't know if he was the cause or not.

Time passed with no change, and he couldn't be quite sure whether it was minutes or hours that he sat there beside her. He couldn't move.

Through all this, he stayed by her side. Everything else was like background noise. He hardly noticed the beings that came in and out of the room. The door opened and closed as humans came in to check on her, as members of the Restitution came in to ask him questions about the mission, and as the interns did their rounds.

He didn't hear when they spoke to him.

He didn't care.

He'd done this.

His nefre pulsed with a deep pain that was boiling in the pit of his stomach.

He was the reason she was fighting for her life.

Time passed.

How much?

He wasn't quite sure...and he didn't really care about the outside world to find out.

He stayed by her side, staring at her face for moments on end.

It looked like she was just asleep. He wished she'd wake up.

It was because of this preoccupation that he saw the first signs of movement.

It was her nose that scrunched up first. Then her fingers moved.

Ajos held his breath.

She was there.

She was back.

Relief shot through him, but he didn't dare to speak.

Keh-reh-nah groaned and twisted a little as her eyes flicked open and she squinted.

"Wha..."

For the first time in what must be hours, his shoulders sagged a little with relief.

But that was short-lived for another fear bubbled in the pit of his stomach.

How would she react when she realized he was the reason she almost died?

It seemed to take a moment before she realized she was awake and then she tried to sit up, grimacing as her body protested.

"Stay still, Keh-reh-nah." He used a hand to press her gently against the gurney once more and her eyes flicked to him.

That's when he found he was holding his breath. Waiting.

"Ajos..." she whispered before her body fell back against the gurney. "I thought..." Her bottom lip quivered a little and she took a deep breath. "It's so cold. I thought—I thought those bad guys got me again."

"Never."

She shivered underneath his hand. "It's so cold."

Ajos frowned.

Cold?

She was burning up.

"Please," she whispered. "I'm so cold."

She stretched toward him and Ajos' eyes widened a little. Immediately, his nefre began to pulse, spreading need throughout him and he almost snarled at himself.

"Please," she whispered again, as another shiver went through her.

She wanted him to comfort her not qef her but his body didn't know the difference.

Something else wrung inside him as his instincts moved faster than his thoughts and he climbed atop the gurney to lie by her side.

She didn't hesitate; she settled against him, but she was still shivering.

She needed his warmth.

Without thinking about it, Ajos began stripping, throwing his garments to the floor below.

"Me too," she whispered as she tried to remove hers.

He helped her with that, slipping the small tunic from over her head and letting it fall somewhere on the floor. Then he pulled her toward him, settling her against him so she could take from his warmth.

A sigh left her body as she snuggled against his chest.

"Thanks," she whispered.

He couldn't answer.

His throat worked but no words came out.

This was...

This was too much for him to process all at once.

It felt...forbidden.

"Where are we?" she asked.

Did she not feel any different? She'd been unconscious for days.

"Back at the base," he managed to answer and as she moved against him some more, her naked skin rubbing against his.

"We made it back? I don't remember leaving the forest after—" she paused and he felt her stiffen.

After they mated.

Maybe she didn't remember...

"You went unconscious. I took you back to the ship."

"Oh," was all she said.

She snuggled into him some more. "I hope you don't mind me doing this. You just feel...so good."

Ajos' throat moved again. So did she.

What had he gotten himself into?

Life would never be the same after this.

...after she revived fully and came to her senses.

...after she decided to leave him.

Her words came back to him immediately. She wanted to forget him.

He was a warrior, yet that single line could make him crumble.

He tightened his arms around her then, pulling her closer to him.

She was his mate, but she'd never know.

He would always be there for her, but he could never tell her.

This was forbidden for he didn't deserve any of it.

It seemed...

It seemed the gods had meted out their ultimate punishment.

He was to find the one that completed him...yet, he was to remain incomplete.

As Keh-reh-nah sighed against him, Ajos pulled her even closer.

If this wasn't the lifetime of torture that he had imagined, he didn't know what could be.

24

———

WHEN SHE WOKE UP, HE WASN'T THERE.

Kerena squinted, her eyes coming into focus.

A fleshy nose moved close to her face and if she had the energy, she'd have shrieked.

"You're awake," Aker said, moving from so close to her face.

Kerena lifted her head a little. She felt groggy and her stomach growled.

She was famished.

To add to that, her head felt like she was carrying a ten-ton weight on top of it and her entire body felt like she was encased in a block of ice.

Not to mention the pain.

Her entire body ached.

Fuck!

It didn't feel that bad when she'd woken up and Ajos was there.

"What the hell is wrong with me?"

It was more a statement than a question, but Aker answered anyway.

"Some kind of infection. One that we are yet to determine how to treat properly."

Her gaze flicked on a spot of color in the otherwise white room and she focused on it.

The spot of color soon turned into a defined shape and she realized it was the flower from that strange plant.

Ajos must have taken it up when she'd fallen unconscious.

"V'Alen brought it just a few minutes ago. He said it belonged to you," Aker said, his gaze following hers.

Oh.

So not Ajos then.

Kerena swallowed the lump of disappointment that suddenly formed in her throat.

Aker moved around the room, mumbling things to himself as he looked at a data pad. He reached for a vial with some blue fluid and turned toward her.

Kerena eyed the thing. "What's that?"

"I call it my 'reenergizing serum.'" His nose moved and his face scrunched up in such a way, she assumed he was smiling. "It will make you feel much better. Ajos said you were unconscious for three days so you need the energy."

What?

"Three days?"

Aker grunted. "And another two days since you've been in here."

Had it really been that long? She felt like shit but...five days?!

"Yes." Aker took up a device that looked like a huge needle and attached it to the vial. "You were in a critical state when you arrived." He paused. "I am surprised and...*thankful* that you survived. We have lost enough refugees."

Her eyes widened at that, and for a moment, she thought he was referring to losing some of the other humans.

"All of your kind are accounted for. Mostly okay."

Kerena let out a breath. "Mostly?"

Aker took that moment to bury the vial into her arm.

She hissed and his nose moved. "I apologize but surprise seems to work better with these things."

The injection site stung a little and Kerena watched as the strange blue fluid disappeared into her body.

"You said mostly okay?" She brought it up again. "Are there some women who're critically ill?"

"Well..." Aker removed the vial and dabbed her skin with what felt like a moist cloth. "Most of the women are fine. We are having trouble connecting with the one that was awake while in stasis. She is still...unresponsive."

Between the strange feeling now spreading through her body and the brain smog, Aker's words didn't connect immediately.

"Wait..." Kerena finally said. "Wait, what? Awake?"

Aker's nose moved.

"Well, I guess I can tell you. Athena didn't want to alarm anyone until we found out we could help the female." He paused as he removed a pen-like device from his pocket. "There is one female that was rescued. She is...numb. She was stuck in stasis but awake, kept alive only by the stasis pod. The Arois, Yce, says her mind is frayed. He cannot even connect with it. I am afraid..." He sighed and if his face could communicate sadness, this must be it. "I am afraid of her chances of survival."

Kerena blinked, her mouth slightly open in shock.

Her mind immediately went back to the lady she'd seen in the room all alone. The one with the dead eyes.

It had to be her.

The horror of the situation made a hole open up in her chest. She couldn't imagine how utterly terrified the woman must have been all alone in that dark stasis hold for how many months.

The fact she was even still alive...

"Can I see her?"

Aker's nose moved.

"We're restricting contact for now. Only a few people get to speak to her. For obvious reasons."

Kerena nodded, a sigh making her shoulders heave.

She understood.

The woman's mind was fragile enough.

As she rubbed the back of her neck, Aker's nose moved again as he moved the pen-like device in front of her eyes.

"The serum is working," he said.

So it was.

She was sitting upright now, and it didn't feel as if her body wanted to fold in two.

"Can you stand?"

"Only one way to find out," Kerena replied as she slipped off the gurney.

As her feet touched the floor, they felt like jelly for a few moments before they literally infused with strength.

"Good," Aker approved. "I need to take you to the lab for some tests. Come with me."

Kerena nodded and took the first few steps toward the door.

The flower caught her eye again and she took it up.

Five days, and it hadn't wilted.

She frowned at it as she followed Aker from the room.

"WHERE THE QEF IS SHE?!" Ajos roared, not caring about the humans that whimpered at the sound of his voice or the Taiq'ud intern trembling before him.

He'd told them to keep Keh-reh-nah in the room till she recovered, and he HIGHLY doubted she'd recovered already.

He'd tried to keep away.

He'd forced himself to leave the room after she'd stabilized. Keeping out of the med bay had been hard enough. Not to mention, the heat was still upon him.

Just one taste of Keh-reh-nah had not been enough.

He'd known that. He'd even injected triple doses of metcer cells, hoping to quell his need, but it was hardly working.

"Sh—she—" The intern's nose was trembling so much it looked like a female pleasure device on the Taiq'ud's face.

Ajos growled and reached for the small male, his anger getting the best of him.

If the little weakling didn't tell him where they'd taken his mate, he was going to—

"Calm down, brother." Someone touched his arm and the contact only made his rage grow. Ajos turned his head slowly to glare at the offender and Xul removed his hand from his arm. "She is with my Athena and Aker at the laboratory. They are running some tests on her."

Ajos dropped the Taiq'ud in his grasp and stalked from the med bay. No one stood in his way, but he could feel all their eyes on his back, and he didn't qrakking care.

He was seeing red.

He'd told them to take care of her.

He'd trusted them to.

Yet, they were moving her about when she was clearly ill.

When his arms found their way around Aker's throat, the medic better have a good reason why he couldn't have run the tests in the med bay.

If they made her relapse...

The walk to the laboratory took ages and as he approached the building, Ajos stopped dead in his tracks, his fists clenching and unclenching.

Rage filled him, steam was probably releasing through his pores.

"Oh, hello, Commander." Iceon's ears perked when he saw him.

Ajos growled and Iceon's ears immediately lost their perkiness and fell flat on his head. "Commander?"

Ajos stalked forward and before Iceon could do anything, Ajos felt the male's throat between his fists.

Power surged into his arms as he lifted Iceon off his feet.

"Commander?" Iceon gripped his arm but did not fight back. Maybe out of respect or maybe because of his rank, because he knew the male could defend himself.

"What. The Qef. Were you doing. In the lab?"

Iceon blinked. "That's a bit personal,...Commander."

Ajos growled again. The male obviously didn't know how close he was to snapping his neck.

He knew Iceon was attracted to Keh-reh-nah. He'd seen the way the male had been looking at her when they went to the sky tower.

"You should be at the sky tower."

"Yes, but I had...business to take care of here. I would have gone already too if the human females didn't come in. I found it hard to leave when—"

He didn't want to hear the rest.

Ajos threw the male and he crashed against the laboratory's door. The door split in two, falling in on itself as Iceon's large body skirted across the floor to bump into the long legs of a pale female.

Ajos' breath came hard from his body as he looked up slowly, his eyes following those legs.

He knew those legs. Remembered them wrapped around him.

Keh-reh-nah stared back at him, her mouth open, her eyes wide.

He was vaguely aware that there were others in the room.

In the blurry background of their surroundings, something the bright color of purple fell from her hand and into one of Aker's many large receptacles laid out on the table.

"Ajos?" His name came from her lips and for a moment, he was sane again.

Ajos blinked, his throat moving as the world around them slowly came back into focus.

His nefre pulsed and shivered with the agitation of unspent emotions.

He wanted to kill something while, at the same time, he wanted to take her into his arms and be gentle with her.

"What the fuck?" He assumed the other human there, Xul's mate, Athena, said that.

He wasn't quite sure. He didn't really care.

He heard Iceon groan and let out a series of expletives himself.

And then, there was another exclamation.

"Raxul!" Aker pushed past the two females, his nose working like a piston as he leaned down to look at the vial by Keh-reh-nah.

The contents of the vial were bubbling dangerously as they ate up Keh-reh-nah's flower.

Some guilt flooded into him. She liked that flower, and his lack of control had caused her to drop it.

"Ajos?" she said his name again and his throat moved once more, unable to form words just yet.

"Iceon, are you all right?" The other human asked the Ochair as he rose to his feet.

He could feel the Ochair's wary gaze on him and knew what the male was probably thinking.

Again, he didn't care.

He could only think about the one person in his sights right now. Keh-reh-nah.

She looked okay, as if the past few days hadn't happened.

For two days, he'd stayed with her as she shivered against him. He'd held her tight, never leaving her alone for more than a few moments.

He doubted she remembered any of that, but that wasn't the point.

The point was that each moment he'd spent with her had made his decision to leave her side even the more difficult.

"Are you okay?" he finally asked, his eyes on Keh-reh-nah.

He watched her mouth close as her brows furrowed a little. She, too, had a wary look on her face and he hated to see it there.

"I'm fine." She forced a smile. "Aker gave me something. Some kind of serum. Didn't you, Aker?"

She glanced at the Taiq'ud but Aker wasn't paying attention to any of them.

Instead, he rushed across the room, throwing instruments this way and that before he grabbed something, opened a drawer that hissed as cold air was released from it, and retrieved a thin disc with what looked like goo on top of it.

"What's that?" Keh-reh-nah asked.

"Stay away from it. It is highly contagious. It is a sample of Tasqal tissue."

"Eww, why the hell do you have that?" Athena heaved, holding her stomach as her face scrunched up at the sight of the disc's contents.

"I've been testing different things on it," Aker said as he placed the disc on the table and rushed toward the still-bubbling receptacle near Keh-reh-nah. "I'm not a good fighter, so I contribute in the only way I know how: medicine and research." He paused as he took a sample of the bubbling fluid and carried it carefully back to the disc holding the Tasqal tissue. "I've been working on something to eradicate the Tasqals. Something to take them out quickly. But, so far, I have not been successful. My formulation is missing something. But...if we can find a way to take them out biologically..."

Ajos took a step forward, his gaze finally leaving Keh-reh-nah for a moment.

Aker's words interested him.

If they could take out the Tasqals using some form of biological warfare...it would change the game considerably.

Iceon stepped out of his way as he came to stand by Keh-reh-nah and she glanced up at him for a moment before her gaze returned to Aker.

Everyone seemed to hold their breaths as Aker placed a few drops of the fluid unto the tissue.

At first, nothing happened but Aker grabbed his pocket microscope and peered down at the thing.

Silence enveloped the room.

"Raxu..." The medic finally whispered.

"What?" Ajos asked.

Aker lifted his head slowly. "It worked."

25

"What do you mean, it is *healing* it?" Kerena stepped forward, only to feel Ajos' warm touch on her arm.

She turned to look at him.

He was sweating and his eyes still looked wild.

He was still sick, obviously.

His eyes dropped to his hold on her before he released her slowly. "Don't go close," he said. "Tasqal tissue is contagious."

Yes, Aker had said that.

She nodded but heeded his words. Athena picked up her line of questioning.

"*Healed* it?" Athena asked.

Aker had his head over what looked like a crude magnifying glass.

For what felt like minutes, he said nothing more and Kerena glanced at Athena.

The woman shrugged.

"Raxu..." Aker finally muttered. "The concoction seems to be fighting the disease, though, the effect is slow." He looked at Kerena. "That flower. Where did you find it? Was it something you had with you from your planet?"

"N-No. It was on Choria G622. I brought it back with me."

Aker shook his head vehemently.

"Impossible," he said. "We've tested samples from every plant known on that planet. None of them produced this result."

Aker began pacing before he came towards her and grabbed her arms.

Beside her, a growl rumbled in the air and she looked up to see Ajos looking murderously at the doctor.

If what he did to Iceon was any indication, he was unstable, and she didn't need him hurting the one being who seemed to have the answer they all needed.

Taking Aker's hands, she gently removed them from her arms and frowned at Ajos.

They'd have to talk about this.

She wasn't his property, but he sure as hell was acting as if she was.

"That flower," Aker said, pulling her attention away from the still-glaring minty-teal alien, "does not exist on Choria G622. I am sure of it."

Kerena blinked at the doctor, her mind buzzing.

He might be right.

Back on the planet, they'd been walking for some time and she hadn't seen any flowers at all.

They had only bloomed after her blood had touched the roots.

Kerena's eyes widened a little as it all came together in her head.

She'd taken the flower because she'd wanted a better chance of studying why the plant had reacted to her that way. It reminded her of a parasitic plant, like the Rafflesia or corpse flower. But now, with Aker's words, there was even more to it than that.

"My blood..." she muttered.

"What?" Athena asked. "What about your blood?"

"The flower bloomed because of something in my blood," she said. "Maybe something in my DNA caused the reaction."

"Bloomed?" Aker stepped away to stare into the receptacle that had been bubbling. Only the pollen from the flower remained untouched at the top of the fluid.

Using a utensil, he reached in and scooped the pollen out.

"Yes, it bloomed right in front of me," Kerena said. "I'd never seen a flower grow that quickly." She paused. "Actually, I'd never seen a plant behave like that at all."

"What do you mean?" Athena asked.

At that, Kerena gave them a rundown of what happened. How she'd been pulled away and how she'd gotten injured, her blood falling on the roots to create the flowers.

"Maybe the plants on Choria G622 are sentient." Iceon chuckled a little, trying to lighten the situation, but his chuckle only got a growl from Ajos.

He sobered immediately but Kerena frowned at his words.

She'd never considered anything like that before.

Wind blew inside from the destroyed door, lifting the pollen from Aker's receptacle into the air.

Almost immediately, Kerena rubbed her nose followed by Athena.

For a moment, Aker tilted his head their way.

"The pollen..." he said.

"What about it?" Athena asked.

"Do all humans react in such a way to pollen?"

When Kerena glanced at Athena, she found the woman looking back at her as well.

"No," they answered together.

As they said this, Athena staggered a little and leaned against the table, a cold sweat breaking out over her forehead.

"Raxu," Aker said, turning to Kerena. "How long were you exposed to this flower?"

"A while," she murmured as she rushed over to Athena. "Are you all right?"

"I don't know," Athena said.

"Iceon, bring her to the med bay immediately. Tell the interns to administer the same medication I gave to Kerena."

Iceon nodded.

"Hurry," Aker said as he moved across the room, depositing the rest of the pollen into a dish that he closed tight. "I suspect I have found the cause of your illness, Kerena."

"The pollen?" Kerena's eyes darted to Aker as Iceon lifted Athena in his arms and rushed from the lab.

"Precisely."

AKER DREW some of Keh-reh-nah's blood to run the tests he needed, all the while muttering to himself—most of which Ajos didn't understand.

"If there's something in my DNA, or human DNA for that matter, that the plants react to, then I want to help with studying it," Kerena said, rubbing her arm as Aker pulled the last vial of her life blood that he needed.

A growl rumbled from him at her words.

"No," he uttered, and she raised those beautiful brown eyes to his. For a moment, he was lost in them until he realized they were glaring at him.

"No, *what*?"

Even in his agitation with everything and everyone around him, he felt somewhat rebuked by the tone of her voice.

She was angry too, about *something*.

"You are not doing that."

"What? You can't tell me what to—" She stopped and took a breath, closing her eyes for a second. "Why?"

It was simple. Didn't she see?

"The flower makes you ill. You almost died. There is no way you're going to put yourself in more danger just to help us win this fight." He glared at Aker. "We will find another way."

Keh-reh-nah stood and took a few steps toward him and Ajos could feel his throat move, a pulse running from his nefre straight down to his genital pouch at her nearness.

Qef.

He only had one metcer vial left.

He'd have to get Aker to generate some more.

"And if there is no other way?" She glared up at him.

So small, yet she managed to look defiant.

Her shoulders were set, her mouth was in a thin line, and her gaze was hard, unmoving.

"You don't get to tell me what to do. I am a member of the Restitution now and I'll contribute in the best way I know how." She turned to Aker. "I'm a botanist. Plants are my thing. I'm sure I can be of assistance."

Aker's nose moved before he jumped a little in glee. "Perfect! I welcome the help! Between the med bay and the lab, I don't get to do much research. This will be positive, indeed."

A growl rumbled from Ajos' chest as he glared at the qeffing Taiq'ud.

Aker stuttered. "B-but of course we'll take precautions. You are still not healed. It is the serum giving you energy now. I'll give you another along with one more dose of medicine so you can go back to the med bay to get some rest."

He moved to one of his tables and began preparing the vials. "We'll look into getting some protective gear for you as well, if you don't change your mind about working with me here."

Keh-reh-nah grinned. "Why would I change my mind?"

Aker glanced his way and Ajos narrowed his eyes.

He was pretty sure he knew what the male was thinking.

He would do him the same way he did Iceon if he needed to. But Aker shook his head and said instead, "Well, it is a boring duty. It is all research."

Keh-reh-nah grinned some more. "That's my job. It'll be like I am still on Earth."

Staring at her, Ajos felt something move within him.

The thought of risking her life just to discover whether this flower was the miracle they were looking for...the premise brought her joy.

She felt useful...a bit like how he felt when he first joined the Restitution.

Who was he to demand that she lose that happiness?

Aker stepped forward and administered the medication.

"Now to take you to the med bay. Ajos—"

"On it."

Ajos reached forward and swooped his arms underneath Keh-reh-nah and she yelped a little in surprise.

Walking forward through the broken door, he glanced back at Aker. "I'll have that fixed for you," he said.

Aker didn't hear. He was already back at his table, looking at his experiment.

For a few moments, there was silence as he walked, only the foot-steps of the other beings that walked the streets around them reached his ear.

"I can walk, you know," Keh-reh-nah finally said.

"Nonsense."

He felt her body rise and fall against his in a sigh.

"Hey, this isn't the way to the med bay."

He glanced down at her and wished he hadn't.

The light of the star hit her eyes in such a way they shone. Her lips were moist as if she'd just wet them, and her filaments were blowing around her head like a halo.

Ajos swallowed hard, his genital pouch pulsing.

Qef.

"I'm surprised you know the layout of the base already."

"I'm learning," she said. "Where are we going?"

"Home."

"You mean, *your* home?"

Her words stung, even though they shouldn't. But she was right.

She wasn't going to stay there with him and even so, if he was to open himself to her being his mate, he would have to get new quarters.

"Yes," he muttered.

The door opened as he reached his bunker and V'Alen stood at the inside.

"Ajos," he said, his eyes flicking to Keh-reh-nah.

"V'Alen."

"Kerena," V'Alen said next.

"Oh, hi, V'Alen. I—"

She didn't get to finish because he was already heading into the quarters.

"Thanks for all you did getting us home, V'Alen!" Kerena shouted and Ajos growled a little.

"How do you know V'Alen did anything to get us home."

"Well," she said, "you were a little...indisposed the last time I saw you on that planet."

Despite himself, Ajos huffed out a chuckle.

He was by his room and the door was opening in the next second.

"Computer," he said, "adjust for Keh-reh-nah."

He set her down on his bed as he felt the temperature begin to change. As soon as his arms slipped from her, he turned from her.

"Rest," he managed to say as he stepped toward the door, but her next words had him frozen.

"So that's it? You're just going to leave me here like that?"

Ajos' throat moved but he couldn't turn to look at her.

He could feel her glaring at him.

"What do you wish for me to do?" he managed to say.

She breathed out a hard breath. "I don't know. Look at me maybe?"

He leaned his head against the door.

He couldn't do that.

The whole reason he'd turned toward the door was because his control was hanging by a thread.

A small palm landed on his back and Ajos shuddered.

He hadn't realized she'd moved from where he'd set her on the bed.

"What is happening to you?" she whispered.

"I'm fine." His voice wasn't his.

It was deep. Gravelly.

His body trembled underneath her touch.

"Liar."

He turned on her then, so fast that she stumbled and would have hit the ground if his hands didn't grasp her back.

He pulled her into him, bringing her dangerously close. So close, he could feel every curve of her soft body against his.

"Ajos?"

Her eyes searched his face but before he could say a word, his body responded as his head dipped and his mouth closed over hers.

26

———————

Somehow, they stumbled back on the bed. The mattress he'd gotten for her was still there, and it cushioned their fall.

Pleasure shot through her as his tongue found its way into her mouth.

She didn't know what it was about him, didn't understand why her body lit up like a sweet fire when he touched her, but she was suddenly weak in the knees, having only the strength to hold on to him.

"Keh-reh-nah," he groaned as he nestled between her legs, tearing his lips away from hers to look down at her.

Their breaths came hard, making their chests heave against each other.

"Ajos..."

Fuck, she didn't want him to stop. The last thing she wanted was for him to release her.

"I can't do this," he said, pain showing through the wildness in his eyes.

Disappointment swelled within her, quelling the heat that was spreading between her legs almost immediately.

Kerena stiffened. "What? Why?" She pushed against him.

To be fair, she was annoyed. A bit pissed too.

Had she been stupid to think there was something there between them? Something more than a one-night-stand kind of thing?

Ajos breathed hard and rested his forehead against hers.

In the back of her mind, she realized he wasn't letting her go.

"I can't..."

"You can't what?" She pressed against him again. "You can't kiss me? You can't fuck me?"

He released another breath, and his shoulders shook a little.

He was laughing.

"Oh, I can definitely do that." His eyes focused on hers. "As a matter of fact, it's all I want to do."

Kerena frowned at him.

Then what was stopping him?

They were both adults.

They knew what they were doing.

"I don't deserve you," he said. "I..."

He eased off of her then and sat.

"What are you talking about?"

He didn't answer. If anything, he seemed to go into himself even more.

"I thought..." She let the words die on her lips.

She'd thought they'd shared something in that forest. Something *more*.

He shuddered again and the fleshy fin-like structure at the back of his head looked like it pulsed.

Ajos groaned and walked toward the door, pressing his fist against it.

She was beginning to understand what this was.

She was no biologist but she knew that some species went in heat, with the urge to mate becoming so strong it was overwhelming.

Only Ajos was fighting his—for what reason, she did not know.

She opened her mouth to say something else to him when a thought struck her.

Maybe he was holding back because he knew he was going to leave after this heat of his was over.

"V'Alen is coming," he said as he raised his head.

The door slid open then and the robot man stood in the center of the frame.

"Commander," he said before his eyes slipped over to her.

"Report, V'Alen," Ajos said, a note of pain and annoyance in his voice.

"The device you found," V'Alen began, "I have information on it."

"Report," Ajos repeated, grimacing as he did.

"It is ancient." V'Alen paused and only then did she realize he'd been staring at her the entire time.

Ajos stepped in front of his friend and blocked his view.

"Ancient how?"

"I have scanned it and cross-referenced records within the archives. I found nothing. I had to connect with the archives from my home world. That's when I found...something."

"Go on." There was still that note of annoyance in Ajos' voice.

"It is a relic from the era of the Vikteki..."

There was silence as they both stared at each other.

"That's not possible. Everything from the Vikteki was destroyed."

"Apparently, not," V'Alen answered.

Staring at them, Kerena could see the tension between them and that made her uneasy.

"Is that bad? What's the Vikteki?" she asked.

Ajos turned to look at her, his golden eyes softening a little.

"They were a great ancient civilization that, based on the archives, developed some of the most advanced technology ever to be made in our universe. They knew things that they should not have known, were stronger than they should have been...it is written that their technology was...remarkable."

"They built things that we are only just beginning to understand," V'Alen added.

Kerena's gaze flicked from one male to the other and she brought the blanket around her as she sat up a little.

"So, why do I get the sense that is a bad thing?"

Ajos glanced at V'Alen then looked back at her. "Because the Vikteki were wiped out. Completely. Even with all their knowledge, they could not save themselves."

Kerena frowned. "Save themselves from what?"

Ajos crossed his arms. "We do not know."

Well, fuck.

This world just seemed to be getting better and better.

Kerena's eyebrows rose as she settled back on the bed.

It blew her mind that humans were so behind on things.

They all thought they were safe on their little planet, but...there was a whole universe out there teeming with life.

Kerena blinked. She'd just referred to humans as if she wasn't human anymore.

"What does this mean?" she asked after a few moments.

"I surmise the Tasqals have somehow uncovered some Vikteki tech and have found how to use it to their advantage," V'Alen answered. "It's how they managed to jump right from hyperspace directly into the base and exit as well."

"Qef..." Ajos murmured. "This isn't good. This isn't good at all." He paused. "Send word to all the commanders. We must meet and discuss this."

V'Alen jerked his head before she heard the door slide shut.

Ajos stared at the closed door, his back turned to her and she let her eyes roam over him.

With V'Alen gone, the tension between them suddenly returned.

Her mind went back to what they'd shared in that forest.

She'd never felt such pleasure in her life before.

It felt as if each time he came, a tsunami of pleasure washed from her cervix straight up through her.

Nothing had ever felt so good...

And nothing had ever made her feel so *alive*.

Staring at him now, she shivered a little—more from the fact that it seemed she still had the chills than anything else.

He didn't look well.

The protrusion on his head was still red.

"You need more medicine," she said.

"Don't worry about me, Keh-reh-nah."

Anger washed through her so fast, she didn't see it coming. "Maybe I wouldn't worry about you if I didn't care. Maybe if you left me alone, I could forget about you and then you could forget about me. Then we wouldn't have this problem."

She knew her response was defensive, but the feelings he was inciting in her were confusing.

He turned on her then, his eyes dark, the gold completely gone.

"You wish to forget about me?"

She stared at him, her frown so severe she could feel it stretching her forehead downward.

Kerena blinked.

This wasn't like her at all.

The only time she let her emotions get the best of her was when…

Fuck.

FUCK.

She was falling for him.

But she knew that…didn't she?

Only, she hadn't wanted to face it because she'd had no idea what it meant.

She turned from him then, blinking at the wall as she got her thoughts in order.

"I should go," she heard him say.

Yes, he should.

He was confusing her. Not only that, she suddenly felt open, vulnerable.

You could only get hurt if you cared—she'd learned that lesson many, many times—and fuck her if she didn't care about this tall minty man.

She cared.

A hand touched her back and caused her to shiver.

At his touch, she slipped from the bed, landing on her feet in a move Cindy Clawford would have approved of.

Goddamnit.

Her heart was hammering in her chest as she now faced the door to the bathroom, her back turned to him.

She stared at the white surface in front of her and crossed her arms, swallowing hard.

She'd been abducted from Earth, leaving everything she knew

behind. She'd found herself in the arms of a man she hardly knew anything about, but who drew her to him in a way she never knew was possible. And...she was falling for him.

Falling for him!

And he wanted her too...or didn't. She didn't really know.

It could just be the heat. His actions could just be spurred on by his need to mate.

"I should go." His voice sounded tortured this time, and closer, as if he'd taken a step toward her.

Maybe he didn't know it, but he was playing with her feelings.

"Then why don't you!" She spun on him only to have the breath lodge in her throat.

He suddenly advanced, pressing her back into the door behind her.

His body pressed against hers as she glared up at him, her breaths coming hard.

He planted both arms on either side of her as he leaned down, his dark eyes on hers.

"Because," he said, "despite that it's the right thing to do. I can't seem to leave you alone, Keh-reh-nah."

He leaned down farther. "I told you...there are only two things I want to do..."

Kerena gulped but her gaze never wavered from his. "And what's that."

"Qef," he said as he moved his hand to her throat, grasping it lightly. "And kill."

Fuck.

This should turn her off. It really should.

A tall, powerful alien had his hand around her throat and he just told her, without mincing his words, that he felt like killing something...but the only thing she could focus on was his first word.

For he'd just said he wanted to fuck her...and right now, she wanted him to do just that.

27

AJOS' MOUTH CRASHED INTO HERS AS SHE WENT ON TIPTOES TO meet him.

The groan that rumbled from his chest vibrated against hers and he took her into his arms, his palm settling on each side of her ass cheeks as he lifted her off the ground to plant her back against the door.

She couldn't breathe as she cradled his head and pulled him toward her, the kiss deepening into something more than a kiss, something feral, something full of need.

Her hands settled on the fleshy fin at the back of his head and it pulsed against her fingers.

She stroked it, and Ajos groaned deep into her mouth.

For some reason, the door behind them opened and they stumbled into the bathroom, but Ajos held her fast, and she was mildly aware that they ended up in the shower stall.

Her back was pressed against the wall again as he pressed her to him.

One of his hands found its way into her hair as he held her head and almost painfully, he broke their kiss, panting as he looked down at her.

"Shower," he said and Kerena blinked at him.

He wanted her to shower now? But before she could open her mouth, water began raining down on them.

Ajos pressed her against the wall some more, securing her there as he stripped out of his shirt.

His pants went next and he used his legs to kick them off his feet.

The entire time, he watched her, those dark eyes of his seemingly seeing everything and Kerena bit her lip as her gaze fell down him.

The shadows of the forest had only hidden his magnificence.

His hard chest heaved and when her fingers touched the lines of muscles there, his breath hitched in his throat.

The more she touched him, the more he groaned, till she felt something brush against her slit.

It was hard, wet, the tip smooth and Kerena's eyes fluttered a little at that one touch, that one promise of more to come.

His body was tense as he allowed her fingers to explore him and when Kerena met his gaze once more, it felt like she could drown in the intensity of his gaze.

Slowly, he let her slide down him till she was on her feet. And they were facing each other.

The water from the shower sluiced down them both, soaking her hair and dress and wetting his brilliant skin.

She let her eyes fall, straight to the thing she'd felt earlier, and her lips opened a little at the sight of it in daylight.

It was white. His cock was white.

A stark contrast to his skin, it stood out like a beacon.

Big. White. Thick. And smooth.

There was a slit in his groin, like a pocket that it extruded from and at its base, his balls looked swollen and firm.

His cock jerked at her attention as she reached out to touch it, but she didn't get a chance to.

Ajos grabbed her hand, his chest still heaving.

"You first," he said and before she could answer, he was kneeling before her.

His hands found her hips as he lifted her onto his shoulders, his face immediately buried against her.

"Keh-reh-nah," he groaned and his hot breath brushed against her clit. "I've wanted to do this for so long."

Kerena blinked. Really?

She couldn't form any words though, because his tongue darted out to swipe straight from her entrance to the hood of her clit.

She cried out against him as he began to run his tongue over her bundle of nerves. She gripped his head, bit down hard on her lip, and tried not to scream in delight at the host of feelings suddenly shooting through her.

She was glad he was holding her, because otherwise she'd have fallen because it felt like she'd lost all energy in her body once more.

Everything was concentrated in her center with an intensity she'd never experienced before.

Her moans filled the room, echoing against the walls as she cried out his name.

Vaguely, the thought that V'Alen was bound to hear them crossed her mind, but she didn't care.

All that mattered was the man who'd just closed his entire mouth over her, sucking and moaning her name.

His tongue was hot and smooth, and when he slipped it deep inside her, Kerena bucked against his face as a climax shattered her from inside out.

But even as she came, he didn't stop. He lapped at her slit, drinking every drop of wetness that she produced.

She jerked against him, unable to control her body anymore as each swipe of his tongue sent another shock wave through her.

And when she thought she couldn't take it anymore, he removed his tongue only to slip a finger deep inside her.

She looked down only to see him remove that finger and place it in his mouth.

"So sweet," he said.

Between the ecstasy still coursing through her and her own shyness, she couldn't blush harder.

He placed his mouth over her again and Kerena shuddered once more, her eyes rolling back into her head as she screamed his name again.

She wasn't sure she could take any more.

But Ajos didn't stop.

He kept his mouth over her, his tongue writing a letter dictated but the gods themselves and she felt another climax building within her.

She'd never climaxed twice in one session before him. She hadn't been promiscuous, but none of her exes had been able to manage such a feat.

Heck, some of them couldn't even get her to orgasm once.

But this was the second time Ajos was doing it, and he hadn't even entered her yet.

He groaned then, his body shuddering underneath hers too and when he finally released her, and her feet touched the floor, she saw the streams of his own climax hanging from his tip.

He'd come...from giving her pleasure.

The thought only made her heated.

Ajos moved forward to grasp her again, lifting her off her feet once more and this time, she was face-to-face with him.

She could smell her musk on his lips and see the pure lust in his eyes.

He gripped her hips tight as his eyes settled on hers.

"Keh-reh-nah..."

It seemed like the only word he could say but she understood his meaning.

He needed her.

He needed her now.

"I'm ready," she whispered before joining her lips with his.

With a groan, Ajos surged upward, the tip of his thick rod forcing its way past her lips and deep inside her.

The fit was tight, but his cock found its way, taking the path it had carved so many times before.

Kerena screamed into his mouth, she couldn't help it, but neither could she let go of him.

She kept their lips sealed, forcing him to swallow her screams as he pistoned into her.

Her entire body was trembling and when she felt that swelling at the base of his cock rise within her, stretching her even more only to culminate at the tip of his cock, her memory came back just before the pleasure burst within her.

She was ready for it this time—remembered it from that night when it had happened first.

It felt like his cum was a drug.

Her eyes rolled back in her head and she couldn't see.

Sight didn't matter.

Thoughts didn't exist.

Only feelings.

And she was feeling everything.

Her body jerked, her breasts bouncing as his rhythm continued.

Vaguely, she could feel his spend running from within her, washed away by the water raining down on them, and vaguely, she realized one thing.

This all felt too good to be true.

And if it felt too good to be true...chances were...

It was.

28

<hr>

THREE DAYS PASSED AND THERE WAS NO SIGN OF AJOS.

It's like he'd completely disappeared from the base.

Kerena kept her head high, her shoulders straight, as she went about the day-to-day.

After that last time in the bathroom, he'd held her all night, but a part of her had known it was the end.

The end of something that hadn't even begun.

The end of something that could have been great.

But she couldn't dwell on could-haves.

There was only one reality now: she was on an alien planet, in the middle of a war, and she had a chance of helping make things better not only for the aliens who'd been affected by the terrible scourge called the Tasqals, but for the humans like her who'd been taken as well.

Kerena stretched, a yawn leaving her lips as she slipped off the seat and moved over to the other side of the table in Aker's lab.

The kind doctor had found her a sort of hazmat suit that seemed to be working.

He'd locked the pollen away as well.

Research was slow and she hadn't discovered anything new yet, mainly because they needed more flowers in order to get anything really started...and to get more flowers, she'd need to go back to Choria G622 and expose herself to the contaminant, the plant.

So, for the past three days, she'd been observing the cells of the Tasqal sample that Aker had, only leaving the lab to head back to the med bay to sleep at night.

Athena's husband and his team had worked out some temporary housing and some of the females had already moved into it, so there were quite a few beds available in the med bay, to the point that she didn't feel like she was taking up resources and could sleep without guilt at night.

There was no way she was returning to Ajos' crib.

Not after he'd disappeared.

Something wrung deep inside her at the thought, and she didn't realize that she was no longer alone.

"You're so busy. Find out anything?" The female voice reached her ear and Kerena turned to find Alaina smiling at her.

Pushing her feelings behind her, Kerena met the woman's smile with one of her own. "Nothing yet."

She peered down into the strange microscope. "Don't come close. They say this thing is very contagious and you're not wearing a suit."

In the corner of her eyes, she saw Alaina raise her hands. "Don't worry about me. It's not my sort of thing anyway. I'm more interested in robotics and machines. I wasn't any good with biology."

"Oh? You studied robotics?" Kerena lifted her head.

"Basically." Alaina smiled again. "I am a...was an engineer." She sighed and there was a note of sadness there. "I'm used to keeping busy. It's great that you found something to do here." She met Kerena's gaze. "You're lucky you've made friends with one of them. The others all seem to be staying far away from us."

Lucky, she said.

Ha.

She didn't feel lucky.

Her heart felt torn.

"So," Alaina continued, her face brightening once more. "What are you working on?

"Uh." Kerena shook her head. She really needed to stop thinking about him. "Just trying to see if we can find a way to fight the bad guys." She looked down into the microscope once more. "I may have found something that has an effect on their cells, but we're not sure yet. We'd have to create a stronger sample. Isolate whatever is having an effect on the Tasqal cells, and begin further testing from there."

"Did you see them? The Tasqals, when you went on that planet?"

Kerena shook her head. "No, thank God. But Aker has an image."

She moved over to Aker's control panel and pressed the button she'd seen him press to bring up the hologram.

The image of a huge toad-like creature sprung up before them.

Alaina shrieked. "Oh my fucking God, that's hideous."

Kerena chuckled. She'd had the same response.

Alaina stepped forward slowly, her eyes wide. "This is what took us away from Earth?"

Kerena nodded. "With help, yes."

"Fuck."

"I know."

For a few moments, Alaina just stared at the image, the huge dark eyes of the Tasqal seemingly staring back at her.

"What effect is your experiment having on its cells?"

Kerena sighed. "I'm not really sure. It seems to be...*healing* the cells."

"Healing it?" Alaina frowned.

"Precisely." Aker's voice reached their ears as he entered the lab, his feet carrying him quickly.

He moved over to the receptacle the flower had fallen into and he stooped so he could look into it.

"We need more," he said.

"I know. But there's only one way to get it." Kerena stared at the doctor.

Alaina stepped forward, her gaze moving from one to the other. "You're not planning on heading back there, are you? You almost died."

Kerena looked at the woman. "I know."

"And that doesn't scare you?"

"A little." She looked back at Aker and understanding seemed to pass between them.

"I'll radio the dock," Aker said. "They will prepare a ship."

KERENA LET out a breath as she looked up at the small airship. Aker had only managed to get this one on short notice, and it seemed it was only big enough to carry two passengers.

She turned to glance at Alaina by her side and that's when she saw him.

How could she miss him anyway?

Tall, minty-teal...he walked through the space as if he owned it.

He was dressed differently today, and even with the scowl on his face, Kerena couldn't take her eyes away from him.

Ajos.

His eyes met hers, the spun gold raking over her before he looked away dismissively, and something inside her fell and cracked into a million pieces.

She watched as he walked to stand right by her, his eyes on Aker the entire time.

"This is the ship?"

Aker looked up at him. "You arrived quickly."

"I had nothing better doing at the moment."

He was ignoring her, but worse than that, his words stung like salt in a wound.

Nothing better doing.

He hadn't seen her in three days, yet he was off doing nothing.

He seemed healed too, better. No longer was his head red or his mood testy.

Kerena's throat moved, a lump forming in her throat.

It was clear to her then.

It had just been sex.

That's all.

She was a big girl. She'd known what she'd been getting into.

Still, it hurt.

When had she become so...*weak*? So easily affected by things?

"You," he said, his voice so emotionless, it took her off guard when she realized he was referring to her.

For a moment, she couldn't speak, then her anger flared.

"What?" She mirrored his tone and saw him frown a little.

How the fuck did he expect her to react? If he was cold, she could be too.

"Give me the vial with your life blood."

She narrowed her eyes at him and handed the small package to him.

They'd decided it was better that she send a sample of her blood instead of her being physically there.

No one wanted a repeat of what had happened before. Who knew how the plant would react to her when she returned? It was better to play it safe.

Ajos took the package just as another alien, a huge one with horns on top of his head, came from the other side of the ship.

"Ready?" the alien with horns asked.

"Always, E'lot." Ajos grinned and Kerena felt more pain and hurt within her.

She didn't realize she was scowling till Alaina touched her arm and asked what was wrong.

Kerena shook her head.

"Nothing," she answered, her eyes still on the minty-teal alien.

How dare he.

The one name E'lot glanced at them before hopping into the ship and without a backward glance, Ajos hopped in behind him and the door closed.

Pain swelled inside her as the engine of the craft started and they had to step away.

"Hopefully, they will get the samples and return without much trouble," Aker said.

"Mmhm," Kerena replied.

"I'm heading back to the med bay," Aker said.

"Me too," Alaina replied. "I'm kind of trying to help out. You know, keep busy like you are." She winked and Kerena forced a smile.

"Yea, I'll come by in a while," Kerena said, her gaze focusing off at nothing. "I just...need a few minutes."

The other two muttered something she didn't hear, goodbye till later probably, as they walked off together.

Kerena started walking, not sure where she was going and not really caring.

She was walking in a straight line. She'd find her way back.

The last few moments just kept repeating over and over in her head.

He'd been so...cold.

It kept repeating in her head.

The way he'd looked at her...there'd been nothing there.

Nothing.

She didn't know how long she was walking, but the surroundings soon changed.

There were more buildings on either side of the road here. More aliens too...and some of them turned to look at her as she walked past.

She got it.

She looked strange to them.

They looked strange to her too.

Whatever.

Crossing her arms across her chest, she kept on going, a frown on her face as she berated herself for her own stupidity. How could she fall for someone who could dismiss her so easily?

She kept reminding herself that it was just sex but...

Her heart wouldn't listen.

Her heart was a stubborn fool.

Ahead there was a fork in the road and Kerena paused, looking left then right.

Maybe she should turn back now. She didn't want to get lost.

She was about to do just that when something hit her over the head.

She was only able to register some shock before her body slumped and her world went dark.

29

"I told you to hit it lightly! If we kill it, we'll be in deep, deep excrement."

"This was your idea, fool."

"Yes, but qrak…I didn't think it would actually work."

"I told you they had *hard* skulls."

The voices were whispering but still, they sounded loud.

"It's waking up."

"Qrak…what do we do now?"

"Hit it again."

"No! You fool. The Tasqals will want it alive. If you hit it again, it might die."

Kerena blinked, the blurry forms of two beings coming into view.

"And how do you suppose we get the sample to them? You said you knew someone. Where is he? He was supposed to meet us hours ago."

Hours?

Kerena grimaced as she tried to rise, but soon found out she was restrained.

Her wrists were tied to something behind her and her back was pressed into something hard.

Her feet were free though.

"I don't qrakking know! But this is the one chance we have. If we give them this sample, maybe they will leave us alone."

"And you're sure nobody saw you do it? What if we get caught?"

"She was alone. No other humans saw and only those who are a part of the rebellion know."

The rebellion? What rebellion?

He'd said it like they were talking about another rebellion, one different from the one the Restitution was fighting.

"Ok, at least you did that right."

"Oh, shut up."

There was a moment of silence.

"We can't have a war on this base. Time is running out. I saw the opportunity and I took it."

The other one grunted. "I know. Where would we go after this?"

"Right," the other one agreed.

Kerena blinked some more and the forms of the aliens came into view.

Purple skin. Four arms.

They were of the same species and they were both staring at her.

Fear shot through her.

"Where am I?" she asked, her mind coming online quickly. "What do you want from me?"

The aliens looked at each other and fidgeted, giving her the impression they weren't really confident in what they were doing.

But their words had communicated as much.

"Be quiet," one snapped and the other turned away from her.

"He should be here by now," said the one that had turned away. "Maybe he got caught."

The other one laughed. "Caught how? The commanders and the other idiots who fight with them know nothing about the rebellion."

"Yes, but..."

They both went silent, and Kerena took the opportunity to look around.

It seemed as if she was in someone's home. One that was a stark contrast to Ajos'.

She frowned at the thought of him and forced herself to focus.

This house looked like the inside of an old pub.

There were wooden furnishings, and she was tied to a pole that supported the roof.

She'd never seen this place before and fear went up her spine at the thought.

No one knew where she was.

"What's the meaning of this?" she asked.

She needed them to talk. She needed all the information she could use.

One of the aliens glanced her way but said nothing.

"I've done nothing to you. Why the hostility?"

This time, she got a response.

One of the aliens stalked toward her, his face twisting cruelly. "Nothing?" he asked.

She held his gaze even as she struggled with whatever they'd used to tie her hands together.

"It is because of you why our world is ending."

Kerena frowned. "Based on what I've heard, it was ending before."

"Well, you and your kind have made it worse!" the alien shouted. "If it weren't for you, so many of us would not have died. The Tasqals would not have attacked the base. We would have been safe."

The flawed logic was too much.

"They would have attacked you anyway, one day," she said, trying to keep her voice level. "Surely, you know this."

"Don't speak to it. And be quiet," the other alien cut in and the one in front of her eased back.

Kerena released a breath she hadn't realized she'd been holding.

If he had gotten violent...

Glancing around her, she did the best thing she could do. She tried to find something to help her escape.

No one knew where she was.

No one knew she was in trouble.

And no one was coming to save her.

She'd have to get out of whatever this was on her own.

Hours passed and Kerena's body sagged against the pole. Her wrists burned after trying so hard to break free and she was sure she'd broken some skin.

In the time that passed though, there was one big change: the aliens who had her hostage had grown increasingly agitated.

They were pacing now, both of them, their heads glancing toward the door every now and then.

Whoever they were working with had still not shown up—not that she wasn't happy about that.

It was buying her time to get out of her predicament.

And she needed that time because the outcome was clear.

She was going to be sent to the Tasqals.

The image Aker had on his computer of the beasts was enough to drive fear into her.

She didn't need to meet one in person.

And she was pretty sure that once she left the base, the chances of the rebels finding and rescuing her were slim to none.

Testing the restraints at her wrists once more, she pulled in a breath as they rubbed over the sensitive skin there.

Fuck.

There must be a way out.

That's when she heard it.

A sound by the door.

It was so slight, she'd have thought she imagined it, but it was so silent in the room that she was pretty sure there had been a sound.

Her eyes flew to the two purple aliens.

They were so caught up in their worry, it didn't seem as if they'd heard the sound.

Her lungs started working harder as her eyes focused on the door.

Their friend.

He'd arrived.

Fuck it. She was running out of time.

Her wrists hurt some more as she pulled against the restraints, ignoring the burn.

She was determined to break it, even if it meant tearing off her skin in the process.

This couldn't be the end for her.

She couldn't have survived all this only to be taken to the enemy anyway.

Her spirit left her body as a loud bang echoed into the room. Dust flew everywhere, the lights went out, and it took her a few moments to realize just what had caused the noise.

She could see the dark sky and knew that, somehow, the door wasn't there anymore.

In the dust that rose and now obstructed her vision, something moved.

Something big.

One of the aliens cried out and she heard that cry die on his lips, silenced by the unmistakable sound of bone snapping.

For the next few moments, terror crawled all over her spine.

It was dead silent and then there was the sound of feet scrambling against wood.

The other alien.

He was trying to escape or find cover.

But he didn't get far.

Through the darkness and dust, she could make out the other alien trying to make it out the door, but a hand reached forward and grasped him by the neck, pulling him back.

There were more cries, and something crashed behind her.

Kerena ducked her head, squeezing her eyes tight.

Glass broke, and things fell and then there was silence.

Did the aliens get betrayed? Was she going to get killed now too?

Fear had a tangible feeling.

Thick and heavy, it weighed down her spine and crawled over her like an invisible cloak. She could feel it brushing over her skin as she felt the air shift behind her.

Whoever had taken out the aliens was behind her.

She could hear him breathing now and she didn't know what to do.

She was tied to a pole, weaponless and vulnerable.

The only defense she had, was her mind.

Think, Kerena, think!

"Keh-reh-nah…"

That voice.

Her name.

Only one person said her name like that.

Motherfucker.

"You."

The dim light flickered on and Ajos moved so he was standing in front of her then, the dust settling enough that she could see better.

Ajos stooped, his chest heaving, his eyes roving over her.

He moved his arm toward her before his gaze landed on his outstretched hand.

His entire skin was covered in dark fluid.

He paused and dropped his hand instead.

"Did they touch you?" he asked. "Did they harm you?"

Kerena stared at him.

He looked absolutely…terrifying.

His eyes were wild, and his skin was drawn as if he hadn't eaten in a while.

She didn't know what to think.

"No. They didn't touch me," she managed to say.

"Did they harm you in any way?"

"No," she answered, fear ebbing away to be replaced by anger. "Just…can you release me?"

His chest was still heaving but he moved behind her and soon her hands were free.

Kerena rubbed her wrists as she stood on shaky legs.

She could hardly believe what had just happened.

"Did they harm you, Keh-reh-nah?"

What the…?

Maybe he was more mentally unstable than she'd thought?

Maybe he was bipolar.

"I didn't think you cared." She spun on him, her eyes raking over his body.

He looked even worse than she'd first realized. "I don't know how you knew I was here. I have to thank you for that," she motioned around her, wincing as she saw one of the bodies. It lay crumpled in such a way, it didn't look like something that was once alive.

Realization hit, and she stared at him.

He'd killed for her.

"You don't have to thank me for anything. I should have been by your side."

Kerena blinked. Her anger rising again. "I don't understand you. First you disappear on me, then you appear and pretend as if I wasn't there, now you're back and pretending like nothing has changed between us."

"Have things changed?"

Kerena threw her hands up and headed toward the door.

She couldn't deal with this.

She needed space to think.

Strong arms lifted her before she could even cross the threshold, and she was suddenly over his shoulder.

"Put me down. You have no right."

"I have all the right. You are mine."

His words stunned her, but she still hammered her fist into his back.

"The hell I am."

"You are. I know this now. I cannot run away from it. You are mine and you will always be mine, Keh-reh-nah."

"You really have some nerve." She had the view of his feet and realized he was walking. "Are you just going to leave them there? The dead guys? Shouldn't we call someone?"

"V'Alen already knows. I contacted him just before I entered the room."

"You killed them."

"And they deserved it."

She couldn't argue with that. They were about to sell her off to the enemy.

Kerena released a breath.

"Put me down, damnit."

"No."

"Ugh!"

"Say that again later, when I'm inside you."

That stunned her and made her speechless.

He really did have some nerve.

"You completely ignored me earlier. As if I didn't exist. And now you're coming with this. What am I to you? Huh! Just some booty call?! I realize I may have given you that impression, but a booty call I am not. I thought there was something between us. Something *more*. I don't know how you came back from Choria so quickly but if you think—"

"Was that where you thought I went? I didn't go to Choria G622."

Confused, she realized he was setting her down and that around them was the busy street she'd walked through earlier.

Aliens still walked along it, more than a few of them now staring at the spectacle she and Ajos no doubt made.

"And I don't want to call your booty. I want to *eat* it. I want to be *in* it."

Kerena's eyes widened.

"I want *more,* Keh-reh-nah. You are my mate. And I was a stupid Shum'ai to think I could live without you."

Kerena's eyes nictitated. Her mouth fell open as she looked at the male in front of her.

And she wasn't the only one who seemed dumbstruck.

In her peripheral vision, she could see that aliens around them had definitely stopped to stare.

"What are you talking about?"

"Keh-reh-nah," he said, taking her face in between his hands.

In the light of the streetlamps, a shadow fell across his face and he looked even wilder. "I was wrong."

He wasn't making any sense and even though he'd rescued her, she still felt a bit angry at him.

He'd left her after they'd spent the night together. Then he'd ignored her like she didn't exist.

Next, he'd lied about it.

For a moment, she searched his gaze.

Had the fever gotten to his head?

"I want you," he said, his throat working. "I need you. If you will be mine."

That took her out of her trance and Kerena shook her head, frowning as she tried to step around him.

Ajos grabbed her arm, stopping her from moving.

"Ajos, you are making a scene."

"I don't care. Let them watch."

She shot him a look. "You didn't seem to care earlier either."

Confusion passed across his features. "I don't understand."

"Neither do I." For a moment, she saw his confusion turn to fear in those wild eyes of his.

Shaking from his grasp, Kerena walked off. A crowd parted for her and she felt her cheeks warm.

Shit.

This was bound to spread across the base soon.

Not only that, but the fact she knew she wasn't safe, anyone watching could be her enemy.

That made her wrap her arms around herself.

Heavy footsteps sounded behind her and she knew by the gasps and mumbling that Ajos was following her.

As soon as she was out of earshot of the crowd, she spun and Ajos stopped just short of bumping into her.

There was a worried look on his face as if his world was ending and he didn't quite understand why.

"You know, I've said it before but I'll say it again. You really do have some nerve."

Ajos blinked at her, his chest heaving with heavy breaths as he took her in.

She studied him.

"How did you return from Choria G622 so quickly?"

Again, he appeared confused. "I didn't go to Choria G622, Keh-reh-nah." His golden eyes moved over her face.

Why was he lying?

"I saw you," she pressed.

Still, confusion played over his face before it slowly melted away. "You saw Akur."

"A-who?"

"My brother."

Kerena blinked at him as he glanced around them.

"This is not the place to speak." He moved so fast, she was in his arms before she could even open her mouth. "Come, I have something to show you."

30

In silence, he took her through streets she'd not yet walked on and past buildings she hadn't yet seen.

She was pretty sure he wasn't taking her back to his place or even back to the med bay.

Yet, all she could do was look up at him as he carried her.

As the shadows played across his face, she couldn't help but think he was beautiful.

He was a handsome guy...and it annoyed her.

She should be angry with him right now. Instead, she was silenced, confused, and a bit anxious. She still hadn't faced the effect being captured had had on her.

Every now and then, he looked down and caught her staring, and she was sure she saw his mouth twist in what could be a smile.

That's when it dawned on her.

She didn't think she'd ever seen him smile before.

"Ajos." She called his name and he looked down at her, the gold in his eyes seeming to churn as his pupils adjusted when he looked at her face. "Where are you taking me?"

"Home," was all he said, and Kerena glanced around them again.

Maybe the aliens that had kidnapped her had carried her to a section of the base that she didn't know because everything still looked unfamiliar.

"This doesn't look like the way home."

His chest moved then, and she was sure he chuckled.

"It will be."

He came to stop in front of a building before he pressed a button and a part of a huge column opened up.

Ajos stepped inside and white light lit up the space.

He pressed something else and suddenly they were being lifted.

Kerena held her breath as she stretched her neck to look around.

"This is..."

"A lift. It is taking us home."

The elevator opened and Ajos took a few steps down to a door where he scanned his hand.

The door opened and he stepped inside. It was pitch black within, but he walked as if he knew where he was going.

After a few steps, he set her on her feet then let her go.

Looking around, she couldn't make out a thing in the darkness.

But then the lights came on and her breath hitched in her throat.

It was a living room and she only knew because of the way the furniture was set up. She'd have surely missed that fact otherwise, because the entire space was filled with flowers, vines, bushes, and shrubs.

It was like a living jungle within a room.

Kerena's eyes widened as she took one step forward, her mouth falling open.

"Where are we?"

"Home." Ajos' voice came from behind her and she turned to look up at him. "Your home...and mine."

Kerena blinked. "I don't understand."

Worry passed over his face again and Ajos took a breath.

Kerena's eyes moved over him.

In the light, he looked even worse than she'd thought before and she was beginning to realize those dark marks splattered all over him was the blood of the two aliens that had kidnapped her.

"Ajos—"

"You're mine," he began. "I know that now. I knew it before...but I tried to ignore it."

"You ignored *me*," she said.

"That was Akur, my twin brother."

Kerena's eyes widened. "You said you had a brother. You didn't say he was your *twin*." She searched his face for any sign of deceit. "Identical?"

"Unfortunately." Ajos sighed. "I'm pretty sure it pains him that he has the same image as the damned."

Kerena frowned. "What does that mean?"

Ajos reached forward and took her hand. "Come, I'll tell you while we wash."

He led her to another room that was obviously a bedroom judging from the bed nestled within the "forest." He led her from there to another room—the bathroom.

Kerena gasped.

Above, it looked like she was looking up into the open sky. She could see the stars through the roof.

"How..." she whispered.

"Do you like it?" Ajos' eyes moved over her face as if her answer mattered to him, and Kerena was momentarily at a loss for words.

"This is like a dream home..."

He smiled then, a full-on smile that made her breath catch in her throat.

Somewhere behind the vines, he activated something, and water began literally raining down from the sky.

"Keh-reh-nah," he said. "I have to tell you something."

With the "rain" falling down on them, soaking them both, she could almost feel the atmosphere around them change.

"Many moons ago, I was sent with some females from Tonvuhiri... traveling across the stars to our mother planet for the joining ceremony." His throat moved as he swallowed and his eyes darted away from her to focus at nothing. "Everything seemed okay. Shum'ai females are...delicate...so they all rested in stasis pods for the long journey. Nama," he said, "my sister, was with us."

Kerena blinked, waiting for him to continue.

"She...died."

He still wasn't looking at her, but there was so much pain on his face that Kerena knew he was battling something deep within.

"I could not save her. She begged...and I could not." Pain crossed over his eyes. "Losing a female...a sister...is a blow to any Shum'ai's lineage. Females are gifts. They alone can carry on the family line by bearing young. And I..." Another breath shuddered through him. "I couldn't save her. It would have been better if I had been the one to die."

"How did she die?" Kerena whispered.

He finally looked at her then. "Her stasis pod failed."

The similarity wasn't lost on her.

When they'd first met, she'd been stuck in a stasis pod. She'd almost died in it.

"Is that...is that why you've been so *nice* to me."

Through his pain, he smiled a little.

"A little—at first. And then..."

He paused and his throat moved again.

"And then what, Ajos?"

"I thought the gods were punishing me." He moved toward her and pulled her to him. "I joined the Restitution as penance for what I allowed to happen to Nama. And then...you came along." He touched her hair. "This beautiful creature that I'm drawn to. This beautiful creature that I've bonded with."

He took a breath. "I want you, Keh-reh-nah. I *need* you."

The pieces were slowly falling together. The house. The "forest" within the rooms. Everything he was saying...

Was he really saying what she thought he was?

"I thought..." she whispered, allowing herself to reach forward and touch him. Her fingers brushed over the skin of his cheek and Ajos closed his eyes to her touch, leaning toward her hand.

"You disappeared for three days..."

"I had to." His golden eyes met hers again. "I begged the gods to show me a sign..."

"And you got that sign?" She searched his gaze.

"Yes."

"What was it?"

He smiled a little then, but he didn't answer.

Kerena released a breath. "This is a lot to digest."

Ajos tilted her chin up so she was looking at him.

"Being without you felt like walking toward death itself." He paused. "I think I know now. I am not being punished. You are a gift from the gods themselves."

Uh, she wouldn't exactly call herself that, but which girl wouldn't take such a compliment?

As Ajos' lips crashed against hers, Kerena allowed the tension she'd been holding within her to fade away, and she sagged against him a little.

"I want you, Keh-reh-nah," he said. "I hope you want me too. Tell me you'll give me a chance." His breath was warm against her lips. "Tell me you'll give *us* a chance."

Kerena trembled. His words were powerful.

"I want you, Keh-reh-nah," he repeated. "Do you want me?"

"More than anything," she whispered—an admission, even to herself.

31

Ajos' cock slipped inside her for the third, no, fourth, or maybe fifth time?

She'd lost count now. He groaned as he pressed her pelvis into his so hard, her clit rubbed against him with each thrust.

Sweet ecstasy filled her as he kneaded her breast underneath his palm.

Her cheek was plastered against his chest, his fresh wintery scent wafting into her nose like a thick musk.

Ajos pummeled into her until she couldn't take it anymore and as she screamed his name, her orgasm flooded through her like a warm unending wave. In the midst of the sweet ecstasy, she leaned into his neck and nipped him lightly.

Ajos groaned, slamming into her one last time and she felt his seed rise from his base to flood her channel.

The effect caused another immediate orgasm and even as her body stiffened then trembled, she wondered how she was able to keep them coming.

She felt limp, but so, so sated.

For a few moments, he held her there, his cock still buried deep inside her.

"I don't think I will ever get enough of you," he murmured.

"You better not."

Ajos chuckled and slipped from inside her, brushing against her leg as he moved to lie beside her.

His chest heaved at the same rate hers was, and she couldn't help but giggle when his eyes met hers.

Around them, the leaves of the foliage seemed to sway, affected by her happiness.

"I don't get how you can still be hard."

"It will go down."

"But we had like, *five* rounds."

He glanced at her. "Human males do more?" He began moving. "I can go again."

Her eyes widened as she pressed against his chest, another fit of giggles moving through her. "Heck, no!"

Ajos chuckled and dropped his head on her chest, idly rubbing his nose against her nipple.

This was hardly believable. But it felt...right.

Planting a kiss on his head, she rubbed the protrusions he told her were called his nefre and he shuddered.

"Stop that...unless you want me to spin you over and mount you again."

Kerena smiled.

"We should go." Her smile slowly faded.

They'd been bad. Wholly ignoring the fact that he'd killed two beings, destroyed a building, and that they'd gone missing.

She doubted anyone knew where they were and she knew Alaina and maybe even Aker would be looking for her.

She *had* told them that she'd be going back to the med bay and she hadn't turned up.

"Ajos..."

"Eh?"

"How did you find me?"

He stiffened suddenly.

"Nobody knew where I was. Nobody knew I was taken...how did you know where to look?"

"You are my mate...I just..." He paused and raised his eyes to hers. "I cannot explain it. I followed my instincts."

Kerena frowned a little. "How did you know I was taken though?"

"Something felt...wrong."

He rested his head against her again and left it at that.

But she was still confused.

"You came after me because something *felt* wrong?"

"You are my mate, Keh-reh-nah. I will always be there for you. It is my oath."

Kerena frowned some more.

"You keep saying I'm your mate."

He lifted his head then, his golden eyes calm. "Because you are."

"When did that happen?"

"Don't you feel it?"

She blinked because, for some strange reason, she knew exactly what he was talking about.

Something felt...*right* with Ajos.

Just then, a loud bang ricocheted off the walls as the door to the bedroom was flung in.

A scream left her lips as Ajos dived over her, covering her completely.

There was a pause and then someone said, "Qeffing qrak!"

"He's fine and the human looks...safe." She recognized that voice.

It was V'Alen.

"V'Alen?" she asked, trying to see around the minty-teal hulk that was covering her.

"Brother, you must learn to control yourself," said the other voice.

It sounded just like Ajos.

Realization dawned.

"GET OUT!" Ajos roared so close to her ears, she was almost deafened.

"Happily," V'Alen said. "I, for one, do not wish to see any more of your nether regions."

Ajos growled and Kerena couldn't help but giggle.

He'd covered her but his ass was in view of their visitors.

Moving her head a little so she could see around him, she realized his brother was still standing there.

It was so strange looking at him. The exact image of the man lying on top of her.

"Akur," Ajos growled. "I know you're still there. Get. Out."

"Unlike V'Alen, I see that ass every day. Doesn't faze me. I have the same one."

Ajos let out a growl of annoyance.

Kerena stared at his brother.

The entire time he talked to Ajos, Akur had his eyes on her, a strange look in his eyes.

"Qef you. Get out."

Akur's eyes finally moved to his brother. "You are needed in the conference hall." His eyes slid back to her. "You too, suini."

Ajos stiffened against her, his head raising a little as he turned to look at his brother.

They locked eyes and something passed between them that she couldn't see before Akur left the room.

As soon as Ajos was sure his brother was gone, he relaxed against her a little, muttering something underneath his breath.

"Qef..."

"What...what did he just call me? What does 'sweeney' mean?"

Ajos raised his head to look at her. "You heard that?"

Kerena nodded.

"Sister." Ajos' gaze studied her face. "He called you sister."

Kerena slipped into the new tunic Ajos had gotten for her. A sort of knee-length dress with a band she could tie around the waist to make it fit better.

There was still the issue of having no panties, but she was getting used to going commando.

When they finally dressed and exited their new apartment, Kerena was surprised to find V'Alen and Akur waiting outside.

Akur had his arms crossed as he leaned against the balcony, his hard eyes on his brother—eyes that turned curious when his gaze slid to her.

"Ready?" Akur asked.

She swore Ajos rolled his eyes.

He didn't answer. Instead, he took her hand in his and began walking toward the elevator.

"You could have knocked. Or called. You know, like a civilized being."

"Civilized?" Akur chuckled. "I'm not the one who's been throwing people around, attacking innocent sky tower technicians like a maniac, bashing doors in, and, wait, not to mention KILLING two refugees and destroying their dwelling in the process. So don't talk to me about civilized, brother." Akur looked at her. "Although, I do understand now why you've been such a pain in the ass."

Ajos frowned at V'Alen. "You told him all of that?"

For the first time since she'd known him, V'Alen looked surprised.

His eyes opened a little farther than usual in shock.

"Why on earth do you think I would do such a thing?"

Kerena's head snapped to the robot man.

"Why on earth?" she repeated.

V'Alen blinked at her. "I have been learning human terms."

She chuckled then. "Don't mind Ajos, he's just mad you saw his ass."

"It was not a pleasurable experience."

Kerena chuckled again and Akur joined in.

Ajos narrowed his eyes and pulled her toward him as they stepped into the lift.

Akur and V'Alen piled in behind them, causing a tight fit.

Ajos leaned down as the lift descended, his lips brushing against her ear.

"If I recall, you didn't think my ass was so funny a few minutes ago." He nibbled her ear and her breath hitched in her throat. "You were too busy screaming my name to laugh."

Kerena's eyes widened and she glanced at the other two males in the small space with them, sure they heard Ajos' words.

Akur was frowning at nothing but V'Alen's eyes darted from her and she was sure, with his enhanced everything, he'd heard every word.

As they exited the lift to the street below and began walking, she turned to glance at the two males walking behind them.

"A meeting? For what happened last night?"

"More or less." Akur held her gaze and again she felt that uncanny feeling. It was like staring into Ajos' eyes, but not.

How did she not realize that before?

They took another direction she didn't know and Kerena looked around.

This part of the base seemed more *developed*. More buildings were here and not as many people were walking on the streets.

As a matter of fact, it felt like they were on the business side of the base.

"This is the central hub. Most of the decisions are made here." It was as if Ajos read her mind.

The buildings all had that brown color, formed out of the earth itself, but the streets weren't just made of mud hardened by many years of footsteps. These streets were lined with what looked like bricks.

They were walking for a few more minutes before they came upon a singular cylindrical building and stepped inside.

It was a huge lift, but instead of going upward, it went down.

Darkness enveloped them and the lights came on.

The ride was short, lasting only a few seconds and soon they were on their feet again, walking down a corridor to a singular set of large doors.

The doors opened and Kerena blinked a little.

She had expected a meeting, but she hadn't expected *this*.

In front of them, were rows and rows of seats all forming a circle. Several dozen aliens were already sitting inside and as her eyes moved over the group, they landed on a familiar face.

Athena sat there with Alaina on one side and her husband, mate, Xul, on the other.

Around them were those same aliens and the other women who'd led the rescue of the stasis hold.

There were a host of other aliens that she was sure she'd never seen before, too.

Alaina waved at her and Kerena smiled but when her gaze met Athena's she was sure there was some tension there.

Something was wrong.

Ajos led them to some free seats and then silence enveloped the room.

"What is this?" She leaned into Ajos and whispered.

"Annoyance," he said, albeit unhelpfully.

Movement caught her eye and she watched a tall alien that looked like Jack Skellington minus the nightmare pumpkin head effect walk down toward the center of the room.

There was a raised platform there, and the alien stood on it.

The alien took a breath.

"Now that the commander has graced us with his presence," the alien shot an eye in their direction, "we may begin."

He took another breath. "It has been brought to the council's attention that two Krinqrids were killed in their home in the last dark cycle."

Murmurs went through the group of seated participants and Kerena glanced Ajos' way.

His frown deepened.

"It is needless for me to remind you all that this is a serious crime. Not only is there unrest within the population of refugees from the explosions, but I am afraid these killings have caused quite a stir, and understandably so." More murmurs and he paused. "The refugees are losing trust in us."

"Who killed the Krinqrids and why?" someone asked.

"Well, they're a bit of a nuisance and a dishonest species. I am not surprised someone has killed two of them," someone else said. "More will probably come."

More murmurs and she felt Ajos stiffen beside her.

Kerena bit her lip.

"It doesn't matter who did it or why. You know the law. No one.

And I mean, no one, can deliver their own justice. That is what the council is for."

Kerena glanced at Ajos.

His jaw was clenching and unclenching and only when she touched him did some of his tension ease.

There was worry in his eyes though, and she had to admit, that scared her a little.

"We ask that the guilty one reveal themselves," the tall alien said. "Punishment will be light."

"Punishment?" she whispered.

"It depends on the species, but they will probably do something that hurts a lot," V'Alen whispered beside her.

"Reveal yourself now," the tall alien said. "We know who you are. Have some dignity and come forward." The alien turned and looked directly at Ajos.

Kerena's eyes widened a little.

They knew it was him.

They were going to punish him for something he did to save her? Were they dumb?

Before she even considered it, Kerena stood.

There was a gasp and Ajos grabbed her arm.

"Keh-reh-nah," he hissed. "Sit."

"I did it," she said.

The tall alien looked shocked.

"Impossible," he said, but something in the way he glanced around made her believe he wasn't entirely sure.

"Why? Did you see who did it?" she asked.

The tall alien frowned a little. "No, but we have reports from bystanders that Commander Ajos," he stressed on the name, "was seen leaving the vicinity with a human female."

"That's me," she said. "I'm the human female. I did it."

The tall alien opened his mouth but Kerena cut him off.

"And before you continue, let me speak."

The tall alien's mouth slammed shut and he glanced behind him, she assumed, at his other council colleagues.

A murmur went through the group of seated beings.

"Keh-reh-nah, what are you doing?" Ajos hissed once more.

"Saving your ass like you saved mine," she hissed back.

"Okay," the tall alien caught her attention. "Approach. You may speak."

Fuck.

Her knees suddenly felt weak but holding her head high, Kerena walked down to the center of the room.

Even though the platform was raised, she felt small standing on top of it.

The tall alien moved out of her way to give her some space.

Kerena took a deep breath.

"There is no way she took out two Krinqrids," someone said.

"Silence!" the tall alien shouted. "Let the human speak."

Nodding at the tall alien, Kerena began.

"Last night, I was walking alone." She looked around and made eye contact with as many beings as she could. That would make her story seem more believable. It would inspire trust that she was speaking the truth. "I was hit over the head and lost consciousness."

There was a growl and her eyes darted to Ajos.

She gave him a hard look and his brother rested his hand on his shoulder.

If she was going to do this, Ajos needed to keep his shit together.

"When I woke up, two purple guys with four arms—"

"Krinqrids," the tall alien corrected.

"I'd rather call them assholes." Kerena frowned and someone chuckled. "When I woke up, I heard them talking about meeting someone who was to take me away to the Tasqals as a sort of peace offering."

There were loud murmurs at that, and through all that noise, she heard another growl. Ajos was probably starting to see red again, and she tried not to look at him.

"What did you just say?" the tall alien said.

Kerena repeated and there were more murmurs.

"How do we know she speaks the truth? The Krinqrids are dead. There is no one to question."

The tall alien cocked his head at her, willing her to answer.

"I have no reason to lie." And she hadn't lied...yet. She'd told them the truth.

There were a few more murmurs before someone asked something. "They attacked you?"

"They would have. Whoever they were to meet was late and I was beginning to think they didn't know what to do with me. They had communicated that their plan was a secret and that the commanders, and the council," she added, "didn't know about it."

Eyes darted around the council members.

"If their friend didn't turn up, they didn't know what to do with me." She'd surmised that on her own. "I did what I had to do. Otherwise, I wouldn't be here right now. I passed out again after I, uh, killed them. Commander Ajos found me."

The tall alien frowned.

"Passed out?"

"Yes."

"I can confirm that." A voice rang out and she turned to see Aker in the crowd. She hadn't noticed him there before. "This is the human who has gone through extensive physical strain to have made it even possible for us to have something that reacts to the Tasqal's disease. It was this same human who helped retrieve the strange device from the fallen Tasqal vessel."

More murmuring and Kerena smiled a little at the doctor.

"This human?" The tall alien beside her asked, eyeing her with disbelief.

"Yes," Aker answered.

"And you can confirm that this...feeble-looking being has the propensity to kill two grown Krinqrids?"

Aker's nose moved. "The humans have cells within themselves that attack each other. I am sure that is enough proof that they are a vicious species."

Kerena choked on a laugh and cleared her throat instead.

The tall alien blinked.

Someone stood up. Another tall alien like the one beside her.

"This is a farce of a trial. We don't care about the qrakking Krinqrids. If the human is telling the truth, which we can assume she is judging from the character of most Krinqrids, then we can forgive her for the basic instinct of defending herself. Now," he said, "tell us more about what happened to you and tell us more about this...weapon."

Murmurs of agreement rang out and Kerena glanced back in Ajos' direction.

He settled back in his seat, his eyes on her, and she smiled a little.

It had worked better than she had planned.

32

—————

For what felt like the next three hours, she and Aker were drilled for information.

It turned out that this new development with the flower she had accidentally found was like a ray of hope to all the commanders.

Akur joined in, saying that he had managed to harvest more of the flowers using her blood and that brought more conversation.

Judging from her background, or probably because she was the discoverer of this new plant, she was tasked formally with leading the research with Aker.

She was exhausted by the end of the three hours and suddenly she felt herself being lifted off her feet.

"Wait, what are you doing? We aren't finished discussing this," the tall councilor said.

"It will have to wait. You have exhausted my mate and that is not your job. It is mine." Ajos settled her over his shoulder.

The councilor's mouth opened and shut.

"Your mate?" Xul stood from the seats, his eyebrows rising on his forehead.

"Do you have a problem with that, Commander?" Ajos asked.

Xul's face split into a grin. "No. It's about time you got some—"

Athena's hand flew over his mouth and she looked mortified.

288

If blood wasn't rushing to her head from the way Ajos was holding her, Kerena would have laughed.

"Go, Brother," Akur touched Ajos' shoulder. "I will stay here and help Aker as much as I can with these *ongoing* questions." He stared pointedly at the councilor. "Rest well, suini," he leaned down so she could see his face and she saw a smile in his eyes.

Kerena nodded and then she was moving.

Ajos didn't speak and neither did she as he took her back to the lift and it began to rise, taking them above ground.

The dirt bricks that paved the road were her view as he headed back to their apartment.

Their apartment. It still didn't feel real.

"You know, you have to stop doing this Tarzan and Jane thing." She chuckled. "I can walk."

"I don't want you to walk." He squeezed her ass. "I like your ass right here. I can smell your sugar even now."

Kerena's mouth opened in shock and she felt her cheeks grow warm.

"You can smell me?!"

"And you smell so, so good, Keh-reh-nah. My tongue and cock are both twitching. They want your sweetness."

Kerena blushed harder. "Put me down right now, Ajos Khattull!"

He stopped walking for a second before he squeezed her ass again.

"No."

"Ugh!" She feigned annoyance.

"You know my name."

Kerena blinked. "Yes."

"Did I tell it to you?"

"I'm not sure."

Fuck. She only remembered, somehow, from that time that she'd been snooping on him while in the shower.

"Does it matter?"

"Yes," he said, and her fingers brushed against some flowers.

She didn't realize they'd made it back so quickly.

"It matters because now I know," he said.

"Now you know what?" she asked as he set her down on the bed.

"Now I know you cared enough about me to go snooping into my records."

Kerena licked her lips. "Do you mind?"

"No, but I should still punish you."

"Oh." There was a mischievous look in his eyes and she bit her lips this time. "How?"

"I know just the thing."

Slipping his hands down her thighs, Ajos grabbed the sides of her dress and pulled it up over her lips.

This time, he licked his lips as he looked down at her and the hunger in his eyes made her heart begin to flutter in her chest.

Ajos settled between her legs as he buried his face into her inner lips, inhaling deep.

It was so carnal, so dirty, but it made her instantly wet.

As he took his first taste of her, his tongue swiping out to lick her, a groan rumbled through his chest.

"This," Kerena panted, her palms fisting the bedding in anticipation of what was to come, "this doesn't feel like punishment at all."

"I've changed my mind, Keh-reh-nah," he growled, and she had to chuckle. "I could never punish you."

"Why?"

"I've decided to pleasure you instead."

"Why?" Oh, why didn't she just shut up and take it?

"Because." Ajos met her gaze and something visibly changed within him.

He climbed up her till he was face to face with her, his gaze boring into hers.

"For many moons, I walked a dark path alone, haunted by my past," he said. "You've changed that for me. You've given me purpose to live."

His words made tears form in her eyes and she reached a hand to caress his cheek.

"My, Keh-reh-nah," he said, bending so his face was buried in the soft flesh of her neck. "You're everything I want but everything I don't deserve."

As Ajos wrapped his arms around her, pulling her close, Kerena knew one thing with clarity.

He was wrong.

In the small amount of time, he'd become her world as much as she'd become his. He was strong, loyal, and he had a good heart. If that wasn't deserving of her love…she didn't know what was.

Destiny couldn't have given her a more suitable mate.

A NOTE FROM A.G

Whoo, what a ride! (No, I'm not talking about Ajos...okay, now I am.)

I hope you loved Ajos and Kerena's story! The plot thickens with our rebels fighting for the Restitution and I can't wait for you to see where it goes.

It feels great being able to expand on this world and that's all because of you.

For that, thank you <3.

I don't know who the next book will be about yet. I have an idea but it's not concrete. I was inspired by too many of the side characters (some in my head that weren't even mentioned in this book, haha).

If there's someone's story that you want to read about, let me know on Facebook or send me a message through my website at agwilde.com.

Once more, catch you on Facebook or at the back of my next book!

Till then, happy reading!

A.G.

OTHER BOOKS BY A.G.

Captured by Aliens

Xul

Crex

Yce

Kyris

Kyro

Riv's Sanctuary

Riv's Sanctuary

Sohut's Protection

Ka'Cit's Haven (COMING SOON)

ACKNOWLEDGMENTS

Special thanks to my little booboo, my darling Feen. You and your sister push me to be a better person every day and make me work harder. Because of you, I can't give up.

IF YOU ENJOYED THIS BOOK...

If you enjoyed this book, please consider leaving a review because it would make all the difference.

ABOUT THE AUTHOR

A. G. Wilde is an avid reader, a gamer, a lover of all things space, alien, and sci-fi.

She is addicted to intense romance, irresistible heroes, and deliciously naughty things.